W9-AXA-026

THE PRICE OF FREEDOM

3 1526 05116272 2

WITHDRAWN

THE PRICE OF FREEDOM

Rosemary Rowe

This first world edition published 2017
in Great Britain and the USA by
SEVERN HOUSE PUBLISHERS LTD of
19 Cedar Road, Sutton, Surrey, England, SM2 5DA.
Trade paperback edition first published
in Great Britain and the USA 2018 by
SEVERN HOUSE PUBLISHERS LTD

Copyright © 2017 by Rosemary Aitken.

All rights reserved including the right of
reproduction in whole or in part in any form.
The moral right of the author has been asserted.

British Library Cataloguing in Publication Data
A CIP catalogue record for this title is available from the British Library.

ISBN-13: 978-0-7278-8742-9 (cased)
ISBN-13: 978-1-84751-869-9 (trade paper)
ISBN-13: 978-1-78010-932-9 (e-book)

This is a work of fiction. Names, characters, places and incidents
are either the product of the author's imagination or are used fictitiously.
Except where actual historical events and characters are being described
for the storyline of this novel, all situations in this publication are
fictitious and any resemblance to actual persons, living or dead,
business establishments, events or locales is purely coincidental.

All Severn House titles are printed on acid-free paper.

Severn House Publishers support the Forest Stewardship Council™ [FSC™],
the leading international forest certification organisation.
All our titles that are printed on FSC certified paper carry the FSC logo.

MIX
Paper from
responsible sources
FSC
www.fsc.org   FSC® C013056

Typeset by Palimpsest Book Production Ltd.,
Falkirk, Stirlingshire, Scotland.
Printed and bound in Great Britain by
TJ International, Padstow, Cornwall.

To John and Linda – lb and sil – with much love

FOREWORD

The novel is set in the dying weeks of AD193, when Britannia was the most remote and northerly of all the provinces of a Rome still rocked by the events of a tumultuous year. No less than three Emperors had been overthrown within the last twelve moons: first the corrupt and cruel Commodus, then the austere and careful Pertinax (presumed friend and patron of the fictional Marcus in this tale), and finally his successor, Didius, who effectively bribed his way into Imperial power with promises of money which he could not pay. Even now the situation was extremely tense, the most recently acclaimed new Emperor, Septimius Severus, was still fending off two remaining pretenders to the purple: one, Pescennius Niger, the governor of Syria, was currently engaged in armed rebellion, while the other was the governor of Britannia itself. For the moment – as the story suggests – his loyalty, and that of the legions under his command, had been bought by the courtesy title of 'Caesar' and a promise that he would succeed as Severus's heir. (A hollow promise, as later events were to prove.)

Meanwhile, Severus was undertaking what we might now describe as a 'charm offensive': proclaiming that he was the 'avenger' of the murdered Pertinax, the last 'true' Emperor, whose reputation he was eager to restore and whose supporters (like Marcus) he set out to woo, by sending personal legates with messages and gifts to the most influential of them 'throughout the Empire'. There are claims that this continued 'despite flood and storm' until the defeat of Pescennius in late 194, and this is the assumption on which this story turns.

It may be exaggeration: travel in winter was extremely arduous, and sea travel in particular was rare and hazardous (as witness the unseasonal voyage and shipwreck of St Paul), indeed most captains would refuse to put to sea in any threat of storm. However, legates and other official travellers (including the

Imperial post) did have the authority to compel a ship to sea, so that the arrival of a legate in the winter months – although unlikely – is not impossible.

Nor was road travel easy. All major routes were military ones, built by soldiers for the army's use, and – though still difficult in bad weather – paved roads made long distance travel possible, but in winter older tracks were often near-impassable. In low-lying areas, flooding was an annual event and whole areas – now drained – were turned to swampy bog. Ancient Celtic settlements had made this fact a source of self-defence – only a local could find the way across the marsh or safely estimate the tides (still true in some coastal areas today) – and in isolated places this tradition probably remained, as the siting of Darturius's property suggests.

On major roads, official travellers (of any rank) might use the 'mansio' a kind of military inn, where facilities were generally good and horses might be changed. Civilian inns were much less welcoming: one was likely to share a bed with fellow travellers, let alone a room, and bedding (difficult to clean) might not be changed for months. The food was basic, there were bugs, and sanitary arrangements were rudimentary, at best. But fleas, filth and overcrowding were the least of the hazards one might face. Many establishments were notorious – like the one encountered by Libertus in this tale – little better than a bawdy house, where crime and robbery were commonplace.

The centres of population which were linked by these main roads, varied in size and status and sometimes purpose, too. Glevum (modern Gloucester) was an important place, thriving with shipping, trade and industry and a centre for regional civic government. This meant that it was almost certainly responsible for the collation and return of tax for the surrounding area, with contributory tax-collection being conducted in a number of small towns, including the semi-fictional Uudum in this tale. (Semi-fictional, because it is assumed to be approximately where Woodchester is now. The 'chester' suggests a Roman army base nearby, and medieval sources give the name as 'Uudchester', but there is no evidence that such a name, or civic settlement, existed at this time.)

Tax collectors were notoriously unpopular, of course, although the system had been much reformed. The early 'licences' – effectively contracts which required tax collectors to submit a given sum to Rome, but permitted them to set the tax at any rate they chose – had been replaced by a regulated system, in which the publicanus received a fixed percentage, and tax collecting had become almost respectable. However, failure to produce the requisite amount would result in an inevitable fine, seizure of all property and – if necessary, the sale of the publicanus into slavery. This system was likely to be rigorously enforced – since, in the case of shortfall in the tax, the members of the local curia (in this case, Glevum council) were legally required to make up any deficit themselves.

The sale of licences was not confined to tax. Official permits were required for the extraction of precious minerals, and other natural commodities. For the most part the state reserved such profitable activities for itself, but small-scale private operations might be licensed, on payment of a fee, at the discretion of the magistrates. One such commodity was salt – (called 'sal' in Latin: it was so valuable, it was even used as payment to the legions at one time, from which the word 'salary' derives). There were large and profitable salt-extraction enterprises in East Britannia, owned and operated by the state (using slaves, of course), but there is also evidence of small-scale evaporation pans and kilns elsewhere in the province, which appear to have been in (largely unsuccessful) private hands. This is the presumed status of the imaginary saltern which features in this story.

Latin was the language of the educated, people – especially in the newly founded towns – were adopting Roman dress and habits, and citizenship, with the precious social and legal rights which it conferred, was the aspiration of almost everyone. However, most inhabitants of Britannia were not citizens at all. Many were freemen, scratching a precarious living from a trade. Hundreds more were slaves – mere chattels of their masters, to be bought and sold with no more rights or status than any other domestic animal. Some slaves led pitiable lives; a slave in a kindly household, ensured of food and clothes, might have a more enviable lot than many a poor freeman starving in a squalid hut. All the same, slaves – especially senior ones who were often given small gratuities by guests – might spend a life-time saving their 'slave-price' to buy themselves free, though some masters either confiscated tips (slaves officially owned nothing) or else continually increased the sum required until the servant was too old to work.

Yet Celtic life and customs continued to exist, most especially in country areas, and many poorer families, living in native settlements well off the major roads, might have little contact with Roman ways at all, except for essential trade and business purposes. Slavery was less universal in the Celtic world, being traditionally reserved for conquered enemies or – as in this story – as a temporary arrangement in payment of a debt. However, by the second century, Roman practices were spreading everywhere.

Real freedom, naturally, was reserved for men. Respectable Roman women married very young (twelve was not uncommon and fourteen was usual) and thereafter were expected to produce a family, and spin and weave – though not cook, since the household almost certainly had slaves to do that task. (Slave-girls, of course, were the possessions of their masters to be used as he desired – any resultant children might be sold, or simply killed.) Although individual Roman women might inherit large estates, and many wielded considerable influence within the house, they were excluded from public office and a woman (of any age) was deemed a child in law, requiring a man to speak for her and manage her affairs – a father, husband, or a legal 'guardian'. Poorer 'free' women worked beside their men, or – like the inn-girls in this narrative – otherwise found ways to keep themselves alive.

Celtic females, like Aigneis in this narrative, had one advantage over their Roman counterparts: by tradition they had the right to choose themselves a mate, or at least to refuse to marry a man they did not like – although, as the story suggests, economic necessity might dictate otherwise.

The rest of the Romano-British background to this book has been derived from a number of (sometimes contradictory) pictorial and written sources as well as artefacts. However, although I have done my best to create an accurate picture of the times, this remains a work of fiction and there is no claim to total academic authenticity. Septimius Severus and events in Rome are historically attested, as is the existence of Glevum and the basic geography of Britannia. The rest is the product of my imagination.

Relata refero. Ne Iupiter quidem omnibus placet. I only tell you what I heard. Jove himself can't please everyone.

ONE

It was a distinction I could have done without. In fact, I have carefully resisted nomination to the town council over several years, on a number of occasions and on a variety of excuses.

But when my patron, Marcus Aurelius Septimus – the senior local magistrate and one of the wealthiest and most powerful men in all Britannia – decides on something that he wishes you to do, in the end it is folly to resist. Especially when he seems to feel that he is offering a favour, and makes it clear that he'll be affronted if you don't accept.

I finally succumbed the evening he invited me to dine – though even then it was more or less an accident. Perhaps I was too dazzled by the occasion to be fully on my guard, though I should have suspected his motives from the start. Being asked to feast with Marcus at his country house is a signal compliment for any citizen, and for a mere Celtic tradesman like myself it was absurdly flattering – it had happened only rarely in all the years since I'd become his *cliens*, and then it was either because he needed me (usually as a witness or something similar) or because there was a huge public banquet, where I had the lowest seat.

This time, however (according to the courier page who brought the message to my roundhouse door) it was a private feast, arranged on sudden impulse in honour of a distinguished visitor who had arranged to call. It would be held the very evening this personage arrived – which was to be the next day following – and I was one of a small and specially selected group. Furthermore, I was confidentially assured, I was to be seated on the left hand of my host, 'in recognition of recent services' – the second highest couch position in the room. It was an unlooked for honour and – naturally – had the desired effect.

I was ridiculously pleased (I must be credulous!). I sent my acceptance back by the same messenger, and duly presented myself on the appointed night, dressed in my best toga, and scrubbed and barbered by my slave-boys to within an inch of death – this on the orders of my dear wife, Gwellia, who was in a state of high excitement even greater than my own.

She even wrapped my warmest cloak around me, as I left, with her own two hands, sending my attendant servant – whose job that should have been – to fetch and fuel the little oil-lamp we would use to light us home. 'Now, husband, don't be later than courtesy demands! It is threatening to be frosty later on, and you know how Marcus's feasts can linger on!'

I nodded. Gwellia was always fussing over me, but I had come to the same conclusion for myself, however unconvivial an early exit might appear. It was almost Saturnalia and the nights were dark and cold, so – though Marcus's country residence was not half-a-mile away – at this time of year returning to my roundhouse would be a daunting walk, on a chilly forest lane when there might be wolves about. Any of Marcus's visitors would understand at once, though my host was apt to be lofty about such trifling concerns.

Even he, though, had shown unusual thoughtfulness today. He was not offering me accommodation overnight, of course – as he always did with visitors of higher rank, or with further to travel in the dark – but he had arranged for one of these more privileged diners to send his private litter back (after it had delivered its owner at the feast) to transport me to the villa while there was still sufficient light. Not home again, obviously – by that time it would be too dark for the bearer-slaves to see – but the arrangement would save me half the walk and I accepted gratefully.

It meant, moreover, that I could wear my toga there, instead of having to put it on when I arrived. That would have been impractical if I'd been on foot. The unwieldy garment is not designed for lengthy walks in wind and rain, least of all on aging citizens like me. Mine always threatens to unwind itself at the least exertion – to say nothing of what the muddy winter track would have done to my newly-laundered hems.

So I arrived at the villa gates in style, in a handsome curtained litter borne at a brisk trot by four handsome boys in scarlet uniforms – with my poor slave, Minimus, swaddled in a cloak and padding after them – exactly as if I were a wealthy man myself. The gatekeeper (a burly giant whom I vaguely knew) flung the gates open at once and waved us grandly through. I decided that he hadn't realised it was me!

Dismounting at the front door of the house, I was met with similar elaborate and unaccustomed courtesy. Practised hands relieved me of my cloak, a dining-wreath of flowers was pressed onto my brow, my little slave was taken off to the servants' quarters for entertainment and his own repast while I was shown at once into the atrium. A tow-headed young man in a similar wreath and pale green *synthesis* – that useful combination of tunic and toga which the Romans often favour for dining-purposes – was there before me, seated on a stool and nibbling delicately at a plate of sugared plums.

He looked up as I approached and waved a sweetmeat at me. 'Citizen Libertus! Greetings! How good to see you here!' He patted a vacant stool beside him. 'You found my litter and bearers satisfactory, I trust?'

I beamed. So this was the man I had to thank!

'Quite excellent, Titus Flavius,' I replied, with genuine pleasure as I took the proffered seat. 'Thank you for making them available.' I had other reasons to be grateful to Titus Flavius: a year or two ago, when I'd found myself facing an impromptu court of curial magistrates – accused of a wholly imaginary crime – he was the only councillor who listened to my pleas and spoke in my defence. I knew that he had prospered, but I had not seen him since, though in his careless but flamboyant way (how can a man look slightly dishevelled in a brand-new synthesis?) he seemed in splendid health. I murmured something civil to that general effect.

He nodded. 'Marcus has been very welcoming – even permitted me to share his bathhouse when I came. We had a long talk while we were being oiled and strigiled clean. Very entertaining. He's getting changed for dinner, now. He won't be very long.'

I gave an inward grin. Marcus, like any wealthy Roman, always left his visitors to wait a little before he deigned to come – how long, depended on the relative importance of his guests. Not that any other diners seemed to have arrived, which was unwise of them, I thought: Marcus was almost certain to be displeased that they were late.

It was not necessarily deliberate, of course: when the sun is covered by thick winter cloud, it is very difficult to judge the hour of day, and no host would ever be specific as to time, in any case. Not everybody has a water clock, and hour-candles are notoriously vague. But, for whatever reason, it seemed the other guests had not arrived, and though a servant was already taking off my sandals so he could rinse my feet – although having come by litter they hardly needed it – there might be quite a pause before we all went in to dine.

As if in answer to this unspoken thought, a slave appeared from nowhere with a plate of plums for me. I took one, gingerly. Sugared plums are a delicacy, of course – replacing the more customary figs or dates – but Marcus's feasts are famous for the variety and richness of the food, and I did not wish to dull my appetite. Besides the things are rather difficult to eat. (I was right to be cautious, honey-crystals cascaded down my toga-front, but the plum was so delicious that I found myself reaching for another, nonetheless.)

Titus gave me a conspiratorial smile as I attempted to brush the crumbs away. He waggled his broad fingers to signal to the slave, who instantly appeared with water and bowl to wash our sticky hands, while Titus spoke above his head, as if he wasn't there. 'Excellent, aren't they, citizen, those plums? I don't know how his cook-slave manages these things. Makes one look forward to what else may lie in store!'

I nodded, my mouth too full of sweetened fruit to speak. When I'd swallowed, I managed to reply. 'Do you know who else is joining us?'

He looked so startled that I was surprised myself. 'But, citizen, surely there are just the two of us? Did Marcus not explain as much to you?'

'Not in so many words,' I answered. 'But, on reflection, I should have understood.'

Now, of course, I understood too well. Having the second highest guest-position in the room is not so great a compliment when there are only two of you. On the other hand, it was an honour to be here at all, in the company of a citizen of rank, and Marcus had taken some trouble to supply the honey-crusted fruits. I took another one. I was clearly going to earn it, later on – I was not invited for the pleasure of my company, or to make up numbers as I'd originally supposed. That was obvious. I was here for a purpose. But what, I wondered, did my patron want me for?

Titus seemed to realise that I was mystified. 'You've heard the dreadful news about the *curia*, I suppose?'

For a moment I did not take it in. Council matters did not affect me very much, but there were often scandals – somebody had taken a bribe too openly, or one of the magistrates had been notably unjust. I was about to shake my head, more interested in my plum than gossip from the town, but then the implication dawned on me. My patron had often called upon me in the past to help him find the truth behind unfortunate events, which might otherwise have been embarrassing to his role as magistrate. Well, I thought wryly, now I knew what I was doing here. There was doubtless another such assignment awaiting me: some investigation into the curia which would keep me from my pavement-making trade, and which Marcus would expect me to be honoured to accept. (It never occurs to him that I have family to support.)

Trying not to sound depressed, I said, politely 'News?'

'Serious news!' he told me, convincing me that I was right in my surmise. 'It has not been generally announced, though it happened days ago, but – between the two of us – there's been an accident and several of the councillors were killed.'

Between the two of us? There were at least a half-a-dozen servants in the room, waiting with towels and bowls of water, or trays of drinking goblets and jugs of watered wine. Titus, like any Roman, seemed not to consider that slaves were sentient, with the use of ears and tongues. But it was too late now – they had heard what he had said, and I was playing at being an important Roman visitor myself. 'Only perhaps it was not an accident?' I prompted, taking another sugared sweetmeat as an advance reward.

He stared at me. 'Oh, on the contrary, there is no doubt of that. The curia were invited back to dine at the town house of the Priest of Mercury, when a brazier got knocked over in the kitchen-block, it overturned an amphora of olive oil it seems, and there was a dreadful fire.'

I had not visited the house, but I knew where it was, and had heard its fine appointments spoken of – an expansive and expensive residence, close to the eastern gate, with private courtyard garden at the front and stables to the rear. There was even an impressive fountain just within the gates, which could be glimpsed when they were opened to admit a guest. All paid for by a wealthy marriage, people said – though the Priest of Mercury came from no mean family himself.

And now there'd been a fire. I had not heard the news – I had been very busy for the last half-moon and had not time to listen to the gossip of the *colonia* – though I thought that I could guess what caused the blaze. Conflagration is always a hazard in any town, but those who do not pay their fire-guild dues are apt to find their premises at more than usual risk – sometimes even appearing to spontaneously combust! Even the wealthy do not seem exempt.

'He wasn't a member of the fire guild?' I enquired, hoping Marcus didn't want me to investigate the guild. (I paid my own subscriptions to them regularly, of course – but I know what it is to have a fire. The upper storey of my premises was once badly damaged in a blaze, which is why I no longer live above the shop but have moved to my present roundhouse, several miles from town. On that occasion it was certainly an accident, but I did not want it happening again just because I'd managed to irritate the guild.)

Titus Flavius raised a brow at me. 'Silvanus? Oh he's a wily fellow, he belonged all right. The guild brought buckets, and fought to quell the blaze – there is a fountain in the courtyard, as perhaps you know – and the slaves pulled down the stable-thatch before the fire could spread to that. But several of the bedrooms round the courtyard caught alight – there was a wind that fanned the flames. The wooden window-shutters and hangings went roaring up, and with the beds and bedding, the wing was an inferno in no time at all and the whole house filled with smoke. People had to grope to find the exit route, and it was almost impossible to breathe. Most of the guests and the priest himself escaped, but it was dark of course and in the commotion it was not clear if everyone was out.'

I could see where this was leading. 'And not everybody was?'

He shook his head. 'Several of the Priest's most valuable slaves were lost – all the kitchen staff, we realised that at once – the fire was so intense that some of the servants' corpses were reduced to ash and never found. But when it was safe to go inside again, the bodies of three senior councillors were discovered, in a passageway.'

'In suspicious circumstances?' I ventured, and added, as he looked at me appalled, 'since those corpses were recognisable and not consumed by fire?'

'Hardly suspicious. They weren't burned, it is true, but they had obviously been overcome by fumes. All three were elderly, and could not move as quickly as the rest of us. It seems they must have turned the wrong way in the smoke. The priest's chief steward realised they weren't with us, when we reached the street, and he went back to look for them – but died in the attempt. His body was discovered not very far from theirs, though it seems he was less fortunate and had been badly burned. It was only his rings and slave disc which told us who it was. Poor fellow, he had been saving for his slave price too.'

I blinked at him. 'You speak of "us" – so you were there yourself?'

'Oh indeed,' he answered. 'Did I not explain? Most senior members of the curia were there, discussing how we might fill the current vacancies – we'd already lost four members from ill health and death this year. So this event has been a dreadful blow. Glevum council has only fifty seats – unlike some larger cities which have the full hundred, just like Rome – but we were already several members short, and this has made it worse.' He turned his attention to the fruits again – so as not to have to look at me, I guessed. 'Marcus is very anxious to make up the list. As senior magistrate it's his responsibility.'

'Oh ho!' I muttered. Suddenly this was beginning to make dreadful sense. 'Surely he doesn't hope that I am going to stand? I've had this conversation with him several times before. I don't have the necessary size of property in town, I'm not a wealthy man, I've been a slave and I'm not of Roman birth – let alone patrician lineage. I lack every qualification.'

Titus selected another sugared plum and grinned at me. 'Would you not be willing? We could do with men like you. You are intelligent and honest, you are a citizen, and as for servitude – you were a Celtic nobleman by birth, I understand. Strictly it is being *born* a slave which is the bar. And the property requirement is easily arranged, Marcus has a flat in mind for you, I think. It was confiscated from another councillor, so it clearly qualifies. It would be gifted to you as a present while you lived – and revert to your patron afterwards. It's very well-appointed and luxurious, I believe, and the furniture is in it, so there won't be that to find.'

I knew the town apartment that he meant. Marcus had suggested the self-same thing to me before. The place was luxurious all right – intended to impress – and had belonged to a man who committed suicide.

'But I don't want to be a councillor,' I said. 'It always surprises me that some men are so keen, since the council is responsible for tax.' Responsible, in the sense that local centres are required by law to send due tax to Rome, and more to the local garrison for its maintenance. Usually, of course, that means collecting it, and there are tax collectors charged with doing so, but if that fails – as has famously happened once or twice elsewhere – the councillors themselves are personally liable. 'I don't have the money to agree to that.'

Titus waved a cheerfully dismissive hand. 'Oh, Marcus would indemnify you, I am sure. You could make that a condition of his nominating you. In fact. he suggested that very thing himself. And for once, I do agree with him. The curia needs people of your calibre – it's too full of men who simply want the fame or – worse – hope to profit from awarding contracts here and there.'

I nodded gloomily. Bribing officials is against the law, of course, and if money changes hands it is discreetly done, but everybody knows that gifts and favours are frequently required before a valuable civic commission can be won. 'You and Marcus have obviously worked it neatly out,' I said. 'But Titus, I know nothing of such things – and I don't want to know. I'm just a humble workman with a trade to ply. I've never held a public office in my life. Everyone knows that. Even if Marcus did suggest my name, I can't imagine that it would have much support.'

Titus signalled for the slave to bring the towel again, and beckoned to the boy who held the jug of pre-prandial watered wine. 'My dear Libertus, you are an innocent. You really don't know anything about the council, do you? If you were his nominee you could hardly fail.' He held his fingers out to have them washed again. 'If the Emperor Caligula could once have his horse created senator, don't you think Marcus could get you onto the curia?'

I frowned. 'Is it true about Caligula? I've heard it said, of course.'

Titus made a wry face. 'Who knows the truth? But that's what rumour says – and I, for one, don't doubt the principle. If you are Emperor you can do as you please.'

'Whereas the rest of us—' I gave him a dark look – 'can only do what our superiors ask us to? But I can't agree to this – if anything happened to Marcus, which the gods forbid, I would be stuck with it, and ruined. Once you're on the council, you have to serve for life. It's worse than slavery – at least a slave can hope to buy his freedom in the end. It's not like being an Imperial Servir for a year or having a joint position like a *duumvir* . . .'

I looked at him for some response but he made none at all, though he obviously knew exactly what I meant. Only the Imperial priesthood and the dual municipal magistracy are annual posts – though even they can lead to a seat on the curia later on.

'Not like a Servir or a duumvir? Well, Libertus, my old friend, that's most convenient,' Marcus's voice came booming from the door, sending me leaping from my stool to offer him a bow. He laughed. The shock he'd caused me was deliberate of course – a man like Marcus never usually enters un-announced. He looked magnificent, handsome as ever in a yellow dining-robe, the gold embroidered bands around the hem subtly echoing his handsome torc and rings, though the blond curls beneath the dining-wreath were these days touched with grey.

To my astonishment he approached me first – though I was the lesser ranking of the guests – extending his right hand for me to kiss. But as I bowed to touch his seal-ring with my lips (full kneeling obeisance is not required when one is a dinner guest) I saw him glance at Titus with a wink, and began to wonder if my patron had been nearby all along, listening and awaiting his moment to appear.

His next words confirmed it. 'It happens that the post of duumvir is what I had in mind. One of the current pair has unfortunately perished in a fire – Titus no doubt mentioned the affair – and a replacement is needed urgently.' He turned to Titus. 'Titus, my friend, you have done splendidly. You may tell the curia tomorrow that I've found a candidate. Libertus Flavius Severus will stand.' He beamed at both of us. 'Now, that's enough of business. Shall we go and dine?'

TWO

I t was a splendid dinner – or it should have been. Marcus had taken considerable pains to serve food that I enjoyed – an appetiser of curd cheese and nuts and eggs, and choice of main dishes which included simple things, like braised pork and leek, or chicken with white carrots in red wine and cumin sauce. None of the dormice or partridge tongues which I have known him serve at public banquets, no showy sow's udders or stuffed peacock's brains. Everything was cut into small portions, too, so that it was easy to pick up with the fingertips and there was no need for a *scissor*-slave to attend and carve things on the spot – though Marcus had one, as I knew from former feasts.

Furthermore, his beloved *liquifrumen* (that Roman sauce of fermented anchovies, which I heartily detest and which he has created for him to a personal recipe) had not been added to every dish beforehand, but was offered separately in a jug. There was no doubt that I'd been treated like an honoured guest in this.

As it was, however, I scarcely tasted anything and actually had to compel myself to eat. From the moment Marcus made the opening offering to the gods all I could think of was the prospect of becoming duumvir, and how much I did not want it. Fortunately, Marcus didn't notice my lack of appetite, he was too concerned with his own exciting news: the impending visit of an ambassador from Rome.

'I shall have to hold a special feast here for him, next, I suppose,' he said, propping himself effortlessly on his left elbow while his right hand daintily dipped a ham-and-fig ball into the jug of sauce. 'Though there will have to be a few more guests at that affair!' He laughed. 'All the same, Libertus, my old friend, as a "top-couch" guest at a banquet-feast of mine, you can regard yourself as being in distinguished company.' He popped the morsel neatly in his mouth.

'A private legation from the Emperor himself?' Titus said, reaching for the breadbasket and selecting a piece of flatbread to mop juices from his plate. 'And at the darkest and stormiest time of year, when so many ships prefer to stay in port? You must feel greatly honoured, Excellence. This is in recognition of your services to Pertinax, I suppose?'

I was glad of the intervention, which relieved me of the necessity of answering. I was not really accustomed to eating lying down, and I always find it difficult to manage with one hand – even with a dining-knife to help with spearing things – let alone attempting to talk at the same time. So I simply nodded to show I understood, and went on thinking my own gloomy thoughts while my patron prattled on to Titus, about this visit and his fortunate escape.

I knew the gist of it, in any case – as no doubt Titus did, though he was contriving to look appropriately rapt. Marcus had been telling the story to everyone for weeks.

'I was really in deadly danger for a little while,' he said, lifting a fragment of spiced goose up on his knife, 'when Pertinax was murdered by his Imperial Guard. He was my personal friend and patron, as I'm sure you know, and when that usurper Didius seized the Imperial crown – or, rather, bribed his way to it – there were dreadful stories about what he was doing to Pertinax's friends – exile and ruin was the least of it. I was in mortal fear that he would reach me here. But now that Severius Severus has taken charge, it is the supporters of Didius who are fleeing for their lives.' He bit the morsel expertly from the blade.

'And the new Emperor is setting out to re-establish links with potential allies in the provinces. As witness this personal ambassador to you!' Titus knew exactly the right flattering thing to say. 'He was always a supporter of Pertinax, of course. He has even re-established him in the pantheon, I hear – like all the other Emperors who've been acclaimed as gods.'

I busied myself with a little pastry parcel of cooked ham and figs. I had my doubts about the motives of Severius Severus. His famed 'accession' – though clearly a relief from my patron's point of view – had been achieved by marching on the capital with an army at his heels: whereupon the perfidious Imperial Guard, outnumbered and faced with a superior force, had conveniently changed allegiance yet again, declared that he was the rightful Emperor and 'executed' Didius before the day was out. Not quite the 'rational transition' that Marcus boasted of.

And that is not the end of it. Severius is not the only pretender to the purple, even now, and he is currently working to defend what he has won: mounting what he calls 'a punitive campaign' against one former rival candidate, while wooing the governor of Britannia with promises, in return for his support and the dropping of his own Imperial claim. A proclamation in Glevum, only recently, announced that 'Governor Albinus is to be known as Caesar from now on, by order of his Divinity the Emperor Severius, as a token that the said Governor is Severius's heir, to whom the rank of Emperor will pass.' Yet Severius has children, in particular a son. If I were Albinus, I thought gloomily, I should be sceptical – and careful to employ a poison-taster I could trust.

Marcus, though, had no such doubts. 'Do you suppose that I should provide dining-slippers for the banquets when this legate comes?' he said to Titus, as the servants cleared away the remnants of the meats and proffered us clean napkins with which to wipe our lips before the table of sweet courses was brought in. 'In Rome one always leaves one's shoes off at a feast, once the slaves have washed one's feet, but in Britannia it is too cold for that. Here in the villa, one might manage it – we have the hypocaust to heat the floor – but I don't want to create an awkward precedent. Other councillors will wish to honour him as well, I'm sure, and try to outdo each other in providing feasts.'

And no doubt, as a reluctant duumvir, I would be expected to attend them all and listen to endless speeches of mutual flattery. I gave an inward groan. I would have to improve my technique for reclining-dining before then. My left elbow was already aching from supporting me. I moved myself discreetly a little on the couch to try to ease my toga-folds and free my eating arm, which had somehow got trapped in the material. Titus and my host were still busily engaged in discussing the proper etiquette for entertaining an Imperial ambassador, so they did not notice my discomfiture, but I had an ambition to taste the honey-cakes.

Raising my weight had solved the problem and I stretched out a hand, but before I could take a morsel from the dish, the feast was interrupted by a servant appearing at the door, and banging stridently upon a gong.

'The lady Julia!' the slave announced into the startled silence which ensued. I looked at my fellow-diners in surprise. Marcus, I saw, was frowning like a thundercloud.

'Lady!' he thundered, as she came into the room. 'Why do you honour us with your presence in this way?' The words made a half-pretence of courtesy but he was clearly furious.

This arrival, obviously, had not been pre-planned. It is not unusual for the lady of the house to be present at household banqueting, but on intimate occasions like this when all the guests are male, Julia – like many matrons of her class – usually elects to dine apart. ('Civic business does not interest me,' she once told my wife. 'And very often I am simply in the way – the men can speak more freely if I don't attend.') Clearly that had been her intention for tonight – she was not even dressed for company: in fact, it looked as if she might have been preparing for her bed. She wore a plain pale-blue tunic with no jewels of any kind, and her hair was pulled back in a simple braid. Her face was bare of her usual make-up, too – no white powder to emphasise her skin, no kohl around her eyes or carmine on her lips – and she looked tired and strained, though to my eyes she was still extremely beautiful. (Her little attendant was a pretty girl herself, but beside her mistress she seemed unremarkable.)

Titus Flavius would have risen instantly – and so would I, of course – but Julia gestured us to stay reclining where we were. She came to stand across the table, straight in front of us and bowed her head to Marcus, but she did not smile. 'Husband, I regret to interrupt you in this way, but there is an urgent messenger.'

Marcus levered himself a little more upright, so that he was leaning on one straightened arm. 'A messenger? At this hour?'

'Indeed.' She met his eyes. 'Some members of the curia had news this afternoon – long after the courts had finished for the day – so disturbing that they called a meeting there and then, and decided that you should be told without delay. Their messenger has ridden through the dusk, and only dismounted when it got too dark to see. He has come the last part entirely on foot. He pleads for audience.'

Marcus was still glowering. 'Surely this can wait till we have finished here? I do not wish to be discourteous to our guests. Obviously, I cannot send a message back tonight. Tell the servants to prepare a bed for him, out in their quarters would be best, I suppose, and see that he is fed. I will see him when we have finished here. We can do no more this evening – whatever it's about – so I'm sure that will suffice. He can take my answer back as soon as it is light.'

Julia allowed herself to smile. 'I have already given instructions to accommodate him, as you suggest. However, I think that you'll want to hear his message straight away. Grave news – or I would not have interrupted you.' Her husband still looked doubtful, so she came around to him and bent to murmur something in his ear.

'Dear gods! You're sure?' Marcus almost leapt up from the dining-couch. 'And all of it is gone?'

'I only tell you what the messenger has said.'

Marcus snatched off his dining-wreath, impatiently. 'In that case, I will do as you suggest. I'd better hear the story from his lips.' He seemed to remember his duties as a host. 'Pardon me, citizens, for deserting you – but I must go and speak to this messenger at once. In the meantime, Julia, have them serve the wine. Keep our guests amused. I'll be back as soon as possible.' And he strode out of the room, leaving the servants looking mystified.

Julia took charge with commendable aplomb. Notwithstanding her unsuitable attire, she took the place that my patron had vacated, reclined gracefully upon one elbow and signalled for the banquet to proceed. A large silver bowl of the finest watered Rhenish was brought in, accompanied by a pretty little slave-boy with a flute, who began to tootle for us while – in the absence of Marcus – Titus made the required libation to the household lars.

There was an awkward silence, during which I made a little offering to the deities myself, discreetly swirling the liquid so it splashed across the rim. I am not a follower of the Roman pantheon, preferring the more ancient gods of river, tree and stone, but one never knows, and this evening's problems were clearly Roman ones. A man can't be too careful with the gods.

Julia noticed. She helped herself to a handful of dried apricots, then turned to smile at me. 'You seek divine protection?' she enquired. 'So Marcus has persuaded you to stand as duumvir? He told me earlier that he intended to.'

This was clearly an attempt at normal conversation, but it was bizarre. It's rumoured that when Emperor Commodus had a feast, he sometimes ordered executions to take place while they ate – strangely cruel ones, like having a bald man smeared with honeyed crumbs and pecked to death by birds – as an entertainment for the banquet-guests. And those invited used to talk of anything – the weather, the cost of slaves, the latest style in beards – rather than mention what was happening in front of them. It felt a little like that, as I answered Julia – as though our host had not, strangely, disappeared.

'I am to stand as candidate!' I said. 'Not that I had much choice in the affair.'

She gave me a sympathetic smile. 'I warned him that you might not welcome the idea – though Gwellia would like it, I am sure.' She saw my doubtful look. 'What wife would not be glad to see her husband recognised? To say nothing of the clothes and shoes she will acquire. All the tradesmen of the town will be competing for her custom, very soon, if . . .' She broke off, as the gong rang out again and the little flautist faltered to a stop.

'His Excellence, Marcus Aurelius Septimus!' the usher cried, as though he were announcing a new arrival to the feast, and there was my patron standing at the door. He was looking anxious and his face was deathly pale, and he was absently running his ring-hand through his tousled curls. In his other hand he held an open writing-block: the message it contained had clearly shaken him.

'My friends and fellow citizens,' he said, 'I'm sorry to interrupt the feast, but I think you should hear this, Titus – it affects the curia. You too, perhaps, Libertus – for other reasons – though you're not a member yet. The news is serious. It concerns a tax official from a small town south of here – Acacius Flauccus – you may have heard of him?'

'But of course I have,' I cried, jumping up so quickly that I almost spilt my wine. 'He is coming to my workshop very soon, to discuss the patterns for an extensive pavement in a house he plans to buy. I'm expecting him tomorrow if the roads permit.' I looked searchingly at Marcus. 'I understood you'd recommended me.' But he did not reply.

'A large commission?' Titus asked.

I turned to my fellow diner in relief. 'I am hoping so. His steward arranged the visit, not half-a-moon ago. He explained that his master was planning to retire, and had agreed to buy a villa on the other side of town but wants to add a bath-suite to the property, with mosaic floors throughout. No doubt there'll be a lot of haggling, but – if he finds a pattern that he likes – it should be a handsome contract in the end.' I keep a range of patterns made up on linen backs, so that clients can select and mix the elements: the usual ones were far too big to send, but I'd made up some tiny samples for him to choose between. 'Unless of course he wants a whole design bespoke – though that would naturally cost a good deal more.'

But my patron shook his head. 'I fear, Libertus, that there will be no contract of any kind at all. Acacius Flauccus was found dead this afternoon. It rather looks as if he's hanged himself.'

THREE

I was startled. So startled that I allowed the slave to pour me another cup of watered Rhenish wine. I don't, in general, drink a lot of wine of any sort: I don't much care for it in any case, and it always gives me a headache the next day, but this evening had been so full of strange events that I was suddenly glad of it's warming bitter taste. Perhaps that's why I could not think of anything to say.

It fell to Titus to express my thoughts. 'Dear Jupiter!' He frowned. 'I suppose this information is reliable? Acacius Flauccus is not simply dead? Did I not hear that he was ill in any case?'

'Ill?' I stared at him. My tongue was strangely reluctant to form words, to my surprise, but I forced it to comply. 'His steward did not mention that to me!'

Marcus gave me a look which conveyed, as clearly as if he'd said the words aloud, that it was unnecessary to share private news with tradesmen like myself. All he said, however, was, 'All the same, it's true. Flauccus caught a fever a moon or two ago. It left him very weak, and he's never really recovered since. He wrote to the curia to explain as much, and was applying to be permitted to resign his post mid-term. The council decided to allow him to withdraw – that's why he was coming to Glevum, now – to meet his successor and render his accounts.'

I nodded stupidly. Of course, the licence to operate as a *publicanus* would not officially expire until the Kalends of Mars (which in ancient times was reckoned the beginning of the year, and is still the moment when the public tax falls due – as even a humble property-owner like me is well aware!).

Titus was saying, thoughtfully, 'I remember. His letter was read out to the curia and it was all agreed, though there was some argument about who should be permitted to buy the licence in his stead. Not everyone approved the candidate. We were discussing it again, the day that fire broke out. Though that would not affect Acacius Flauccus, naturally, except that we agreed to send a message requiring him to come to Glevum as soon as possible and pay in the money he'd collected up to now.'

'Presumably tomorrow was the suggested date?' I said. 'That would make sense of his arranging to see me.'

'Exactly!' Titus answered. Then he frowned. 'Perhaps we set conditions that were too hard for him. The roads can be atrocious at this season of year, and the journey would be harsh, especially for a man who is not in the most robust of health. I trust it was not the thought of that which drove him to the act?'

Marcus shook his head. Julia had relinquished her position on the dining-couch, but he did not come back to join us and recline on it. Instead he sat down on a nearby stool and motioned for a slave to bring him wine. When he seized the cup and drank it at a draught (something which no well-bred Roman would ever generally do) I realised how seriously he was disturbed.

He signalled for a napkin with which dab his lips. 'I don't think the curia can blame themselves,' he muttered bitterly. 'This was discovered beside him on the floor.' He held up the writing-block. 'An open writing-tablet – one of Flauccus's – with a message crudely scratched into the wax. "Gambled everything and lost. I could not take the shame". Since there was no sign of any money in the house, I think we must assume that was indeed the cause.' He passed the block to Titus who stared at it white-faced.

'Gambled everything?' he gasped. 'Official takings too?'

'Official takings in particular.' Marcus sounded dazed. 'The coffer-chest was found beside him, open on the floor. The receipts for the taxes he'd collected were still there. The record-scrolls were on the table – all unrolled. But the money . . .' He groaned and dropped his head into his hands.

Julia came to stand beside him. 'Husband, I've been thinking ever since I heard. How can they be sure he hanged himself? Might it not have been a robbery? Someone could have rigged the corpse up afterwards to look like suicide?' She put a tentative hand out to him but it was shrugged away – though Marcus is unfashionably devoted to his wife. Further proof, if I required it, of his state of mind.

'Woman, do you not suppose that I had thought of that?' he roared. 'The man was a tax collector, after all!'

He had a point, in that. Publicani are never the most popular of men – less hated than they used to be, of course, before the Emperor Augustus reformed the licences. But still detested, as a general rule. Flauccus had no doubt made many enemies.

'There are probably scores of people who would be glad to see him dead,' Marcus went on, more peaceably. 'But it's obvious that he'd pre-planned this whole event. Everyone believed that he was on his way to us – his personal effects and furniture were stored, and the place made ready for his replacement to move in. He'd even sold his servants, or his steward, Loftus, had – that very day in fact – thus ensuring that Flauccus would be in the house alone. Briefly, but long enough to kill himself. And no one but himself could have arranged for that.'

'And all this excited no remark, because Flauccus was to come to Glevum, anyway?' Titus was not really asking, he was marshalling his thoughts.

'Exactly so – and everybody thought he had. His carriage was even seen to leave the property. It was his private carriage, naturally enough, and the man who saw it leave simply imagined it was bringing Flauccus here, together with the tax money.'

'Without an escort?' Titus was amazed.

'That was my reaction, but Flauccus never employed an escort for longer than he must. He apparently insisted that a mounted guard simply drew attention to the fact that there was something of value in the coach, and invited an attack. There were members of the local guard post detailed to escort him once he was on the road – as usual for anyone carrying public funds – but he tried to avoid it whenever possible, and only submitted when he was leaving town. That's been his preference ever since he held the post – and it was his risk, of course, since he was liable if any money went astray.' He groaned. 'Or so we had supposed. We had not reckoned on this development.'

'But surely,' Titus said, 'an escort would have been mandatory today? Scores of miles on a military road, where rebels and bandits are constantly a threat?'

'And he had requested one, but the time of departure was yet to be confirmed – so no one suspected anything amiss. Furthermore, Flauccus had told the guards that he had a few last payments to collect before he left – that was supposedly why he could not be exact about the hour – so if his carriage passed, it would occasion no remark. None of the guards remembers seeing it go by but no one can be sure. They would not have challenged it – there was no question of requiring a toll.'

'One can see how that would help Flauccus plan this suicide,' Titus put in suddenly. 'With the coachman gone he had the house entirely to himself. Loftus would return to lock the premises, ready to follow his master on horseback, and then to surrender the key to the curia here. It's an official residence, I think, and will pass to the incoming publicanus when he takes up the post?'

I found myself nodding, rather stupidly. 'That's why Flauccus needed a villa here?' I said, to show that I was listening, though the Rhenish was doing strange things to my tongue. I took another sip.

'The new man should have been the one to find the corpse.' Marcus ignored my interruption. 'I think that was the plan. But when Loftus got back to the house – with the money from the slave market – before he locked the doors he made one last inspection of the property. He found his master in his study dangling from a beam, with a stool beside him which had been kicked away. And this writing-block and the empty coffer-box beside him on the floor.' He gave another groan. 'You can see what that means, Titus, I am sure. The curia will have to make the missing taxes up.'

Titus Flavius was looking flushed and stern. 'Perhaps we must accept that he committed suicide. But that does not prove he wasn't robbed. If the gold was taken from him while he was still alive, wouldn't he be liable to repay the missing gold himself, rather the burden falling on the curia?' Titus was warming to his theme. 'In which case, perhaps we should be looking for a thief? If someone has the gold, it could be recovered yet.'

'And the message on the wax? The steward is convinced it was his owner's hand – he recognised his master's writing-block.'

A thought was stirring in my befuddled brain, but before I could voice it Titus did so first, 'And the steward can be trusted?'

'Flauccus thought so,' Marcus sounded sharp. 'Loftus was the steward that he sent to me, asking for my recommendations for a mosaicist. On that occasion he was handling a large amount of gold, in relation to the purchase of the Glevum house. And – quite clearly – he did not make off with that.'

'No sign of any shortfall in the price?' Titus pointedly enquired. 'Villas are expensive in this area. Especially ones that are already built.'

It was a sensible question, but Marcus waved it loftily aside. 'Probably we'll find that Flauccus overspent, and gambled money from the treasury to make it up. Besides if Loftus took the tax money, what's become of it? And why not take the proceeds from the sale of slaves as well – which was in itself a considerable sum?'

'And Loftus had that with him?'

'So I understand, together with a tally of how he sold the slaves – proving that he'd been at the slave market since dawn. And that's another thing. Why, if he was guilty, did he not disappear – instead of drawing attention to himself by rushing to the nearest house to ask for help, and – incidentally – to send us messages?' My patron shook his head. 'I think we must accept that Flauccus hanged himself for exactly the reason that he gave and – what's more – that he planned it in advance.'

'What has become of Loftus?' I managed to enquire.

Marcus shrugged. 'A prisoner in the nearest army post, I understand – there's a small detachment guarding a river crossing quite close by. The man he ran to for assistance is a wealthy citizen, and he called them in – so, as well as sending messengers to us and raising the alarm, they seized the steward and took him in for questioning. No doubt a wise precaution – though I know my friend Libertus won't agree with that – but I understand it has not yielded anything so far.'

He was right in thinking that I would not agree. I have often warned him of the uselessness of using torture as a means of arriving at the truth: often the victim will agree to anything, simply in order to make the torment stop. More can very often be achieved by the offer of reward for useful information.

But I was too depressed to argue and I simply shook my head and voiced the only question which occurred to me. 'So what happened to the carriage?'

Marcus stared at me.

'You said it had been seen to leave the property, and may have passed the sentry at the river crossing, too. It didn't come to Glevum – as far as we're aware. So where did it go?'

My patron shook his head impatiently. 'It will no doubt be discovered abandoned in a lane – with the horses missing, I should not be surprised.'

It must have been the wine that made me still persist. 'I wonder if Flauccus's coachman was among the slaves he sold – or if someone else was hired to drive it on that day? I'd like to talk to Loftus, though it's no concern of mine. And it's too late now, in any case, no doubt.'

Marcus rose and placed one hand upon his chest, raising his other arm theatrically towards me, as though presenting me already to the curia. 'Libertus, you make me proud that I've selected you to be a duumvir. Of course you must speak to Loftus, I'll arrange it instantly – the messenger shall take a letter from me, at first light. I'll see you're given lodgings both in the town and on the way, and provide you with a warrant, given under seal, asserting your authority to question anyone and enter the premises where Flauccus used to live. If you discover anything, you'll let me know at once.'

I had not meant to volunteer for anything like this. 'But how would I travel?' I bleated plaintively. 'It's much too far to travel on a mule and, though I have an ox, I don't possess a cart. Besides, I've no idea where I'm supposed to go.'

Marcus – who was looking much less strained, I thought – came and took his place between us on the couch. 'It's a tiny place called Uudum, to the south and east of here – scarcely more than a few houses, a temple and an inn – it mostly exists as a tax-collection point.' He took a handful of dried fruit and nuts and tossed it down his throat. 'I'll see that you have transport – my private gig, perhaps. A little faster than your ox or mule, I think!' He laughed. 'Speaking of which, it's getting rather late. I'll send a pair of servants to light your way back home. Can't have our new duumvir savaged by the wolves! The messenger tells me he could hear them, in the dark. Now, just one last performance by the flautist, possibly?'

I nodded, and pretended to go on sipping wine while paying due attention to the little music-slave, whose repertoire was charming but too lengthy for my taste. But at last it was time for the slaves to fetch my cloak, bring my lighted lantern and Minimus to me and usher me out into the bitter night.

There were no wolves or bears, I'm happy to report – just a dismal drizzle and a rising mist. With Marcus's slaves attending me, of course, I could not strip off my toga – I'd planned to carry it, when we were out of sight – but now I was obliged to wear it all the way.

When I got home, I found my wife already sound asleep in bed. She'd been engaged in dying wool all day, and there was only the sleepy kitchen slave awake to welcome me. I refused the spicy mead that he'd been keeping warm for me – I'd drunk too much already at the feast – and I was glad to simply sit and let the boy take off my cloak and shoes, unwind my mud-stained toga and bear it off to sponge.

I could hardly wait to lie down on the welcoming warm nest of reeds and skins. All the same, I slept indifferently – over-full and fuzzy-headed from unaccustomed wine. I dreamed that I'd become a duumvir and was at a public feast, but disgraced myself by dozing into my pickled jellyfish.

FOUR

Gwellia awoke me before the sun was up. She pulled the skins and woven covers back and shook my shoulder with a gentle hand. 'Husband, remember you're expecting someone in the shop today. A very important customer, you said.'

I opened one reluctant eye, glimpsed the candlelight and clamped it shut again. 'A customer?' I muttered stupidly. And then I remembered. 'Oh him, he isn't coming after all.' I turned over and tried to snuggle back into the warmth.

'Husband, I know you were feasting at Marcus's last night and you probably have a throbbing head as a result, but you told me only yesterday that this man was due to come. A publicanus, I believe you said, on official business to the curia today, and you particularly asked me to make sure you were awake betimes, because he was likely to stay in Glevum overnight and come to see you early, before the magistrates convene. So I am doing as you asked.'

I grunted that there was no hurry after all.

My wife removed the coverings, more forcefully this time. 'If you continue lying there, you'll miss him when he calls. Daylight hours are shorter at this time of year and the roads are treacherous, so if you hope to gain that contract, you'll have to move at once. Besides, I hope to finish that batch of dye today, and you won't want to be here in the steam and smell. I've already sent the slaves to saddle up the mule.'

I forced my lids to open and tried to focus on my wife. She had clearly been out of bed herself for quite some time. The fire was burning brightly in the central hearth and the smell of cooking honeyed oatcakes filled the house. I gave a groan and shut my eyes again. These cakes are my usual breakfast and I am fond of them, but today the scent of baking made me nauseous. 'I don't feel well,' I muttered and pulled the covers up.

Gwellia pulled them down again. 'And both of us know why.'
She gave me an unsympathetic frown.

She was quite right, of course. I should not have imbibed
so much of Marcus's Rhenish wine. I'd lost a contract, been
out-manoeuvered by my host – and now I had the headache,
too, to blight my day!

'Oh very well,' I grumbled and sat up reluctantly. Tenuis –
the youngest of our slaves – was standing by my side, my tunic
at the ready, and he helped me pull it on over the under-tunic
I had worn to bed, but I waved away the bowl of water that
he'd brought to wash me in. 'I suppose I shall have to get used
to feeling like this every day, if they make me duumvir,' I
muttered, reaching for my sandals as I spoke.

'Duumvir?' My wife was collecting up the hanks of wool
she'd spun; a customer had partly paid me with a sheep, and
it had been her chief preoccupation ever since. We had skinned
it and roasted the most part in a pit, and she'd been busy making
use of what remained – rendering the fat, drying and salting
leftover strips of meat, making combs and soups and needles
from the bones, and putting the leather into urine pots to cure.
Now she was spinning and dyeing the fleece so she could weave.
But I'd caught her interest. 'A duumvir?' she repeated, with a
smile.

'I detect that you are pleased,' I muttered gloomily, 'although
I don't know why. You don't approve of Roman banquets much,
but there'll be lots of feasting to attend if Marcus has his way.
Political chatter with people you don't like and drinking too
much wine. To say nothing of poor digestion from eating fancy
food. Though perhaps I should be grateful for the prospect,
after all. At least we will not starve for want of work. I was
relying on a large commission from that customer today, but
– as I already told you – that won't be happening. I suppose I
had better go and tell Junio as much.'

She paid no attention to the last remark and I realised she
was beaming with delight. 'A duumvir! That's splendid,
husband,' she enthused, waving the slave away and stooping to
do my sandals up herself. 'I always said that you deserved some
recognition from the town.'

'I hope you still think so when you find that civic duties

keep me away from you and busy with Roman business at all hours!'

'How shall I know the difference?' she enquired, with a grin. 'You're always at your patron's beck and call in any case.'

I was reminded that I had yet to break the news to her about the latest task that I had somehow – foolishly – incurred. 'Well, certainly I shall be so for a day or two,' I said. 'He wants me to go down to Uudum – where my erstwhile client lived – and talk to his household about what happened there. Probably tomorrow – there are things to be arranged.'

'All the way to Uudum?' She was frowning, suddenly. 'So something serious has happened to your customer? I supposed that he had simply been delayed.'

'Serious?' I gave a hollow laugh – which made my own head spin. 'You could say that, I think. I said he wasn't coming – and that's because he's dead.' She was looking doubtful, as though I might have dreamt the whole affair, so I told the story as clearly as my addled brain allowed.

'By his own hand?' she murmured.

'It seems so,' I agreed. 'He left a note confessing what he'd done – gambling with the tax money and losing it – and a message came to Marcus, while I was there last night.' Her doubtfulness had given way to consternation now, and I could not resist the opportunity to add, 'Fortunate that I am not yet a duumvir. If I were a council-member now I'd have to help to make up the shortfall in revenue.'

Gwellia sat down beside me on the bed. This was clearly a new and shocking thought. 'If you really do not want the office, husband – and I can see why you might not – there must be things that you can do.'

'Such as what, by all the gods?'

'You can't defy your patron, that is obvious, but duumviri are generally elected, are they not? You'll have to make election speeches to the populace. Simply tell them that you don't feel qualified.'

'Marcus has ways of circumventing that – he's made that very clear!'

'But the people are the ones who have to vote – and social standing is all they think about! Say that you are honoured by your patron's confidence, but you've been in servitude and therefore feel unsuitable for such a noble task. That should do the trick. There are plenty of others who would like to take your place.'

Even in my befuddled state I saw that this was true! Titus might wave aside the fact that I was once a slave, but public opinion is another thing! There would indeed be election speeches – from the steps of the basilica itself – and though I lack Roman training in the art of rhetoric, when I have not had too much wine I can be eloquent. I would dissuade the town – politely – from acclaiming me, and there was nothing that Marcus could do to alter that. A simple, but effective strategy.

'There are times when I don't deserve you,' I said, thickly to my wife. I tried to pull her to me but she shook me off.

'Don't be silly, husband. You'd have thought it out yourself, if your brains weren't fuzzled by drinking all that wine! Now try and eat some breakfast and get off to the shop. It seems you've already lost one customer today, and – especially if you avoid election as you hope – we'll still require to eat.'

I gave a sigh of protest. 'I don't think I'll bother with the shop today,' I said, shuddering at the thought of travelling anywhere.

'Then you can chop some wood to feed the dye-house fire. I'll have to keep the hut warm to help dry out the wool when this next batch is finished – and that will be the last. I would ask the slaves, but they're not skilful with an axe. If you're here, you will get it done in half the time.' The thought of working with this headache made me groan aloud but she paid no attention. 'So that's decided. But if you're not going to town, you'd better explain affairs to Junio,' she said. 'No doubt he's already waiting for you at the gate.'

Junio, of course, is my adopted son, who works with me, minds the Glevum workshop when I am not there, and lives in the roundhouse enclosure next door to mine with his young wife and growing family. Generally we travel together into town – sometimes with me riding on the mule and Junio on foot – but always discussing the projects for the day. And he would be anxiously awaiting my arrival now, expecting to go and meet our customer before the courts convened.

I signalled to Tenuis to bring back the water bowl and to his amazement I plunged my head in it. That helped a little, and I struggled to my feet. I still felt slightly squeamish, and peculiarly detached, but I managed – at Gwellia's urging – to take an oatcake with me to force down, as I struggled out to meet the dawn.

Last night's cold wind had blown the rain away, but the rising sun this morning seemed unnaturally bright – though Junio did not appear to notice it. He was waiting on the corner of the lane, outside the gate to my enclosure, as he always did, wrapped in a hooded cloak. He greeted me at once.

'Good morning, Father, you look terrible!' was his cheerful salutation. 'Are you not feeling well?'

I shook my head, and wished I hadn't. 'Too much Rhenish wine at Marcus's last night.'

He laughed unsympathetically – and far too loudly, in my view. 'Ah! The consequence of wine. Boiled snails and onions, that is what you need – I had to prepare them for my previous master when I was very young. Better than the fried canaries that his friends preferred. I'll slip into the market for the ingredients and cook some up for you when we reach the workshop, if you like. Roman maladies require a Roman cure.'

The thought of boiled onions made my fragile stomach heave, and I made a face at him. 'I'm not going to the workshop. There's been a change of plan,' I said, just as my slave Minimus appeared with Arlina, the mule.

'A thousand pardons, master, I had trouble catching her.'

It was almost a pity to tell him that she would not be required.

He gave a rueful grin. 'I wondered if you might not want her after all, given the gossip in the servants' hall at Marcus's last night. I was sure Acacius Flauccus was the man you were to meet, but the mistress told me to go and saddle up the mule, and it was not my place to argue.' And he led the animal away.

'Gossip?' Junio enquired.

'Marcus has no notion of slaves as having ears! There was alarming news and he discussed it openly. But it isn't simply rumour, I'm afraid.' I told Junio what had happened at Uudum yesterday. 'Marcus wants me to go down and investigate,' I finished, ruefully. (I didn't mention that I'd accidentally half-suggested it.) 'As soon as possible, I rather think – certainly within a day or two, though it will take him a little time to make arrangements, I suppose.'

Junio sucked his breath in. 'Great Minerva!' he exclaimed. 'All the taxes gone! Do you want me to come with you?'

I shook my head again – forgetting that this had an unfortunate effect. 'Better if one of us is here to mind the shop, since we've lost a large commission . . .' I let the words trail off, as a small figure came running towards us down the lane. One of Marcus's pageboys, by the uniform – indeed, as he came closer, I recognised the face. It was one of the escort party which had seen me home last night.

'Citizen, Libertus,' he blurted breathlessly, as soon as he was near enough to speak. 'I bring a message from his Excellence.' He fell politely to one knee, though the lane at the corner is full of dust and stones.

I motioned to the lad that he could rise. 'Tell me the message.' I saw his doubtful look and said, reassuringly, 'You can speak before this citizen, he is my son.'

The page glanced doubtfully at Junio's work-tunic, but evidently decided that I must know my own son's rank. He cleared his throat and recited – in sing-song fashion – the words he'd learned by heart. 'Greetings from Marcus Aurelius Septimus. You are requested to call on him today.'

'Again?' I must have been fuddled to have spoken that aloud – one did not question Marcus's requests. 'Something further has arisen?'

The pageboy shook his head. 'Citizen, I fear I cannot tell you more. His message was simply that he wanted you to come as soon as possible – no later than an hour from now, if that's convenient.'

An hour! How did my patron expect me to calculate the time? There was not even any sun today, so that I could gauge its progress through the branches of the oak tree opposite. I would simply have to guess. And it wasn't in the least convenient, of course. But this time, I had the wit to simply nod.

'At least that gives me time to get my toga on,' I said – as much to Junio as to the messenger. 'It will have to be my old one, I'm afraid, although it's patched and mended and frayed around the hems – my best one is wet and muddy from last night.'

'Shall I take that to the fullers?' my thoughtful son enquired. 'I'll ask him to be quick. You'll want it if you're travelling, no doubt.'

'That would be kind,' I told him. 'I'll fetch it out for you. Though no doubt I shall have to buy another new one quite soon – and have it specially bleached and whitened, at my own expense, if I am to be a candidate – it is what the very word means, after all.' I spoke with bitterness. A chalk-white 'toga candida' is expected wear for anyone seeking election to the curia, though the moment they're elected most of them return to whatever kind of purple stripe they are entitled to. (I, of course, was not of patrician Roman birth and therefore did not qualify for any stripe at all.)

Junio was giving me a startled look. 'So you have finally agreed to be a candidate? Well, a good thing too, and I'm delighted, naturally. But I know how often you've refused the privilege. It must have been particularly potent wine!'

'It's only as replacement duumvir,' I mumbled. 'And only till the next regular election's due.'

He grinned. 'Or so you hope. Though – since it's a joint appointment and the office will be shared – perhaps the duties won't be very onerous.'

I snorted. Merely a responsibility for letting market stalls, the provision of water for the town, and the upkeep of all public spaces, fountains, roads, and drains! But I did not intend to be elected anyway, though I could not say that with my patron's servant listening in!

I told the page to hurry back and tell Marcus I would come – not that there really was any choice, of course – then I turned to Junio. 'I wonder what my patron wants me for? Changed his mind about this trip to Uudum, do you think?'

Junio shook his head. 'Thought of more instructions to give you, more than like. So I had better leave you, and go on into town. Send for me if you need me. In the meantime where's that muddy toga you wanted me to take?'

'I'll fetch it. I left it out to dry.' There were no slaves about to help me, so I hurried off myself and brought the bundle back to Junio. 'There you are. And there is something else that you can do for me. When you get to Glevum, make enquiries – see if any unfamiliar, fancy carriages were observed arriving at the town gates yesterday. Acacius Flauccus had a private one, it seems, which was seen to leave his house – and I'd like to know what had become of it. It was supposed to come to Glevum, so perhaps it did – though its owner was not in it.'

Junio nodded. 'Of course I'll do my best!' I saw the sparkle in his eyes. He has often helped me with enquiries before, and was clearly delighted that I'd asked him now. 'With luck I'll find a sentry on duty that we know,' he said. 'Otherwise, I'll ask the tanner's wife next door – she makes a point of knowing everything, so if anything unusual occurred, like a carriage which contained no passengers, she will have heard of it. I'll call in later on and let you know. But if I am to do all this, without a slave to help, I'll go at once – there's no time to be lost.' And he set off, whistling.

Minimus had come back, panting, to wait for my commands. 'The mistress says that I'm to wait on you. She says there is some wood we are to chop.'

I shook my head. 'Another change of plan. I'm summoned to my patron's as soon as possible. I suppose that after all, I'll have to take the mule.'

I had to smile at the expression on his face though, with my thumping headache, this morning I was not easily amused. I went back into the roundhouse to explain to Gwellia.

She heard me out, and snorted. 'I suppose this means that Kurso will have to chop the wood! And take all morning over it, no doubt. But if you're going to Marcus's you'll need this, all the same. It's an ancient recipe I made to clear your head. I thought you'd need it before you used the axe. I did not want you chopping fingers off.'

She forced me to sit down and swallow the concoction she'd prepared – whole raw eggs mixed with pepper and ground sage, washed down with more water from the spring than I could comfortably drink – while she and Tenuis wrapped wet cabbage leaves around my head. It was most unpleasant but perhaps it helped, for by the time I was ready to set off for Marcus's I was feeling a little more like my accustomed self.

FIVE

I took Minimus with me to lead Arlina down the lane – Marcus would expect me to be accompanied by a slave – and we trotted to the villa as quickly as we could. There was a land-slave standing near the gate, guarding a large and beautiful brown horse, so I left him to deal with Arlina as well, while my slave announced me to the gatekeeper.

Once again I was swiftly let inside, but I was not shown into the atrium to wait, though there was a visitor already there (presumably the rider of the horse, since he was wearing the uniform of a private messenger) kicking his heels beside the family shrine. However, to my astonishment – and his – I was immediately ushered through and out into the courtyard garden at the back.

Marcus was out there, lounging on a bench, wrapped in a crimson woollen cloak against the wind. He was embarrassingly unaffected by the night before – more accustomed to Rhenish wine, perhaps – and apparently absorbed in watching his small son playing with a top, while the nursemaid bounced the baby girl upon her knee and Julia looked on. He looked up as I appeared.

'Libertus, dear old friend,' he said at once, holding out his ring-hand for me to kiss, while with his left he waved the little page impatiently away. 'I wanted to see you before I went to town.'

I made the required obeisance, though I was on my guard. Doubly so, in fact. I had expected a meeting in the public rooms, not an informal audience in the peristyle. This studied lack of protocol was most unusual. And why was I admitted while others had to wait – people possessed of handsome horses, too?

'Patron,' I ventured warily. 'Please excuse my mended toga. My other one has gone to Glevum to be cleaned, but – as requested by your page – I came as nearly to the hour as I could guess.'

He looked amused. 'Don't worry about time. And you need

not have bothered to have your toga cleaned. You'll need a
sparkling one to wear as candidate, of course, but Titus Flavius
has promised to look one out for you – the one he wore when he
first stood for the curia himself. Finest wool and linen blend,
he says, and he proposes to make you a gift of it – since he's
now elected to a permanent seat and obviously will not be
requiring it himself.'

'Then I must thank him for his kindness.' I looked around.
'Is he somewhere here? I understood that he was to stay here at
the villa overnight?'

But Marcus shook his head. 'Too late to thank him now. Titus
Flavius and his litter set off just after dawn – immediately after
I'd despatched that messenger back to Uudum to tell them to
expect you there. Poor Titus Flavius. He hardly stayed to eat
– he was so anxious to be at the basilica betimes. They've called
an urgent meeting of the curia at the second hour, to determine
what to do about the tax. Though there's no reason for such
urgency, as I've instructed Titus to tell them: Flauccus's payment
would not normally be due for several months. He was bringing
it now only because he was planning to retire. We're not required
to render it until the usual date. I've suggested that the curia
does nothing until you've made enquiries.'

'That is hardly likely to assist though, Excellence, if Flauccus
lost the money gambling.'

'Ah that depends what he was betting on. I have every
confidence in your abilities. If you can prove it was illegal –
betting on dice, for instance, outside of the permitted period
of Saturnalia – we may be able to force the winner to repay.'

'If not, it will fall to the curia to make good the loss?'

'You will not be liable to contribute, of course.' He paused
to kick back the wooden top, which had whirled towards us as
the child whipped and whooped. 'You're not elected yet.
Speaking of which, Titus will propose you formally today and
make it known that I'm supporting you – no doubt he will have
done so by this time, in fact. So now you are officially a candidate. We'll arrange for you to address the populace, when you
return from Uudum – though you need not do so, if you do not
wish. The people expect it but it's mere formality. From here
on your election should be virtually secure.'

'I am more than happy to address the populace,' I said with truth. 'But you speak of Titus nominating me. You are not attending the curia yourself?'

He gave me a sly look. 'I shall go as soon as we have finished here. But something has arisen which I must discuss with you. Something of importance, which must be dealt with first.'

The fresh air and Gwellia's potion had improved my throbbing head, but the children's sudden laughter still went through me like a sword. I dropped my voice.

'In that case, Excellence, perhaps it would be wise to find a place where we can speak more privately? There are so many slaves.' I gestured around the courtyard, where at least a half-a-dozen of the household were busily at work, sweeping, weeding or picking kitchen herbs.

Marcus gave me a disbelieving look.

'My own attendant knew exactly what had happened here last night, because it was common gossip in the servants hall.' I went on, daringly. 'The house-slaves had been talking about what they'd overheard. So . . .?'

'Dear Jupiter!' My patron looked quite genuinely shocked. 'You may be right. We'll find somewhere more secluded. Follow me.' He rose and led the way towards an arbour set against the outer wall.

It is indeed secluded at other times of year, when it is half-screened by flowering shrubs and trees, but these – of course – were now completely bare so the place was hardly more private than the bench he'd left. At least, though, we were further from the peals of glee.

Marcus took the central place, ornately-carved and raised a hand's-span above the bench on either side, and patted the place beside him, and – reassured that my head would be appropriately lower than my host's – I sat down carefully.

'There are some additional instructions which you wish to give?' I enquired politely, after a short pause. 'Relating to my erstwhile customer, perhaps?'

My patron gave a laugh. 'Still disappointed in that contract which you lost?' he said. 'Don't worry about that. When you are duumvir you'll be awarding contracts, not accepting them – and that can be rewarding, if you choose aright. Not bribery, of course, but gifts of gratitude. When the time comes, I'll advise you what to do. In the meantime . . .' He gave that laugh again, '. . . since you're going to Uudum anyway, there's an extra little task that I would like you to perform.'

I said nothing, but my alarm must have been written in my face.

'Nothing arduous, my friend – the contrary in fact. I wish you to represent me at a wedding feast, that's all. It isn't difficult. You've done it once before.'

It was true that I had done so, several years ago, but that was when Marcus was on his way to Rome – overseas and physically unable to attend. This was something entirely different.

'It would be an honour, naturally,' I murmured, wishing that my brain was clearer so that I could think. 'But surely, Excellence, since this time you are here yourself . . .?' His expression did not alter so I tried flattery. 'It is your exalted presence which they are hoping for and I am clearly no kind of substitute, even if I bring your no-doubt handsome wedding gift. It would be the talk of Glevum to have you as a guest.'

My patron shook his head. 'Ah but it is not in Glevum, that is the concern. And it's taking place just when the Imperial legate will be here. He will be arriving within a day or two – as I believe I told you yesterday – and I must be here myself. You have heard of Portus Abonae, perhaps?'

'Off the road to Aquae Sulis, I believe.' I had only vaguely heard the name, in fact, but I made a daring guess, 'A river port, I think?' (That was not as clever as I hoped it seemed: 'Avon' – or 'Abon' – means 'river' in my native tongue, and 'Portus' was clearly the Latin word for 'entrance port'.) Presumably that was where the legate planned to land.

Marcus – who does not speak Celtic – looked impressed. 'Exactly so. A thriving little sea port settlement, though dependent on the tides. It's not really in our general jurisdiction here – it's too far south for that – but Glevum is the only court for many miles around that has the authority to deal with licensing.'

I could not see where this was leading, but I gave a little nod. 'So there's something for the Imperial legate to rule on when he comes?'

Marcus looked affronted. 'Nothing of the kind. It lies within my powers to grant official licences, so when one of the local Celtic chieftains applied for one, a year or so ago, of course I heard the case.' He paused, as if expecting some response.

'Naturally, Excellence!' I was still attempting to work out why this was relevant. 'But there were objections?' I ventured, finally.

'I would have overruled them if there were. No one else was likely to apply. The seawater's too diluted by the river, in a general way, but he owns swampy marshland on the seaward side, easy to flood to salt pans and evaporate. The man explained it all when he applied. If he was convinced that he could make a saltern pay, I saw no reason why he should not try. I granted his petition, although I set the price quite high.'

I tried to look astute. 'Half of the expense of salt is carting it around – and most of the useful salt works are miles away from here – so he might have done good trade,' I said. 'But the enterprise has failed?'

Marcus gave a laugh. 'Libertus, what has made you such a pessimist today? The fellow, Darturius, has prospered vastly since – in fact, that is the point. He was so delighted with my part in his success that he sent to me some moons ago, inviting me to attend his daughter's wedding, later in the year. As the guest of honour, naturally. I was sufficiently flattered to accept – though I confess that I forgot about it afterwards. But I've had word just this morning that the date's been set, exactly at the period when the legate will be here.'

So that was it. Portus Abonae – or somewhere near it – was where the marriage feast would be! And he hoped I would attend it in his stead! I forced myself to smile. 'But surely, patron, this was a personal reward?'

Marcus raised an eyebrow. 'Oh, he'll understand that an Imperial legate must take precedence. Sending a prospective duumvir will meet the case, I'm sure.' He broke off as a little slave came hurrying towards us from the direction of the house, carrying a platter of fresh figs and bread and cheese.

'Master, a thousand pardons. The kitchen has just learned that a citizen has called.' It is usual to offer something to a visitor, of course, but my fragile stomach was rebelling at the sight. Fortunately, Marcus waved it loftily away.

'Not now. My friend and I have important matters to discuss.'

I looked at him, relieved but more dubious than before. So I was 'friend' again! I am fond of Marcus, but friendship doesn't enter into it. He is my patron and I am his humble client – as he was demonstrating by this interview.

'What was I saying?' he resumed, as the lad retreated to the kitchen block. 'Ah yes, the wedding feast. You're just the man to send. As a Celt yourself you will be quite at home.'

Despite myself, I felt a flicker of interest at that. The last time I had attended a Celtic wedding was my own – when I was young and first took Gwellia to wife. 'It is to be a Celtic marriage then?'

I could envisage it: the 'hand-fasting', in which the couple's linked hands are bound with cords, then the lovely ritual of the oathing-stone, where they jointly hold a pebble while they make their vows, then 'liberate' it to the ancient gods by dropping it into a running stream. All followed by a hearty feast of roasted ox and warm, spiced mead. There might be worse occasions on which to be a guest.

'I shouldn't think so.' Marcus dashed my hopes. 'She's marrying a Roman citizen. Gnaeus something, I forget the details. Twice her age and widowed but looking for an heir – the girl's freeborn, of course, so there's no bar to wedding her – though I confess I'm surprised he chose a woman of no rank at all. Doubtless her dowry plays a part in it. Her father has extensive property.'

Another awkward moment, while I considered what to say. As a Celt the girl would have the right to turn her suitor down – unlike a Roman bride – and this was not a love-match, by the sound of it. But perhaps she hoped to help her father to preserve his lands by this strategic union with a wealthy widower. (That was quite possible. Portions of many traditional estates have been 'required for army purposes' and either purchased for a fraction of their worth, or simply annexed if the owner would not sell. It has been a source of friction with native landowners – not unconnected with the presence of rebels in the woods.)

'It's brackish marshland on the coast, of course,' Marcus went on, answering my question before I uttered it. 'Not much use for raising animals or crops. But with the salt licence . . .'

'Its value has increased enormously,' I said. 'So both the father and this Gnaeus are grateful, I suppose?'

'With reason! Their good fortune is entirely due to me.' Marcus is not given to false modesty. 'And my non-appearance will not alter that. So I'll send their messenger straight back to them, with a letter explaining everything – and tell them that you're coming in my place. The only question is when you will arrive. How long do you imagine you will need to be in Uudum on the way?'

I shook my head. How could I answer that? 'It all depends on what there is to learn. I want to talk to Loftus and see the house at least. Enquire about the gambling, as you yourself suggest. And perhaps examine Acacius Flauccus's body too – just in case there is something I could learn.'

Marcus shook his head. 'I've already sent a message to the local army post telling them to hold Loftus until you arrive, and not to press him any more till then. I'm sure you would approve. And it should be possible to see the corpse, as well, unless of course the funeral has already taken place.' He saw my startled look. 'Acacius Flauccus had no family, and in the absence of the household slaves, I believe the state is taking care of it. Meaning the army detachment in this case. They asked permission in their message to the curia last night, and I was happy to agree – provided we are not required to defray the costs. But I'll send word that you would like to see him first, if possible – Darturius's slave can take it, it is almost on his way. Though you will have to hurry, they will not welcome much delay – they'll fear an unquiet spirit, with a suicide.'

'But it will take some time to make arrangements, Excellence, and if you require me to attend this wedding too—'

He cut me off. 'I'm going to provide you with my private gig – till you get to Uudum anyway. I will ask the army to provide you with onward transport then – they will have carts at their disposal, or they can requisition one. And I'll furnish you with a little money for emergencies – though there should not be much expense – and with a warrant to use the military inns. It's only a question of your going a little further on – so works out quite fortuitously, really.'

Fortuitous? A visit to a man I'd never met, down roads I'd

never travelled, at the wettest time of year, only to arrive at
'swampy marshland' in the end – but I dared not say as much.
'Uudum's hardly on the road to Abonae,' I ventured, daringly.

'Oh no doubt there will be all kinds of ancient tracks – though
I don't suggest you use them, at this time of year. Better to use
the military road and take advantage of the *mansiones* – my
warrant will give you access, and you'll find one every twenty
miles or so.'

'An unfortunate time to leave my family,' I went on. 'I
hope it will be possible to return before the Ides. One does
not care to be away at Saturnalia.' When slaves become the
masters for a while, and everyone is occupied with feasts and
merriment, public roads can be deserted and therefore
dangerous.

He affected not to understand. 'Strange time to have a
wedding, but that has been the choice. The bride was hoping
for the January Kalends, I believe – new beginnings and all
that sort of thing – but no Roman will marry a virgin on a
festal day, of course. So they have settled on the day before
the Nones. But if you have finished at Uudum before then, go
straight on to the wedding. I have been offered hospitality
whenever I arrive, for as long as I require it – which, of course,
will equally apply to you.'

And if I had not finished? I thought, privately, doing the
calculation in my head. 'The Nones? But that is only seven
days away.' It hardly gave me time to question anyone about
the missing tax.

'By which time the Imperial legate will be here.' Marcus's
concern was only for the visitor from Rome. 'Though you are
right, of course. To get things done you will want to leave at
once – just as soon as Titus sends this toga to your house. He
promised he would do so before the day was out, so you could
set off this very afternoon, if it arrives in time.'

'This afternoon?' I echoed, appalled.

'My gig is swift so you could reach the nearest mansio, at
least. Oh, and one other thing, when you get to the last mansio
before Portus Abonae, report your arrival to the authorities.
They'll signal to Darturius and he'll send a man for you – the
area is so marshy that people have been lost, sucked into

the sands or carried by the tide, so it requires a local to lead
you on the track.'

My heart sank even further, if that were possible. Bad
enough to have to travel there at all, with weather, bandits,
bears and wolves to think about, without the prospect of being
drowned as well.

Marcus was smiling. 'I'll provide you with a wedding gift
you can present, and all the other items, when I send the gig.
That won't be until this afternoon, of course – I shall be using
it to take me to the curia first – but I'll send it back to you at
once and arrange a hiring-carriage to bring me home again. But
now I have this warrant to prepare, before I leave. And an
answer to Darturius – you may have seen his messenger, he's
waiting in the atrium to take back my reply. And I'd better write
a letter to the Uudum army post. It's too complicated to require
him to learn it all by heart. So, if you have no questions . . .?'

I had a thousand questions, but I dared not ask. My patron
was already rising to his feet. This was a dismissal and I bowed
myself away, leaving Marcus to admire his son's increasing
prowess with the top (I could only guess where he'd seen
whipping skill exhibited).

A page appeared from nowhere and accompanied me back
through the atrium. On the way I glimpsed Darturius's messenger
again – a handsome sulky boy – who was standing by the altar
to the household goods, moodily examining the remnants of
this morning's sacrifice.

He scarcely bothered to glance up as we came in and – seeing
only an aging Celt in a battered toga – he curled his lip and
looked away again.

I hurried out, retrieved my slave and mule and set off home
to tell Gwellia the news. As we approached the roundhouse,
two unpleasant things occurred. We were forced into the bushes
by the sulky messenger, who galloped past us at deliberate
speed and – almost at that moment – it began to rain again.

SIX

There was a pungent smell as we approached my gate, and clouds of billowing smoke. Not a conflagration, as a stranger might suppose, but Gwellia in the dye-house. 'I see your mistress is at work,' I murmured to Minimus as he helped me from the mule. 'Brewing up the oak-bark and acorn-cups, by the smell of it.'

'I hope there are enough,' he answered, ruefully. 'Otherwise she'll send me out to find some more.' He hunched down against the drizzle as he spoke.

Gwellia is always grumbling that I permit the slaves to answer back but – since she was inside, simmering the yarn – I did not feel inclined to reprimand the boy. In fact, I actually laughed. 'This is the final batch, she told me earlier.' I said. 'Besides, she is using Tenuis to help her now. You can hear her giving him orders. So you take Arlina off around the back to graze, then you can attend me in the house. I expect there will still be wood for us to chop.'

Minimus nodded and hurried the mule towards the field, while I opened the enclosure gate and, pulling my cape-hood up against the rain, walked up through the evil-smelling steam towards the roundhouse door.

Gwellia came out of the dye-house to greet me, her grey hair damp and her arms stained brown from handling the dye. Her face was red with perspiration but she summoned up a smile. 'Ah husband, there you are! Kurso's started on the wood-pile. What did Marcus want?'

I sheltered under the doorway of the slave hut opposite and gave her a quick outline of what had just occurred. 'So now – quite apart from this nonsense of becoming duumvir, and going to talk to Loftus about this suicide – I'm required to attend this wedding on his account, as well.'

Her response surprised me. 'Well, a good thing too. It's high time that your patron sent you somewhere nice, where you'll

be treated as an honoured guest,' she said. 'Besides, if it's
part-Celtic, you'll enjoy it, I expect. When is Marcus expecting
you to go?'

'As soon as possible,' I said. 'Possibly as early as this afternoon.
He's going to send his private gig for me.'

Her face had fallen. Clearly she had not expected that I'd go
so soon, but she rallied with her usual practical good sense. 'Are
you going to take a servant? Tenuis could be spared. If so, I'll
find him a cleaner uniform.'

I thought of little Tenuis, who hated travelling, and how
embarrassing it would prove to be if jolting in my patron's
dashing gig caused him to be physically sick. I shook my head.
'Marcus's driver will guard me on the road, and when we reach
a mansio they'll have people there, specially detailed to look
after guests. And at Uudum they'll be specially anxious to take
care of me – Marcus has sent to warn them that I am on my
way, so they'll be expecting me.'

'And this famous salt merchant? Won't he expect you to have
brought a slave?'

'They'll no doubt provide an attendant for me while I'm
there – Marcus would do that if he had a guest, and for his
representative I'm sure they'll do no less. Darturius is even
sending someone to guide me to the house. So I shall have
attendants everywhere I go. Better than having Tenuis crammed
into the gig, where he would only have to crouch down on the
floor. There's only room for one proper passenger.'

My wife looked dubious but she gave a nod. 'No doubt you
are right. I own I would be glad of his assistance here. I haven't
finished salting all the sheep-meat yet. And you won't be away
for very long, I don't suppose? The wedding host won't expect
you to linger afterwards, so you should be home for Saturnalia.'

'I hope so too,' I told her truthfully. 'I wouldn't welcome
spending the "misrule season" on the road – especially if it's
going to rain like this.'

'Well, take your warmest cloak,' she urged – as though I
hadn't intended to wear my *birrus*, anyway. 'The one you're
wearing isn't thick enough. And I suppose you'll have to
take your toga? Though it's acceptable to wear more comfortable clothes when travelling, isn't it?'

'A toga will be expected if I'm representing Marcus,' I pointed out. 'Though it's my second one. At least I won't be trying to walk about in it. And there's little else I'll have to take. A marriage present to deliver, that's all. His warrant will see that I'm supplied with everything, and he's giving me a little cash, he says, in case of unexpected additional expense.'

'I'll find you a cleaner tunic, anyway – wear it under that one and it will keep you warm and you can change them over, when you get there, to look respectable. Your others are both washed and mended, so you can take your pick of brown or green. Don't sleep in both, of course. You'll want to keep one moderately clean till you arrive – though the gods alone know what your toga will look like in the end.'

I nodded. I could wear the extra tunic while I was in the gig and remove it when I went to bed. 'Let's hope this weather clears a little, so I don't get caked with mud. The gig is open, and these are not ideal conditions to be travelling.'

'They are not ideal conditions for doing anything,' she agreed. 'Not even dyeing wool, although it needed to be done. And that reminds me . . .' She picked up a piece of kindling and waved it with a smile.

I sighed. 'You want that wood chopped for the dye-house fire!'

Gwellia nodded. 'Kurso's made a start. You take that toga off and I will air it by the fire, and I'll look out both your tunics. Or rather Tenuis will. I daren't touch your clothing with my hands like this. But while you're working I will heat some soup – you'll be glad of something warming if you are travelling later on.'

The work itself was warming. There was still a half-tree waiting in the pile, and I vented my frustration on the task. Kurso was glad to help me move the logs and give me the stone from time to time to grind the axe-blade sharp, so I had a useful pile of fuel before I realised it. I straightened up and grunted. 'Put the axe away,' and Kurso proudly hurried off with it.

Hard to remember, looking at him now, that he had been so frightened when he came to us, and so used to dodging blows, that he could move faster backwards. I followed him slowly to the roundhouse, aware that I'd unwittingly allowed the rain to soak me through.

Kurso was waiting. 'Master, I'm to tell you that there's some soup there in the bowl. The mistress has gone back to the dye, before the colour gets too strong, and I'm to help Minimus fetch water from the spring, so she can rinse the wool.' He flashed a grin and hastened out again, carrying a pail. He was as wet as I was, but he didn't seem to care.

I slumped down on the stool beside the fire and took off my dripping cloak, which was making little puddles on the earthen floor, though I decided that I'd eat my soup before I changed my tunic – to keep the fresh ones clean. They were laid out and waiting on the bed, while my toga steamed gently on a wooden frame nearby. Gwellia had clearly supervised all this.

She was in the dye-house, now. I could hear her, giving instructions to Tenuis. 'Take care! It's heavy. Make sure you don't drop it on the ground!' I could almost see him, struggling with the stick, lifting the dyed yarn from the steaming vat into the rinsing pot.

I grinned and reached for the bowl of waiting soup. It was delicious – flavoured with the bones of that same sheep from which we'd had the wool. But I'd hardly taken more than a few sips of it before my wife came in. She was wearing a frown which I recognised of old – something had displeased her, and I was responsible.

'Husband there is a horseman at the gate. He says he has a parcel for you. I dared not touch it, I might cover it with dye – and Tenuis is worse. The other slaves are fetching water for the rinse, so I had no slave to send.'

'Meaning I'll have to go and pick it up myself?' I put down the bowl and struggled to my feet. 'I wonder what it is?'

She raised her eyebrows. 'The driver says you are expecting it.' But you've not told me about it, her expression said.

I frowned. 'It can't be my best toga from the fuller yet, and . . . Oh, of course! It will be that toga candida, from Titus, I expect. He promised me he'd send one.' I glanced at Gwellia as I hurried out and saw with satisfaction that she was mollified.

It was indeed from Titus, a parcel wrapped up in a leather cloth and tied with hempen cords. I prised the folds apart without undoing it and saw the cloth within: finest quality, chalked to a whiteness that took my breath away. I nodded to the man who had brought it to the gate.

'Tell Titus Flavius that it's more than I deserve and I thank him sincerely for the gift.'

He raised a brow at me. 'There will be no opportunity for that. My instructions were to bring it here to you, return to the villa and collect some documents and a wedding gift that you are to present, and then come back for you. I am to drive you for the next few days, it seems.'

So this was the gig-driver my patron promised me? I bowed acknowledgement. 'I should of course have known the uniform, but I did not recognise your face.'

It was a face you would remember, in a general way. A big, broad, bearded, flat-nosed countenance – as if its owner had been in a fight – under a mop of unruly dark brown curls. But the massive shoulders, deep chest and muscled arms suggested that this gig-slave would win any such affray.

He smiled, revealing a full set of perfect teeth. 'I'm a recent acquisition by his Excellency,' he said. 'He only bought me half a moon ago. I had a birth name, but they call me Victor now.'

So someone else had thought that he would win a fight! I could not suppress a smile. 'I shan't forget,' I told him, truthfully. 'Thank you for the parcel. Now go, as you've been told, and I'll see you at this gate again when you return. Though, where's the gig? You didn't come on foot?'

He shook his head. 'I've left it down there, where I could tie the animal.' He gestured with a huge, rein-calloused hand. 'We shan't be taking that horse, anyway. I've pushed him hard today. There is a fresh mare in the stables which I've been told to use – I'll get her in the shafts. Apart from that I should not be very long. Nearer a half-hour than a whole one, I would guess.'

In fact it was much sooner. I had hardly drunk my soup before Victor and the gig were at the gate again. He had arranged a sort of cushion on the seat and tied on a kind of awning on a frame to cover me – obviously these were luxuries that Marcus sometimes used. I would ride in more comfort than I had supposed – especially as the rain had almost stopped by now.

'The wedding gift you are to carry, citizen, is underneath the seat. Watch how you handle it. It's very heavy, I suspect it's made of gold.' I looked at the package – it was circular, leading me to guess it was a platter of some kind. I placed my precious clothing-parcel beside it on the floor, where they were (fairly) sheltered from the rain, and Victor helped me up into the gig.

He had other things to give me, though, before we left. There was the promised little drawstring purse of bronze and silver coins – not a fortune, but welcome none the less – which I fastened on my belt where it was conveniently disguised. And finally, the travel document inside a special leather pouch.

It was an open warrant, necessarily, since I would have to use it several times – meaning that Marcus had not devoted a sheet of precious vellum to it, but scrawled on a writing-tablet (the kind which folds in half to make a box) and simply pressed his seal-ring hard into the wax – literally his signature – and affixed another impression in sealing-wax onto the tie. I would have to be careful, as the days went on, to preserve the seals intact – though his crest was burned with poker-work into the outer case, so there could be little doubt as to whose permission it contained. I placed it very carefully beneath the seat as well.

'Ready, citizen?' Victor had climbed into the driver's seat.

I nodded, and waving farewell to Gwellia and my slaves, I sat back in the gig. Victor urged the horse into a trot and we bowled quickly out along the lane and joined the military road that took us south.

SEVEN

I have ridden in a variety of gigs – including a previous one of Marcus's – but this was different.

'Based on a pattern from the Eastern Provinces,' Victor told me as we bowled along. 'Marcus was driven in one, briefly, when he was in Gaul – during his recent abortive trip to Rome – and he was so impressed that he commissioned one himself when he got home. And bought me to go with it,' he added with a smile. 'Takes a practised hand to manage one of these.'

I could see what he meant. It was smaller and lighter than the usual gig – which made it less robust – but the speed of progress was astonishing. So fast in fact that I could manage no reply, so there was little further conversation after that.

Inevitably we lurched and bounced a lot, but Victor was as good a coachman as he claimed, and avoided the worst irregularities in the road, so travel was more exhilarating than exhausting – to start with, anyway. There were even built-in 'comforts' for the passenger – stout supports to cling to, a backing to the seat and provision for that cushion if required – though comfort in a moving vehicle is relative, at best. The flimsy awning, in particular, was not a great success. It swayed alarmingly, showering us with the raindrops it was supposed to save us from, but fortunately the drizzle largely stopped and, though we threw up muddy water as we passed, that did not reach us in the gig. (Although several roadside stallholders were badly drenched, I fear.)

But I could see why Marcus had been so impressed. We were out of the environs of the town and trotting past the fields of the *terratorium* (the extensive farm that produced provisions for the garrison) far more quickly than I thought was possible – though, admittedly, that was also because other travellers moved aside, in deference to Victor's striking scarlet uniform, which marked him as the servant of a citizen of rank.

Even when we reached a contingent of soldiers on the march, there was no question of our taking to the verge to let them pass, as any normal citizen would be required to do. The centurion merely glanced at the unusual gig and Victor's uniform, and moments later was ordering his men to halt and form two ranks, one on each side of the road, while we went bowling down the middle like a triumphant general. I had been ready with the warrant, but there was no need for it.

Victor seemed unmoved by all these tokens of respect, but it was strange to find them accorded to myself – though I'd witnessed them before in my patron's company, and Marcus regarded them as no more than his due. I was getting a glimpse of what life was like for high-born citizens. And for officials like duumviri, perhaps? A tempting notion, but I put the thought aside and concentrated on simply hanging on, as we swooped along.

After a little, though, the first elation of fast progress ebbed and the journey became, like any other, an ordeal of jolting bones and jarring teeth. But there remained one consolation in the speed – it was not long before we reached the nearest mansio.

It was still full daylight, too, when it came into sight, though a dull glow in the west showed where the setting sun was hidden by the clouds. I feared that Victor would drive past and hope to reach the next establishment before darkness fell, but to my relief he pulled up at the gate.

'Better to stop here and not become benighted on the road,' he said, as though he read my thoughts. 'And we have been moving very fast. The horse will be improved by rest and sustenance.'

'And so will I,' I told him, feelingly, though I was a little anxious about presenting myself – a mere civilian tradesman – at a military inn, in spite of the permit I was clutching in my hand.

I need not have been concerned. Our reception was respectful. The merest mention of my patron's name, as Victor dropped down from the gig to hold the horse, was enough to have the sentry scurrying inside, and a moment later the *mansionarius* himself come bustling out.

'Greetings, citizen!' He was a short, fat, red-faced fellow in a burnished uniform – an army officer of course, but clearly one no longer used to marching very much. He glanced briefly at the warrant that I held out to him, but it appeared to be a mere formality. 'You are a client of Marcus Septimus, I see? Welcome to our little mansio.' He fussed about while I dismounted from the gig, ignoring Victor, who gave me a conspiratorial wink.

I rescued the awkward parcels from underneath the seat. They were something of a struggle – especially Marcus's, which was both extremely heavy and difficult to hold – but I refused the offer of an orderly to help. 'I'll manage,' I said staunchly, as I followed the mansionarius inside.

'I hope you will be comfortable here,' the man went on, as we passed through a compact but bustling stable yard. 'This is only a simple roadside staging-post and inn, scarcely bigger than one of the *mutationes* . . .' He paused, looking at me sideways to make sure I understood.

I did. The modesty was false. He was clearly proud of his small establishment. I was only a civilian, but I knew what mutationes were – barely more than little stable-stops where imperial couriers could snatch a meal and change a tired horse. These places were essential to the Imperial Post – with them a good rider might make two hundred miles a day – but they were hardly advertisements for hospitality.

I realised that a compliment was expected. 'Though – unlike them – you do have beds, I hope?'

It was idiotic but he laughed as though I'd made a splendid jest. 'Ah, citizen, we do indeed! We're quite well-appointed, in a modest way! Though other inns have more facilities – for instance there is no bathhouse here. But we offer the basics, as you'll agree, I hope. This way, citizen.'

He set off and I followed him again, this time through a corridor into a larger court, where a series of small rooms led off on either side. One door stood open, showing a narrow mattress-bed within, a stool to sit on, a table for one's lamp and a mat where a slave could bed down at one's feet.

It might be basic but it looked inviting to my travel-weary bones – and a staircase gave promise of more accommodation above. I glanced at the mansionarius, expecting to be shown into the room, but instead I was ushered firmly on.

'I've put you on the west side, citizen, and I'll have a brazier brought – much better to have heating at this time of year – and I'll have an orderly attend you with clean water for a wash and arrange for the kitchen to provide you with a meal. There is a dining area, but perhaps you would prefer to have the food sent to your room?'

I murmured that I was content to eat in the refectory like anybody else.

'Then this is where you'll find it, citizen.' He flung open a door, revealing a long, low cluttered area, with a long central table and stools on either side. Another visitor – a citizen of importance by the narrow purple stripe – was sitting at the far end by the fire, scooping what looked like porridge from a bowl. He looked up without interest and went back to his meal. No reclining called for here, I noted with relief. I nodded. 'Splendid,' and was ushered out again.

'If there is anything further you require, you have only to ask. Send the orderly to me and I will personally ensure that your request is met.' The mansio-keeper was almost bobbing, in his desire to please. He led the way to a wider door at the far end of the court, where he made great play of producing a large key and opening the lock. 'I hope that you'll be comfortable here.'

I shook my head, not in disagreement, but astonishment. From previous experience of military inns, I'd had a clear idea of what I might expect: stabling for our animal, food and bedding for my slave, and very much the amenities that I'd glimpsed elsewhere – a clean straw mattress, blankets and refreshment – for myself. So a room with decorated walls, a luxurious frame-bed, large storage chest and comfortable stool was a complete surprise.

'You'll find rugs and pillows in the big chest opposite. Will this be to your satisfaction, citizen?' He looked slyly at me, then blurted suddenly, 'If so, I hope you'll tell his Excellence as much?'

Was he hoping for promotion to a larger mansio, perhaps? 'It's beyond my expectations. I'll tell my patron so,' I assured him and he went off, gratified.

Marcus himself could scarcely have enjoyed more luxury! I

took off my birrus, sat down on the bed and looked around the
room, still puzzled at such provision in a tiny mansio. So when
the promised orderly appeared soon afterwards, bearing the
washbowl, I ventured to enquire.

'To what do I owe such amazing opulence?'

He raised a brow at me. He was a tall, spare fellow with a
lugubrious face and an air of being ill-used by the world. The
legs beneath the faded red tunic were lean and muscular, and
livid scars across the tanned skin of his cheek and arm suggested
battle-wounds. An auxiliary soldier, withdrawn from active
service, I surmised, and disappointed by this rural posting to
an inn. His voice was gutteral. 'We always keep a special room
prepared,' he murmured, moodily. 'All mansios are supposed
to have one, for the Emperor, if he should happen by.'

'Surely that isn't likely?' I'd visited military inns before, but
never heard of that.

He gave me a pitying glance. 'Of course not, citizen, and
it is generally ignored, especially in little places such as this.
But the provincial governor paid a visit once, apparently, and
arrangements had to be hastily prepared. He wasn't pleased
and he reported it. This room has been kept ready ever since,
in case some other travelling dignitary arrives. It could happen,
I suppose. It's rumoured that an Imperial legate may soon
be visiting the Glevum area.' He handed me the napkin so I
could dry my face. 'But as to why they've given it to you . . .?'
He let the sentence hang.

I understood, now, perfectly. 'I'm representing my patron, an
important patrician whom the legate's visiting,' I said, pacifically.
'I hold his warrant requesting "all assistance" on the road. And
the same goes for my coachman, I assume. I see there is a slave
mat. Is he to sleep here too?' I was divesting myself of my outer
garment as I spoke.

'Oh, you mean the driver of the gig?' He spoke as if such
people were beneath his dignity. 'He's been given a bed-space
in the stable block where he can keep an eye on both the horse
and cart. Someone has already taken him some stew, I understand – and there'll be something else for you in just a little
while.'

I nodded. Army 'stew' is generally porridge with bits of meat in it – what I'd seen the other diner spooning up, in fact – sustaining, but not designed to tempt the appetite. If Marcus's warrant meant a better meal, I would not complain. 'I plan to eat it in the public room,' I said.

He raised his eyebrows at me in surprise. 'Do you intend to put your toga on again? I could help you drape it on, if you desire. Or perhaps you have another you'd prefer to wear?' He looked meaningfully at my parcel as he spoke, and I saw that Titus's toga was emerging from the folds.

I'd not considered the need to dress up formally, but clearly – if I was to be favoured with a special meal – I would have to demonstrate such poor pretentions to rank as I possessed. Perhaps I should have eaten in my room – but it was too late now. I briefly considered the toga candida, but then I shook my head. I dared not stain it so early in the trip.

'What I have is quite sufficient,' I replied, allowing him to wind me into the awkward thing again. 'Now, perhaps you'd lead the way. Supposing that it is a convenient time for me to eat?'

'But what about your parcels, citizen? Is there nothing of value that you need to guard? And that warrant, too, perhaps?'

This was a problem that had not occurred to me. One does not expect to be robbed in an official mansio. Though perhaps the man was right. Marcus's present, for example, was likely to be gold – and therefore well worth the attention of a thief.

'We could of course provide a guard for it,' the man went on. 'I could do the job myself. I'm sure that if you ask the mansion-arius . . .? Shall I take the message that you request a man to watch?' He hardly waited for me to accept before he hurried off – so eagerly, that I was convinced that this was what he'd been planning all along. I wondered what other, less pleasant, duties he'd been spared.

I had scarcely time to spread my birrus out across the stool to dry, and find the promised bedding from the chest, before the door was tapped and opened and the orderly was back, now sporting a breastplate and brandishing a spear.

'I don't know how you come to deserve it, citizen, but the

mansionarius has ordered the kitchen to serve you his own intended meal. I am to escort you to the dining area, and then keep watch on your possessions while you eat.'

He said this with relish, confirming what I'd thought. I made no comment, merely nodded and permitted him to escort me back to the refectory, though it would not have been remotely difficult to find it for myself.

The previous occupant had disappeared by now, and the place beside the fire was set for me instead. A plate and knife had been provided, and a serving-slave was standing by to serve the food for me. I tried to chat to him, in vain – years of servitude had taught him not to gossip with the guests – and after a few monosyllables in reply, I gave it up and turned my full attention to the food.

Clearly the inn-manager did not spare himself. There was a plate of delicious hare-meat stewed with leeks, accompanied by a hunk of army bread, which – washed down with a beaker of sour watered wine – more than satisfied my appetite. The mansionarius himself came in to ask if all was well, bringing a taper as it was getting dark.

'Refreshing, citizen?' he queried as I raised the beaker to take a final draught.

I could have wished for a different kind of drink – the memories of yesterday were all too clear – but I feared to be discourteous. 'That was splendid, thank you very much.' Tomorrow I would ask for water, I assured myself, as he ushered me across the court back to my room again. (Those who merit the Imperial room can't be allowed to move without attendants – I was learning that.)

I did not need an escort to remind me where my quarters were. Scarface was standing self-importantly outside, leaning on his weapon, and he leaped to open the door for me. The promised brazier was glowing cheerfully and a taper was already burning in a holder on the wall.

'I had them light that for you!' Scarface was standing at the door. 'Couldn't have you groping in the dark.' Evidently he'd now appointed himself my special guardian – and would no doubt expect a hefty tip as a reward.

I dismissed him, to his evident dismay, and shut the door

again. I was suddenly and utterly exhausted by my day – though probably the recent wine contributed. I just had time to take my outer garments off and lie down on my fancy Roman bed before I fell into a deep and instant sleep.

EIGHT

I was wakened the next morning by a strident trumpet-call. Stirring, no doubt, but I was not expecting it and I leapt out of bed with a rapidity which would have astonished my good wife. Perhaps it should not have startled me – this was a military establishment, after all – but I had not anticipated that a tiny roadside mansio would sound the dawn *buccina*, like a full-scale garrison. But this one evidently did.

The brazier had burned down overnight and the Emperor's lodgings had grown distinctly cold. Since I was already – unintentionally – on my feet, I threw my cloak around me (fortunately it was largely dry by now) and opened my door to look outside, onto the central court. The dawn was cloudless, and in the chilly morning light there was the trumpeter himself returning to his quarters, carrying his curved bugle underneath his arm. He paused politely when he caught sight of me.

'Can I be of service, citizen? You'd like an orderly, perhaps, to bring a light repast and help you wash and dress?'

I murmured that I would and – not long afterwards – my guard of the night before appeared, in full parade-kit and jamming on his helmet as he came. He did not look glad to see me. Obviously he'd just completed dawn parade and I had interrupted his breakfast plans.

'You wanted something, citizen? I've been assigned to you again.' The words themselves were not uncivil, but Scarface could not have sounded less enthusiastic if he tried.

I told him what I wanted – washing water and a little food and drink – and he went morosely off to fetch what I required. Then with his assistance I quickly washed and dressed (in a toga, this morning I decided, since it wasn't raining now, and I wanted to look official when I arrived at Uudum.) Then, after a hurried meal of fruit and bread, declared that I was now ready for the road. Scarface made no attempt to assist me with my cloak, so with a flourish I picked it up myself and threw it round my shoulders, saying briskly, 'Now, how can I find my driver and the gig? I imagine that they are already at the gate awaiting me.'

'They are indeed, citizen, and have been for some time.' Scarface gave me a thin-lipped, mirthless grin. 'But the mansion-arius would like to speak to you before you leave. A matter of considerable importance, he says. So if you wouldn't mind delaying your departure till he's free? He's occupied at present with another visitor.'

He could have told me this before, of course, and saved me from bolting my breakfast quite so fast, but I tried to react to the news with dignity. 'In that case I'd better let my driver know.'

That little grin again. 'He's already been informed.'

Scarface was being deliberately unhelpful, though doing nothing of which I could actually complain – probably because I'd refused his services last night. No doubt he had been hoping for a handsome tip (and perhaps a dispensation from fatigues today) for standing guard till dawn.

I summoned up a little smile of my own. 'Please tell your superior to let me know when he is free, and I will be delighted to come and wait on him. His office will be more convenient than here, I'm sure, and I expect the mansio slaves will want to clean this room.'

No doubt the mansionarius would have come to me, but I was not sorry to find a task which took Scarface somewhere else, instead of having him smirking at me from the door. It was slightly inconvenient for him, of course – first to take my message to the senior officer, and then return to escort me back to him, when the moment came. At which point he'd be obliged to assist me with my parcels, too.

I was amused to see that Scarface had worked that out himself, because the smirk had vanished and the long-suffering air was back. 'Naturally, citizen. Whatever you command. If you would be good enough to wait?' He set off scowling in the direction of the archway opposite.

I waited, though a little nervously. What could the mansion-arius want? He would hardly require me to delay, merely to enquire if I'd enjoyed my stay. Then an uncomfortable notion

came to me. True, I was not a member of the military class
but, as Marcus's representative, surely no one was expecting me
to pay? If so, there was going to be some real embarrassment
– my patron had not given me sufficient wherewithal.

I was still considering how – if necessary – I could get them
to send the bill to Marcus (and how he was likely to react,
when he learned that he was paying, not the basic rate, but for
luxury lodgings and the commander's special meal) when
Scarface reappeared.

'The mansionarius is free to see you now. I am to take you to
him and assist you with your luggage – if you require my help.'

'I would be glad of it.' I gave him a sweet smile. 'The large
one's heavy.'

It was awkward too, as I had cause to know, but he picked it
up with practised ease (born of marching carrying a heavy kit,
I suppose) and tucked my toga-package underneath his arm.

'This way, citizen!' and he led the way out, through the arch,
into what was obviously official quarters at the back. The
mansionarius was sitting in a little room at a handsome table-
desk, scribbling something on a sheet of bark-paper. The door
was open and he looked up as we approached, waved the orderly
to put my parcels on the floor and rose to meet me with a cour-
teous bow. There was no smile this morning, though – indeed,
he looked concerned. I steeled myself for an outrageous bill.

'I trust that everything was to your satisfaction, citizen?'

I glanced at Scarface, who was hovering at the door. 'I will
be sure to commend you to his Excellence.' I was about to add
that any bill should be sent in that direction, too, when the
mansionarius interrupted me.

'In that case, citizen, I'm sorry that I have to spoil the last
moments of your stay. But there's been unpleasant news. I
know that your intention is to travel south, so I feel must tell
you what I might otherwise be tempted to conceal, at least until
the army have found the men responsible.'

I frowned. 'The affair at Uudum?' News of the tax collector's
death was certain to have spread, but I had expected the gossip
to be all about the gambling and the shame. 'That was reported to
be suicide. Are you suggesting that there might be other "men
responsible"?'

The mansionarius looked puzzled, then gave me a grim smile. 'Ah, that publicanus who hanged himself! A dreadful business, gambling with the tax – and, of course, you're on your way there to investigate. Your driver was boasting of it, to the stable-slaves. But I wasn't talking about that unfortunate affair. This is something much more pressing, I'm afraid. An Imperial rider has arrived this morning with alarming news. The fact is, there's been a traveller found dead on the road.'

'A person of importance?' It would have to be, of course, for the authorities to take an interest. There are so many corpses to be found beside the country roads that little official attention is generally paid – especially in the winter, when supplies are scarce: every year there are dozens of the poor who succumb to age or cold or hunger or disease. (Matters, of course, are different in the town – there corpses are disposed of in the common pit before they stink and become a threat to public health.) 'Not another tax official, by all the gods?' I added.

'Nothing so exalted,' the mansionarius said. 'A curial servant by the look of him. A courier perhaps, since he was discovered miles from anywhere, though he's been half-stripped and beaten, and if he had a horse, it's gone.'

'That might have been the motive for the attack, perhaps?'

'Perhaps!' He gave me a curious look. 'But I would be failing in my duty if I did not warn you that there may be thieves about, and urge you and your driver to take especial care. Rebels possibly, from the condition of the corpse . . .'

'Druids?' I heard the quaver in my voice. So that was it! I am a Celt myself, but the thought of Druid rebels made my blood run cold.

Everyone in Glevum knew about these men. Celtic outlaws, who still refused to recognise the rule of Rome, operating out of caves and forest hideaways – ambushing convoys to obtain supplies and generally harassing the conquerors. Most had embraced Druidism, the forbidden religion (even if – like me – they were not born to it) as a defiant act, and had taken to making a ritual exhibition of any soldiers who fell into their hands. They took no prisoners, though they might permit one person to survive, to stagger half-witless to the nearest garrison burbling of terrible atrocities: victims were not simply killed, but hacked to death, beheaded, and dangled naked from the trees – to be mocked by spectators and pecked at by the crows – while their heads were ritually hung on oaks in sacred groves, as trophies and grisly sacrifices to the gods.

This was the unenviable fate of this poor courier, it seemed. I sympathised, of course – but that was not the reason I was being told. Civilians, too, might meet a grisly death if they were perceived as allies of the occupying power. By wearing a toga, for instance – the very badge of the Roman citizen – and driving in a fancy Roman gig, with a cargo of more togas and expensive golden plate! Not to mention carrying a Latin document identifying the bearer as the representative of the most important Roman magistrate for miles! Never mind that I was a Celtic nobleman by birth, I could not have advertised myself more totally as a potential target for any lurking rebel with murderous intent.

'Druids?' I repeated, quavering.

The mansionarius looked solemnly at me. 'I'm afraid that's what it looks like, citizen. The body has been . . . well, let us say, it's not been left intact.'

Mutilated, then, exactly as I'd feared. And I was about to drive that very route myself. 'But I thought the army had dispersed the rebels now?' I blurted, as though argument would alter anything. 'Forced them to melt off into the Silurian forests to the west?'

'And so they largely have. There's been no attack like this for moons. But – I tell you from experience with the Quadi in Germanica – wherever Pax Romana is forcibly restored, there are always one or two pockets of resistance that remain, and a few determined malcontents who carry on the fight. And this looks like rebel work. Only Druids mutilate a corpse like that. Besides, who else would want to murder a curial courier? A person of no particular account, except that his owners were Roman councillors? He could not have been carrying anything of value, or there would have been a guard.'

Not necessarily, I thought, remembering Acacius Flauccus's attitude to that, but I said nothing except, 'When did this happen?'

He shook his head. 'That's not altogether clear. The Imperial rider was alerted by a goatherd on the road, early this morning while he was riding here. The boy had found the victim lying in a ditch and recognised the uniform as an important one – but it is not clear how long the body had been there. Not very long he thinks – it's hacked about so it is hard to tell.'

'No other witnesses at all?'

'Our rider could not stop to make enquiries, the Imperial Post must get through urgently. He just dismounted and made a swift inspection of the corpse. At first he was inclined to seize the boy and bring him in on suspicion of the crime, but he quickly recognised that it was rebel handiwork, so he left him there on guard and galloped on to report all this to me, while he paused to change his horse. He'll alert the garrison at Glevum when he gets there, too, of course. All local legionary outposts will be notified, and security increased.'

I was following a different train of thought. 'You say the goatherd recognised the uniform as an important one? The victim wasn't stripped?'

'No cloak or shoes, apparently – but a slave disc round his neck. The goatherd couldn't read it, but the rider did. Identified the wearer as "Venibulus, the servant of Silvanus Publicus, the councillor" with the usual instructions to send him back, if found. Presumably from Glevum, though we can't be sure. Though clearly a town that's big enough to have a curia. Unless . . .?' He looked enquiringly at me.

I was frowning slightly. Silvanus Publicus? Wasn't there something that I should recall? I mentally rehearsed the names of councillors I knew. I shook my head. 'I can't enlighten you. Though that does not mean he's not a member of the Glevum curia. I do not know them all.' (I was acquainted with very few of them, in fact, apart from the ones that I'd had dealings with, or those that Marcus entertained from time to time. Doubtless as a duumvir, I'd soon know them all too well.) 'But thank you for your warning. We shall take especial care. Unfortunately, though, we'll have to journey on. I am commissioned by my patron to investigate this suicide at Uudum, among other things.'

He gave me that peculiar sideways look again. 'That is the very reason why I wished to speak to you. Word is being sent to Glevum, as I said before – but meantime I shall have to check on this report and send a party out to search the countryside, to see if there is any trace of where these rebels went. But I have limited resources.' He dropped his gaze and fiddled with the ink-flask on his desk. 'I'm told that you assist your patron with unpleasant incidents and have a reputation for noting things which might otherwise be missed – and that you have dealt with rebel raids before.'

'How . . .?' I began, but the words died on my lips. Victor had clearly been bragging to the mansio slaves again. I would have words with him about it, I thought bitterly.

But the mansionarius was speaking. 'Would you be prepared to travel with my men and advise them of any indications you observe?' He looked up, hopefully. 'It would have the advantage of giving you an armed escort, too.'

Put like that it was a difficult proposition to refuse. So it was that a little later on, I ensconced myself and parcels safely in the gig, and waited while a pair of soldiers formed up either side, and an ox-cart was fetched from somewhere to bring the body back.

The commander of this little band – a blond-haired auxiliary officer, who scarcely seemed old enough to be an optio – came up beside the gig to introduce himself.

'My name is Hippophilus, citizen. I'll be in charge of you. Please instruct your driver not to drive too fast, but allow us to form a phalanx round you at all times.'

I boggled. I had expected cavalry – or horsemen, at the least. This was going to slow our progress very much, with the added disadvantage of the fact that the presence of the army made us more of a target for an ambush than we'd been before.

Hippophilus – a curious nickname, since he had no horse – seemed to read my thoughts. 'My men are trained fighters, fully armed and on alert. Do not worry, we shall march at military pace. It is for your protection. The road runs through miles of forest, south of here. A perfect place for rebels to attack.'

How encouraging! And there were so few soldiers in the escort, too. But there was no escaping it. A barked command brought one last man to climb up on the cart, and I was actually relieved to see Scarface running out, and strapping on a sword. Not that he was likely to be much use in a fight – he was reaching retirement age and hampered by his wounds – but it was an extra pair of eyes, though it left the mansio without an orderly. Obviously this expedition was making huge demands on the available manpower of the place.

'Ready, citizen?' Hippophilus did not wait for a reply. He was already ordering his troops to march. The cart behind us lurched into motion, too.

Victor raised his eyebrows expressively at me.

'Just try not to run them over, or knock them in the ditch,' I said. 'And next time we stop somewhere overnight – be careful what you say! It's your fault I've been co-opted into this patrol – you and your boasting!'

'I'm sorry, citizen,' he said but he did not look contrite. 'I only told them what my master says of you.' He flicked the reins and clicked his tongue to signal to the horse, and we were on our way.

NINE

Our party was now travelling at walking pace – or rather at a brisk, quick march. As Hippophilus had promised, he had his soldiers (since they were not carrying their kit) moving at the faster official rate and the following ox-cart was struggling to keep up with them. However, our gig-mare – accustomed to dashing everywhere as fast as possible – was unsettled and wayward at this change of pace. She skittered sideways, pawed the ground and kept throwing up her head as if in protest at our sluggishness, or perhaps she was nervous of the sharp pikes close to her. Either way, for a little while it took all of Victor's skills to keep us on the road, but gradually he soothed the animal, and coaxed her to obey the rein and settle to a walk.

Hippophilus was right about the countryside. A mile or two south of the mansio the farmsteads disappeared and we were deep in woods. Really deep – the forest hereabouts was very thick – with wisps of mist lingering among the trees where the thin winter sun had not managed to break through. The sort of place that any self-respecting rebel would choose for an attack. I was acutely aware that though our escort was well-armed and trained, the rebels were often just as handsomely equipped – with Roman weapons from patrols like ours, whose previous owners suddenly did not need them any more.

It was not a comfortable thought and I found myself peering anxiously to either side. It was tempting to forget my promise to the mansionarius and simply order Victor to drive swiftly on. However, I managed to suppress my nervousness and remind myself that the place we sought – although said to be remote – must at least be closer than the next official inn, or the Imperial rider would not have made his first report to us. That meant that we should reach it in less than twenty miles.

Supposing that we found the spot at all. I had begun to worry that it might be difficult, and we would have to spend time loitering to search. The roadside verges here were overgrown with ferns and brambles and the ditches full of fallen leaves, so a body half-concealed there might be hard to spot, especially in the mist. And no doubt the goatherd – if he had any sense – would have departed long ago.

Or so I thought. In fact, the location would have been difficult to miss.

We rounded a corner and there in a foggy dip, we knew we'd found the place. The goatboy was very much in evidence, as were his animals, which were roaming in a swarming gaggle up and down the road, and munching on the ghostly bushes half-visible either side. The result was a kind of living road-block – quite as effective as the piles of wood and stones that the army is known to use.

I say 'effective', because – to my surprise – discernible beyond the animals there was a group of people standing in the fog. Half-a-dozen early travellers, by the look of it, clearly impatient at the enforced delay: a pair of itinerant sellers of turpentine and pitch, a peddler with a mule, and what seemed to be a local peasant and his sons, who were armed with sticks and now fully occupied in guarding their laden farm-cart from the attentions of a couple of interested goats.

The goatboy saw us coming and advanced out of the mist. He stalked into the roadway, planted his staff as though it were a spear and raised his hand to us, for all the world like a company commander halting an advance. He was thin, barefoot and ragged and not especially clean, and could hardly have been much more than twelve years old, but he had the swagger of a person twice his age. His pure effrontery was astonishing, but – amazingly – it worked. Hippophilus exchanged a startled glance with several of his men, but there was no roar of protest. He simply brought them immaculately to a stop. And then did nothing else but look at me.

He obviously expected that I'd do the questioning. I was not prepared for this – usually the army like to be in charge of interrogations – but I murmured a command and Victor drew the gig up a pace or two ahead, where I could lean down and talk to the goatboy easily.

'You're the lad that found the body?' I enquired. That seemed an appropriate beginning to the interview. 'The Imperial rider brought us word.'

'That's right, citizen.' The Latin was appalling, but the sense was clear. 'I was ordered to remain and guard the corpse till reinforcements came.' He looked at our escort with an appraising eye. 'Is that all they have sent?'

'You were anticipating more?' I asked him, switching to my native tongue. The local dialects are different from my own, but I can generally make my Celtic understood.

The boy shot an appraising look at me. With my entourage I must have appeared Roman through and through, but I did have a Celtic birrus over my Roman dress. After a moment he relaxed and answered, in the same language. 'The Imperial rider thought that rebels were involved and this—' he used his staff to gesture to the ditch – 'was some sort of official messenger. He said the murder was an outrage against the Roman state. I was expecting half a garrison.'

From the gig I had a view of the spot he'd pointed to. The body was lying face down, halfway in the ditch, his bare feet uppermost. His arms and shoulders had been cruelly hacked about and his gold and purple tunic – the mark of a servant of the curia – was stained with blood and slashed from shoulder-seam to hem. No doubt the reason why the rebels hadn't stolen it, I thought. The head was missing, which was as horrible as I'd expected it to be, and cutting into the plump flesh around the stump of neck a slave disc collar was plainly visible.

I was glad of the excuse to avert my gaze from him, and look hard at the surrounding ditch instead, in case there was any evidence it might offer us – but if there had been trampled foliage (which might have indicated how many attackers there had been) the goats and their keeper – and no doubt the Imperial Post rider too – had tramped all over it. However, the muddy area below the body was stained with half-dried blood, as though there had been pools of it and they had seeped away – rather as a newly-butchered carcass in a market is hung up and left to drain out through the neck. I swallowed hard and looked away again.

'What do you want done with the potential witnesses?' The goatboy's voice cut across my thoughts. He was trying to sound knowing and assured, but his voice betrayed him, breaking suddenly to a childish squeak. 'You can see that they've been rounded up for you.'

'You stopped them, single-handed?' I enquired. He was so innocently presumptuous that it made me smile.

I should have suppressed it. The urchin responded with a cheeky grin. 'Not on purpose, citizen – to start with anyway. It was the goats, you see. I tried to keep them in one place while I was keeping guard over the corpse, but they are wilful beasts. They got away and strayed into the middle of the road – which meant that when that cart came up, the driver had to slow. Then, of course, they smelt the turnips on the back – and there was no stopping them. They were round it in no time, trying to push their noses in, and forced the cart to stop. The driver got down cursing and wanting to know what was going on here, by all the gods?' His imitation of an outraged farmer was a lively one.

'So you explained?' It was a vain attempt on my part to reassert control. I was at a disadvantage, conducting this interrogation from the gig, so looked round for a method of getting safely down. I could see nothing that would serve me as a step, so I glanced back at the escort – hoping for an arm – and was suddenly aware that I'd created an uneasy stir. The soldiers, in almost perfect unison, were looking from me to the goatherd and then back again, and then at one another – as though performing some unlikely drill. They were obviously unable to understand a word and were very suspicious of what was being said.

Scarface, I realised, had been the cause of this. He'd climbed down from the ox-cart at the rear, and come forward to listen to the interview. From his demeanour it was clear that he'd made up his mind that I was speaking Celtic to exclude the troops: at best disguising what the conversation was about, if not actively plotting with a rebel spy. I sighed and abandoned the idea of getting down – he would construe that as consorting with the witness, I could see.

The lad, however, was quite oblivious. 'I did more than tell him, citizen,' he said, answering my previous enquiry. 'I brought him over and showed him what I'd found. It shocked him terribly.'

'And he did not just drive on – and scatter all your goats?' I braved the disapproving scrutiny of Scarface and his friends and went on as before. It was my best chance of getting information from the boy. 'It must have struck him that – if there were rebels in the area – he and his family might be ambushed too.'

'Perhaps it did.' The urchin grinned up at me. 'But it occurred to me that the army would want to question him – he'd been driving on the piece of road the rebels may have used – and there might be something in it for me, if I kept him here. So I threatened that I'd report them if they tried to leave. The whole family had got down from the cart by that time anyway – trying to shoo away the goats from eating all their stock – and at that moment the pitch-sellers arrived. The farmer wasn't letting them go, when he had to stay himself – they were as much witnesses as he was, he declared – and after that it simply seemed to grow. When the others came this way they assumed they had to stop.' His voice gave way again and dropped dramatically. 'So I've done your job and rounded up the witnesses for you – will there be any question of reward?'

I was tempted. A couple of quadrans would have been a fortune to this lad, and his cheerful innocence was irresistible, but I dared not give him money. Scarface would decide it was a bribe. So I shook my head and made a warning sideways gesture with my hands.

To my astonishment Victor took this as a signal that I wanted to dismount, and in an instant he had slid down to the ground and was offering me an arm to lean upon. I managed to do so with my dignity intact (not always easy in a toga in a breeze) and instantly my escort closed in either side – not so much to guard me, I was almost sure, as to limit what I did. I pretended to ignore them, and walked over to the ditch (entirely for show, there was clearly nothing further to be learned) and then turned solemnly to address the little group.

'Well,' I said – in Latin, 'you can see what's happened here. Obviously we'll need to make a search – to see if the perpetrators are still hidden in the woods. Though from the way the blood has oozed into the ditch and drained away, I suspect this may have happened many hours ago.'

It was Hippophilus who spoke. 'He's quite right, gentlemen.

I've seen this sort of thing on the battlefield before. That body has been here a little while.'

Even Scarface was looking half-convinced. I pressed my small advantage. 'This boy—' I indicated the urchin who was still standing by the gig – 'says he has herded up the witnesses for us – rather better than he's controlled his goats it seems.' That earned a general laugh, though Scarface only scowled. However, my little jest had relaxed the atmosphere.

'Over there!' The boy had understood my words. He gestured with his staff towards the huddled group along the road, who were gazing back – as terrified of us as they were of rebel bands. With reason, possibly: the army is not known for being gentle with witnesses to crime, especially those who have nothing to report.

I raised my voice, and hoped that these 'witnesses' could hear me, though my voice boomed oddly in the mist. 'I think they are simply people who were travelling on the road, but we'll need to question them – just to make sure they saw nothing that would assist us in our search.' I turned to the optio. 'Hippophilus, take a couple of your men and go and ask those people who they are, and whether they have seen anything or anyone – suspicious or otherwise – on this road today. If so, make a note of it. If not, just get their names and where they can be found, then let them go – for now. No force, we want them to co-operate. And you, there, orderly—' I turned to Scarface, now – 'go with them. If any witness – like this boy – doesn't speak much Latin, or speaks none at all, come and get me and I'll talk to him myself.'

This justified my use of Celtic, naturally, and the soldiers nodded, though Scarface only scowled. Hippophilus just seemed glad to have a task to do. He detailed two soldiers to accompany him, and set off down the track. Scarface followed them reluctantly.

I turned back to the goatherd. 'My colleagues will find out what those people know, if anything. But you have some explanations of your own to do. You were the first person to discover this. What were you doing here?'

He shrugged his shoulders. 'Moving on the goats.'

'Moving them, from where?'

'Where I had them rounded up last night.' He gestured vaguely to the forest on the left. 'I tie them up each evening, some-where they can graze – though even then you have to used tarred rope to stop them eating it – and drive them on each dawn. I'm hoping to sell a lot of them in Glevum, by and by, and make a little money. Just keep enough to breed from in the spring.'

My knowledge of goats is limited, having only one myself, but I knew enough to ask. 'You can't feed them overwinter where you live?'

He shook his head. 'We don't live anywhere, in particular. My family used to have a farm once, long ago – but there were lots of sons who had to have their share and by the time my father got his inheritance, there was not enough to make a living on. So he took the goats instead – I wanted the horses, but he said that wouldn't pay, they took too long to rear and were too hard to keep. We moved into the woods, but my father's failing and my mother's dead, so there's only me to tend the animals. We live on milk – and now and then a goat – and anything that we can scavenge as we move from place to place.'

I sighed. Just what we needed – a juvenile itinerant who did not know the area. 'So you have not been in the vicinity for long?'

'Just long enough to build ourselves a shelter out of boughs. I've left my father there. I'll come back and we'll stay here for the winter now, I expect – once I've managed to sell the surplus off – because we've found a stream and there is plenty for the goats to eat nearby.'

'Meanwhile blocking up the public road?' I said.

He shot a look at me. 'I generally try to keep them off the route itself, but with the recent rain, the stream has burst its banks, and the verge is very boggy in this dip.' He gave that grin again. 'You don't know much about goats, citizen?'

'I've never herded them,' I told him loftily.

'Well, you have to watch them when the going is slippery. While you're struggling they get away from you and start to climb the trees, and then you'll never get them rounded up again. The younger he-goats in particular. One charged off when I was talking to that courier today and the others followed him. If it wasn't for the farmer's turnips being such a lure, I think I would have lost them – which we could ill afford. I would have had to sell myself to slavery – that would raise enough to keep my father while he lives, and at least I wouldn't starve. I'm good with horses, and quite good with goats.'

'Never mind all that!' I was sympathetic to his plight, but I had work to do. 'The point is, you haven't been along this stretch of road before? You don't know if the corpse was there last night?'

He shook his head. 'I'm sorry, citizen, but I can't help you there. The first time I came here was shortly after dawn, and I only saw the body then because the goats went over there – I told you that they are inquisitive. But they won't touch dead things, and they turned away. Though . . .' He hesitated for a moment, then seemed to make his mind up suddenly. 'I suppose that I had better show you. One of them was chewing this, until he spat it out.' He unclenched the hand that was clinging to the staff and revealed a little silver clasp: a pretty thing although the hasp had broken off. 'I don't know where it came from. Not the corpse, I shouldn't think. Goats will eat the toggles off your leather bag, if you're not very careful, but they don't like anything contaminated with blood. So it may be from his cloak as it was torn away. Or maybe one of the rebels dropped it as he fled.'

He handed it to me – with some reluctance, and I could see why. It was beautifully made, shaped like a little ram's head with long curling horns, and would have brought a *denarius* or two at Glevum market, with no questions asked. I was surprised he'd been prepared to part with it – had he done so out of fear? Or merely in the hope of receiving some reward? Well this time, I could oblige him. I had reason now. I slipped my hand into my toga folds to find my purse and was in the act of giving him a few small coins, when Victor clutched my arm.

'Could I see that for a moment, citizen?' He had been holding the gig beside me all this time but he now handed the reins to the nearest soldier, and held out his palm. 'That silver clasp, I mean.'

I was surprised but I dropped the little ram's-head into it. He turned it over, stared at it a moment, then returned it with a nod. 'I thought as much. I've seen this thing before. I think I know who it belongs to, citizen.'

TEN

'Y ou?' I was astonished. What could Victor know about a silver clasp found on a public road some forty miles from where his master lived? Or, it occurred to me – since Marcus had purchased him quite recently – was this something that he'd seen elsewhere? That seemed too unlikely to be true.

But he seemed quite certain. 'I'm sure of it. It is not an item you'd forget, and I saw it just a day or two ago, at your patron's villa – my master's country house, in fact. In the slave quarters. That curial messenger was wearing it, a blond good-looking chap – the one who had to be given accommodation overnight. It was his belt-clasp and he was very proud of it – he went on boasting so long that he kept us all awake and the chief slave had to tell him to desist. That's why I'm so certain, citizen. It represents a sacrificial ram, apparently, and was a present from his master, a priest who gave it to him as a mark of high esteem.'

A priest. Of course! How could I be so dense? Silvanus the Priest – the Priest of Mercury in Glevum! Titus had spoken of him at the banquet, just the other night. I knew that I half-recognised the name. 'The servant of Silvanus Publicus the councillor.' As priest of one of the major gods, Silvanus would be an automatic member of the curia. (If I had been a duumvir, I thought, all this would doubtless have occurred to me at once.)

I was about to ask Victor if he knew more details, but he circumvented me. 'Poor lad,' he murmured sadly. 'He isn't boasting now.' He peered into the ditch again, more hesitantly now. 'That does look like his uniform, now I consider it – though it's so torn and bloodied that it's hard to tell, and all these curial uniforms are very much the same. And without the head . . .' He made a little grimace. 'It's hard to judge the height. But I'm fairly sure it's him.' He gestured to the ditch. 'The slave disc should tell you. It would even give his name. Something beginning with "V". I think it was.'

I searched my memory. 'Venibulus?'

He stared at me. 'That was the name, that's right. How did you know that? You didn't meet him, as I recall.'

'From the slave disc, exactly as you thought. The Imperial rider read it and the mansionarius told me, before we left.' I had forgotten that Victor wasn't present at the time.

The driver nodded. 'In that case, it is certainly the man. Anyone might steal a belt clasp but that's not a collar you could remove without the key—' he bent over to peer more closely at the corpse, then swallowed hard and backed hastily away – 'not even when you have taken off the head, apparently. It's so tight that hasn't fallen off.'

He was right in that, again. Some slave collars are simple chains, or even leather thongs, from which the slave disc is directly hung, but this was a high-status version, a handsome bronze band that locked behind the neck, with the disc suspended on a solid loop in front. Clearly a very expensive thing.

Victor was still looking mournfully at the murdered courier. 'His poor master is going to be distraught,' he said. 'He's already lost a number of his slaves. There was a fire at the house not many days ago – the boy was telling us. One of his own relatives was killed in it, he said. And several kitchen staff.'

So that confirmed that his owner was the Priest of Mercury! But I merely said, 'To say nothing of three members of the curia!' I don't have the Roman attitude to patrician birth, and I've been in servitude myself, but even I can recognise that councillors are of more importance than their slaves – to the outside world at least.

Victor raised an eyebrow. 'He didn't mention that. He was more concerned to tell us how it affected him. Apparently, the usual curial courier was injured in the blaze – he'd been waiting for orders in the court, and his clothing caught on fire. So this Venibulus was asked to take his place. He was raised with horses and was very good with them – he'd carried private messages before.'

I nodded. Mercury is the patron god of messengers, so who better than his high priest's courier to serve the council too?

But that raised another question. 'So he gained temporary promotion.' (There's more status in being a public messenger.) 'But how did he obtain a curial uniform so soon? He's clearly wearing one.'

'I believe he borrowed it from the injured messenger. He was grumbling that it didn't fit him very well and it would have to be altered if he continued in the post. Though, he didn't like his new appointment very much. His previous life was fairly sheltered and messages were rare, and he was complaining of being expected now to ride out every day, at all hours and often for long distances as well. Dangerous he called it – and it seems that he was right . . .' He broke off as Scarface came loping up to us.

He shuffled to attention, in deference to my toga, rather than to me. 'The optio sends his greetings, citizen, but regrets that there is little to report. None of the witnesses saw anyone, except the couriers, and that's no use to us. The peasant and the peddler both say that the Imperial rider passed them on the road – and the peasant thought he may have seen him riding up and down—' he jerked a thumb toward the victim in the ditch – 'a little after dawn, but he could not swear to it. Says he was too busy loading up his cart to pay much attention. It does not add to what we know, in any case.'

'And the pitch-sellers?' I asked him, though without much hope.

'They have even less to offer. They weren't even on the road for the first hour of light. They stopped to sell and demonstrate their wares to a traveller who wanted to re-waterproof his coach, and after that they saw nobody at all – except a plump young fellow setting bird snares, but he was going the other way. In any case he was on foot and wearing country boots—' he made a little gesture of distaste – 'country boots' are simply bits of uncured rawhide, bound around the feet – 'so he could not possibly have run and got here ahead of th– Ahh! Get away, you stupid animal!'

One of the goats had come softly up behind him and was now balancing its hooves against his back and gnawing at the leather lappets on his uniform.

'Get that creature off!' He flapped ineffectually at it, but the animal merely moved its attentions to the *tunica* instead, until the goatboy noticed and came hurrying across to give it a firm thwack with his staff.

The creature looked mournfully at him with its strange black eyes, spat out the cloth that it was chewing on, and ambled off again. The goatboy followed him.

Scarface reached around and examined the back hem of his tunic. 'Will you look what that animal has done! It has made a hole in the material. What will the quartermaster say?' It was almost comic, but I did not smile because a thought occurred to me.

I called over to the goatboy, using Latin now. 'Would that creature eat a sash or belt, do you suppose? A whole one?'

'Depends what it was made of, citizen. A fabric one, quite possibly, and fairly quickly too. A leather one would take a little time.'

Scarface was still attempting to regain his dignity by pulling his now-tattered tunic down behind, but Victor had understood what I was driving at. 'Venibulus wore a silken sash-belt, a fine expensive thing. You think . . .?'

'The goat might easily have eaten it,' I said. 'Though I wonder why the rebels did not steal it when they could – after all, they took his cloak and shoes.'

Victor raised an eyebrow. 'Perhaps he took it off – tried to hide it somewhere, in the hope he might escape and rescue it. He was proud enough of it and of that clasp as well—'

He was interrupted this time by Hippophilus, who had come striding back to me, accompanied by his men. 'Citizen? I have had my troops examine the verges further on – especially the muddy areas – but if there were ever footprints or trampled foliage it has all been obscured by the meanderings of the goats. And as the *evocatus* will have told you, none of the so-called witnesses can help.'

I looked at Scarface. An evocatus, then! A legionary who had served his time or otherwise been honourably discharged (because of those wounds perhaps?) but had chosen to enlist again. Volunteering as a veteran – only to be sent on special duties to an inn! No wonder Scarface wore a disillusioned look.

Hippophilus was still worrying about the witnesses. 'You're sure that I should not arrest them and take them to the inn? We could arrange to have them interrogated properly. I should like to have something to take back and report.'

'I think not,' I replied. 'I would have been surprised if they had noticed anything. These rebel bands exist by hiding in the woods and they are very skilled at it.'

'As the army knows too well,' the optio agreed. 'But, since there are no traces, what else can we do? I suppose that we could search a little further on. The rebels, like any horsemen, will no doubt use the softer verges, to save their horses feet – but there have been others walking this way since. Not least those wretched goats.'

'I think that you can let the witnesses depart – except the goatherd. I suggest that you detail someone to keep an eye on him – until he gets to Glevum, anyway. Just to make sure he's really what he seems. The vigilance need not be discreet – suggest the guard is for his own protection on the road. Your evocatus, possibly – it seems he has a natural affinity with goats.'

Scarface turned scarlet and seemed ready to protest, but I forestalled him.

'The boy says he's going to market to try to sell his goats. Make sure that's all he does. Do not alarm him, but watch him carefully – and pay attention to any people that he meets.'

'You heard that, Evocatus,' Hippophilus put in, making it clear that he was in command. 'The boy may be a spy. Report to the Glevum barracks, if you discover anything, before returning to your post. They will be able to respond more swiftly than our little group.'

'You are on detachment from the Glevum garrison?' I said. It should have been obvious – it was the nearest full legionary post – but it had not occurred to me. 'Mention my name to the commander there, if you do report to him. He will see that my patron hears of this.'

'It shall be done, citizen,' Hippophilus replied. 'The lad may be working with the rebels, after all. I suppose he is a Celt. Well, my man shall watch him like an eagle and we may find out.'

The evocatus, as I must call him now, was looking mollified – satisfied that there was proper work to do. He glanced towards the goatboy who was now across the road attempting to coax one of his younger she-goats from a tree. For the first time since I'd met him, Scarface grinned at me. 'Permission to call in at the mansio on the way, and find another tunic, citizen?'

He had addressed me rather than his supposed superior. I looked at Hippophilus who gave a tiny nod.

'Permission granted,' I said soberly. 'But keep the boy in sight.' Then, because I could not resist the urge to preen, 'And while you are in Glevum you might care to call on the Priest of Mercury, and tell him that we have found the body of his slave. If he doubts you, show him this as proof.' I handed him the silver ram's-head as I spoke. 'It's a valuable thing, so take good care of it. Tell the priest that he can have it when he reclaims his slave – he'll no doubt wish to make arrangements for the disposal of the corpse. But your instructions are first to take the body to the mansio.'

Hippophilus's ruddy face had fallen in gratifying surprise. 'I heard that you were clever with deductions, citizen—' he glanced at Victor – 'but I never guessed that it would lie within your power to work out the identity of a headless corpse. And so quickly too. You are quite sure of this?'

'The goatboy found the belt-clasp near the corpse, and that – together with the slave disc – convinced me of the facts. You may report it to the mansionarius when you return. You might even suggest to him, with my compliments, that goat meat might make a pleasant addition to the kitchen stores – I'm sure our goatherd would be pleased to sell you one.' I turned to Victor. 'And now, I think it's time for us to be on our way. And they—' I gestured to the 'witnesses' – 'should be allowed to leave.'

Hippophilus nodded, and began to bark commands. The army sprang to action, with a speed and efficiency that was commendable. Two men fetched a wooden ladder from the ox-cart at the rear and (aided by the driver who'd been watching all this while) began to load the body onto it. Two others waved the waiting travellers on along the road, while Scarface went over and murmured to the boy – who shook his head at first, then looked at me and shrugged.

'I don't need protection,' he called across – in Celtic. 'I'm in more danger from rebels with a Roman soldier at my heels. But I hear you've ordered it, so I suppose there's no escape. At least this skinny fellow can help me drive the goats.'

I smiled. Scarface had taken on more than he supposed.

'Ready, citizen?' Victor had already taken back the reins, and now he helped me up onto the gig. 'All this has taken quite a time. We shall need to hurry if we hope to reach Uudum in time to do anything today – and then you'll want to speak to the guard-post before dark, to find our accommodation for the night. That will take us most of the daylight that there is – even supposing we don't run into rebels on the way.'

He climbed up beside me and with a flick of his wrist he urged the gig-mare into an easy stride.

ELEVEN

We drove in jolting silence for a little while, both watchful lest the rebels might still be somewhere near. However, by now there were beginning to be other travellers on the move – men with donkeys, women driving geese and wagons full of wood. We even met a salt cart lumbering past (I wondered if it belonged to my projected Celtic host!) and a group of soldiers making road repairs – so the risk of ambush diminished all the time. Then, at last, we left the woods behind and found ourselves in open countryside, where land-slaves were toiling in well-tended fields, smoke billowed from the chimney openings of poor men's makeshift shacks, and a group of little roadside stalls clustered round the entrance to some ancient farm.

Victor turned to me, and we exchanged a grin of pure relief.

'It can't be far to the next army staging post,' I said.

I meant to be encouraging, but I'd sparked a new concern. 'Dear gods,' he muttered. 'And I learned from the mansio stable boy that the road to Uudum branches off before we come to that.'

We stopped to ask directions from one stall-keeper, an aged Celtic woman wearing faded plaid, and bent almost double with infirmity – or rather, Victor stopped and let me do the questioning. She proved, ironically, to be offering fresh goat's milk to weary travellers and her shrewd eyes looked astonished at my enquiry.

'Well, citizen, if you'd driven another half a mile you would have seen it for yourselves. Just around that corner,' she gestured with the hand that held the pail. 'The route follows a very ancient track, with lots of turnings off, but it's a proper military road these days. So stick to the paving and you can't go wrong – Uudum is the last place that it serves. Would you be wanting a drink, now, to see you on your way?' She smiled, showing gums and two remaining teeth.

I nodded – partly out of pity for her age and partly to reward her for the information we'd received – and we each drank a measure from the battered metal cup she dipped into the pail and handed up to us.

My doubts must have been written on my face. 'Cleaner than the water from the stream, and more sustaining too,' she told us, as we wiped our creamy lips. 'Fresh-milked this morning.' Then, to my astonishment, she named a shocking price – I should have asked before we drank, of course – and I parted with another four *dupondii*. If I went on like this I'd have no small coinage left.

Victor raised an eyebrow at me as we drove away. 'She may be old but she is still as wily as her goats! Which reminds me – do you really think that goatboy might have been a rebel spy?'

'One cannot be too careful,' I replied. 'Though, I rather liked the boy and I hope he's innocent. But there's something troubling about this whole affair.'

'I suppose his presence was a little too convenient. Goats which helpfully trample everywhere, and obliterate completely all tracks? To say nothing of the way he kept us talking there – and incidentally stopped the other road-users as well?' He looked thoughtfully at me. 'Might that be a distraction to allow the rebels to escape?'

I had not taken Victor for a thinking man, and I was impressed. 'It had occurred to me,' I told him truthfully. 'That's why I arranged to have him watched.'

Victor nodded. 'I heard you talking to Hippophilus. And I suppose we only have the goatherd's word for anything. It may be that his parent isn't frail at all, but a bandit rebel – the boy admits that his family's dispossessed!' He gave an appreciative whistle through his teeth. 'I knew your reputation, citizen, but you've excelled yourself.'

'I've done nothing of the kind. You have drawn the obvious conclusions for yourself. Though there is one deduction which I'll confidently make – that you speak a little Celtic, as you clearly do. I did not translate that information for the troops!' I was surprised, in fact. Most slaves in Roman households are born to servitude, and have spoken nothing but Latin all their lives. 'You could have asked for those directions for yourself.'

Victor turned scarlet and gave a short embarrassed laugh. 'I understand a good deal more than I can speak, these days, though at one time it was my mother tongue – I was sold into slavery when I was young,' he said. 'Like that poor young idiot we just saw lying dead. Another thing that he was boasting of the other day – as if it is a privilege to be freeborn and poor, and sold to slavery to pay the family's debts.' He shook his head. 'But here's the turning that the crone was talking of!' He urged the gig around it as he spoke.

It was a good road, as the milk-seller had said though, as a minor route in difficult terrain, barely more than regulation width, with scarcely any verge on either side as we followed it down a narrow valley between tall wooded hills. It might have been a pretty journey if the weather had been fine, but the mist was clinging to the hilltops here, and the morning sun had given way to heavy cloud, so the general impression was of gloominess and grey – especially since there were few other travellers about.

We followed the direction of a little stream, which we crossed and recrossed twice on sturdy wooden bridges, each of which had military guard posts to one side, but we were not challenged. Perhaps Victor's splendid uniform and the fancy gig were enough to have us nodded through, though it might have been simply that we were clearly carrying no goods so there was no question of being asked to pay the military toll (which would presumably have swelled the coffers of the tax office that we were heading for).

There was increasing evidence of Roman presence, now – one or two fine villas on the hills and even a cluster of tombstones by the road, though most of the dwellings here were humble ones, including one little group of Celtic roundhouses like mine, inside a palisade, with women spinning at the doors, and incurious ducks and pigs roaming their small enclosure as we passed.

The leaden sky did not permit us to estimate the hour, but – judging by my stomach, which was beginning to notice that I hadn't eaten since my hurried snack at dawn (apart from a few sips of goat's milk, which hardly qualified) – it must have been late afternoon before we reached the outskirts of a proper settlement, surrounded by an ancient earthwork and a ditch.

Here there was a sentry on the bridge, and Victor slowed the
gig and once again permitted me to do the questioning.

'Have we arrived at Uudum, soldier?' I enquired – in Latin
now, of course.

The sentry was a wiry fellow with a thin impassive face, and
muscles in his arms and legs that stood out like knotted ivy-strands.
'This is Uudum.' He planted his pike in front of us and stared
boldly, first at me – wrapped in my Celtic birrus – and then at
Victor and the high-status gig. 'What is your business here?'

I produced my warrant. 'I believe,' I said, with would-be
dignity, 'that you're expecting me. I am here at the request of
Marcus Aurelius Septimus, the chief magistrate of the Glevum
fiscal area, to enquire a little further into the death of his tax
collector here.' I was not entirely certain of this claim, but it
sounded convincing.

And it had the right effect. The guard glanced briefly at the
document. 'Ah, you are the citizen Libertus? You must be a
person of some significance. We've had two separate messengers
about you, in the last two days. Wait here a moment, and I'll
fetch the man in charge.' He disappeared inside the little building
to the side and returned, after an uncomfortable pause, accompanied by an older, stouter man – clearly the duty officer of
this watch party – who swaggered out in armour so polished
you could see your face in it. He did not look as friendly as I
might have wished.

His greeting, though not quite discourteous, confirmed my
impression of unease. 'Citizen Libertus. Welcome to Uudum. I
am the *principalis* here. You wish to interview Acacius's chief
slave, I believe?' The words were clipped and there was a suggestion of disdain – clearly he held himself in very high esteem.

'And to view the body of the suicide, if possible,' I said, trying
an ingratiating smile.

'So I understand,' he answered, with arched eyebrows and a
disapproving tightening of the lips, 'although I confess that I'm
surprised. The fellow has been dead for several days. I would
have been glad to see the corpse disposed of speedily. I do not
want his spirit haunting us.'

'You had arranged a funeral?' I hazarded.

A curt nod answered me. 'The man had no family living to

consult and there's no local burial guild for tax collectors, as there is for slaves. I arranged a simple military affair – well away from town, of course – to get the corpse cremated with minimum delay. And to allay potential trouble too – there is anger against Flauccus from the local tax payers, some of whom have skimped to pay the rates he gambled with.' A sigh. 'But we have deferred the funeral, since you've requested it, though I'd be glad to have permission to recommence as soon as possible.'

'I'm sorry to have occasioned you delay,' I murmured, peaceably. 'But clearly the loss of the tax revenue is of concern to everyone. To yourselves, not least. A large proportion is assigned to army purposes, I think?'

But he did not thaw. 'I do not see how an inspection of the corpse will help?'

'Merely to ensure that it was a suicide, and that he was not in fact strangled and hanged by someone else,' I said. I could see from his face that the possibility had not occurred to him, so I gently pressed the point. 'A disappointed creditor perhaps? And my master is concerned to know what gambling was involved – what was Acacius betting on, how often and with whom.' I looked at him blandly, with an enquiring smile. 'You could not advise me on that subject, I suppose? You probably know the local gambling scene as well as anyone.'

He gave me a thin smile. He knew what I was hinting at, of course. Gambling on dice or board games is forbidden nowadays (except at Saturnalia when normal rules do not apply), but Romans love to bet and soldiers are famous for loving it the most. And no one believes their claims that the stakes are merely chips of wood, though these worthless tokens do ensure that no coins change hands – when anyone is watching!

'We do not mingle with the civilian population very much.' The answer was skilfully evasive, but probably the truth. 'And we don't have local games or circuses where betting is allowed. So I can't enlighten you. Perhaps Acacius's steward can help in that regard. I'll have him brought to you.'

'Brought?' I glanced towards the guard house in surprise. Every such building has a holding cell. 'I understood you'd thrown him into jail?'

'We have him under lock and key,' the man corrected me.

'Uudum is not big enough to have a proper civic jail, and there is no provision for keeping prisoners here, for any longer than an hour or two – after which they generally agree to pay their fines or are given a flogging and moved on somewhere else.'

'And in the case of Loftus?' I enquired.

'One of the Roman landowners has taken charge of him. There are some cells out at his villa that we sometimes use. He had them built for storage, but they are useful for petty thieves and disobedient slaves: we rarely have more serious criminals to deal with, hereabouts. Uudum is generally a law-abiding town.'

I nodded. Poor Loftus would not have had a comfortable few days. I could imagine the makeshift prison very well, because I'd once suffered in such a cell myself: small, airless cubicles without a window space, where the unfortunate might find a pile of straw (at best) to keep him from the cold and damp of walls and floor, while he was fettered wrist and ankle to heavy iron rings. Sometimes a prisoner could not even move his hands to eat, but was obliged to snuffle in his food bowl like a pig, to get whatever scraps his captors chose to fling at him. (Supposing that he could move at all and had not been flogged to within an inch of death. Official torturers are skilled at stopping just in time.)

'Did you interrogate him thoroughly yourselves?' I persisted, wondering if such methods had been used.

The *tesserarius* shook his tawny head. 'We were about to, but we got a message from your patron to desist. So we sent Loftus to the villa cells to stew. A pity, we might have discovered what he knew. You realise that if there's any question of a court case later on – perhaps on charges of illegal gambling – the steward's testimony won't be acceptable unless it can be proved that it was properly obtained?'

Extorted under torture, that is what he meant. And he was right, of course. The Roman legal system chooses to maintain that either a slave will be so loyal to his owner at all times that his supporting words can't be relied upon, or – if his testimony proves his master's guilt – that he is disloyal and simply seeking his revenge. Either way his simple oath is meaningless, so only torment can ensure he speaks the truth.

'Then I shall have to find out what he knows, myself,' I murmured. 'Please have him brought to me. I would like to see the body and the scene of death, as well, so I'd be glad if he could join me there – if that is possible. He may notice changes that another man would miss.'

The principalis heaved another mighty sigh. 'It shall be arranged. I'm under orders to comply with your demands. I'll send a man to lead you to where Acacius lived – he has been laid out on a byre, in what used to be his office there, awaiting funeral – so you can examine both man and building at one time. I wish you joy of it. So, if there's nothing further . . .?'

There was. 'I believe my master asked you to provide me, and my driver here, with accommodation for the night. I take it there's no actual mansio in the town? And to provide me with transport when I move on from here. I'm going to Portus Abonae, as I expect you know . . .'

He had turned back to face me. 'To represent your patron at a wedding there?' the man said wearily. 'Indeed, we were well-informed of that. The second messenger could speak of little else. You are quite right, we have no mansio here, and the mutationis – back the way you've come – does not have beds at all. I've contacted a small civilian inn. It's out of town, but it's convenient, and they can find a room.'

The word he used was '*cubicula*', in fact – which boded well enough. These 'cubicles' are tiny rooms, and rarely offer more than a blanket and a humble palliasse, or an even humbler pile of straw and reeds, and occasionally a pillow if one is fortunate. There is the usual problem with bugs and smells and dirt, and some inns merely have a curtain to divide the space, but the arrangement does afford a certain privacy. Better than a communal room, with just one mattress on the floor which travellers are obliged to share with other customers – drunks, pickpockets, prostitutes, whatever happens to arrive – which is the case in many small establishments.

'Very good!' I nodded. 'See that my driver has directions to the place. He'll need to stay tonight, though I've promised to return him after that. I presume I can rely upon some transport when he's gone?'

'We have an ox-cart, citizen, we use for our supplies. I'll put that at your disposal if you wish. Or there's a man from whom it would be possible to hire a travelling coach, though of course there would be a small expense.'

Meaning that he declined to pay the cost from army funds. I forced a smile again. 'Your ox-cart would be excellent,' I said, and had the satisfaction of seeing his surprise. 'But that's a matter for another day. For the moment, I have pressing tasks – especially if you wish me to release the corpse to your cremation pyre.'

The tesserarius gave another nod. 'I'll find a man to guide you to the house, and send a messenger to have the prisoner brought to you – though I'll have to provide a guard for him, I suppose.'

'You could fetch him on your ox-cart, possibly,' I said. 'That would speed our progress markedly. I don't imagine Loftus is in much state to walk.'

'Or better still, your guide can stay and ride out on your gig, when he has shown you to the tax collector's house. Then he can both direct your driver to the villa and act as escort to the prisoner on the journey back. It may be a little cramped, but it will expedite affairs.' He was clearly proud of having thought of this – leaving the responsibility with me – and for the first time began to bustle into life.

He called over to the sentry, who was busy now talking to other travellers – a fellow with a handcart full of skins, and an old woman with a basket of mushrooms on each arm. 'You there, soldier – when you've finished there – go inside and summon Trinculus. Tell him he's to travel with this citizen, explain what is required, and tell him he's excused all other duties for the time.' He turned to me again. 'I'll have him escort you to Abonae afterwards, as well. I understand that I'm required to provide you with protection on the road, and he can most easily be spared. And that, I think, is everything that you require, so now, if you'll excuse me, citizen . . .' He clicked his hobnailed sandals and disappeared into the guard tower again.

TWELVE

Trinculus, when he finally appeared, was obviously a fairly new recruit. He was young – so young that he could only recently have completed his induction to the ranks – with a mop of sandy hair and arms and legs that seemed too long for him. He wore an ill-assorted uniform: old-fashioned chain mail which did not fit him well, battered greaves, and a breastplate which had many dents in it, as if he'd bought it from a bigger veteran and simply had the armourer hammer it to size. (As probably he had – though I knew from Marcus that the army now issued uniforms to conscripts and volunteers who could not provide their own.)

You would have called him skinny, if it were not for the effects of the training he'd received – there were visible muscles on his arms and legs, and his neck and shoulder area was already unnaturally developed from keeping a heavy helmet up. By contrast his freckled face looked even thinner than it was, with nervous eyes that darted everywhere, and jutting ears that even leather helmet-flaps could not disguise. He wore a general expression of alarmed astonishment, like a dormouse trapped inside a fattening jar.

He hesitated for a moment at the guard-room door, then came across to peer up doubtfully at me. 'I'm ordered to report to you, for duty, citizen.' His voice was a surprise: light but distinctly guttural – from the Germanic provinces, I guessed, though the Latin was as perfect as my own. 'You wish to visit the tax collector's house?'

I signalled that I did.

'Then I will lead you there on foot. It isn't very far and you can take the gig. The street is wide enough.'

'Wheeled transport is permitted?' I was used to Glevum and the regulations there.

He shrugged as if the question was a peculiar one. 'This is a small place citizen – and it's not market day. So, if you'd like to follow?' He did not wait for a response but set off at a lope, and Victor had to quickly urge the gig across the bridge before the young soldier disappeared from view.

Uudum was a small place – smaller than I'd thought from the size of the surrounding earthworks. There was no proper entrance arch, simply a gap in the rampart, and we were in the little town – if it could claim to be called a town at all. No packed houses and apartment blocks here, only a collection of ramshackle dwellings in separate plots, many with chickens scratching in the dirt. There was a smell of tanning in the air, so there was obviously a tannery somewhere, and hammering suggested that there might be a forge, though neither was immediately visible. There appeared to be only a single road across the town, so I need not have worried about losing Trinculus. He was clearly visible, ahead.

Towards the centre of the settlement, the buildings grew a little more tightly packed and, though still effectively a single street – were now backed by a smaller alley running parallel and linked by passageways so narrow a fat man couldn't pass. (Not that it mattered – I saw that many of them were blocked by midden-piles.) Here, too, was a solitary street-stall selling food, and one or two small shops, whose owners glanced up hopefully from their open counters as we passed, but their wares were commonplace: piles of woven baskets, bowls or saucepans spilling out onto the road. There was little else in evidence, except one scruffy wine shop with a tavern at the back (which was open but appeared to have no customers!) and a surprising number of little roadside shrines. There seemed to be one on every corner that we passed, each one to a different deity.

Ahead of us Trinculus was still hurrying along. There were few other people on the street – beyond the fungus-seller and the fellow with the skins that we'd seen at the bridge, and a bored slave scurrying somewhere with a water jug.

Just as I was thinking there was nothing in the town, we came to what was clearly the central area – and here to my surprise was quite a handsome square. Not quite a forum, just an open space, but there was a fountain and a proper little temple on one side, with one or two imposing Roman town-houses standing opposite. On either side there was provision for a row of market stalls, though the only occupant today was a swarthy butcher, who (judging by the prices he had chalked up on a wall) seemed to deal exclusively in different bits of sheep. His solitary customer watched the gig arrive and clearly saw an opportunity for dramatic haggling.

'Call this a lamb's heart?' He picked up the bleeding lump, declaiming very loudly so that we could hear. 'Ancient ewe more like. I'll give you half of what you're asking – and I'm cheating myself then . . .'

But I never heard the outcome. Trinculus had stopped outside a house by now and Victor had brought the gig-mare to a halt.

The driver slid down from his seat to help me to the street. 'I should take your parcels with you, citizen,' he murmured in my ear. 'One cannot be too careful. I'll have to take this soldier to the villa now.' He gestured to Trinculus who was rapping at the door.

It was the largest of the Roman-style houses, and in Glevum would have had an entrance court and gate, but here it simply faced onto the street. It was squeezed between two larger blocks, which might have been market offices or even granaries, though it was hard to tell. (There was no evidence of stairs or side-doors leading from the street so they were not apartment blocks – and Uudum was too small to have a council room or court.)

Trinculus was waiting impatiently for me, making no effort to help me with my awkward load. 'This is the place, citizen. There should be someone here.' He rapped the door again as he spoke, and almost at once it was opened from within.

I had expected a slave or household doorkeeper but – of course – the army had taken charge here now. The man who stood in front of us was a soldier in full kit, who looked from me to Trinculus with dark, suspicious eyes. 'About time too,' he muttered, as soon as the military greetings and the password were exchanged. 'Are you the relief? I've been here all day with no one but the corpse for company.'

Trinculus shook his head. 'I'm only here to guide this citizen – the man from Glevum we were told about. He wants to view the body, and look round the premises.'

The soldier sighed despondently and turned to me. 'Citizen, is it? I'm sorry, sir – I did not realise. With that cloak, I thought perhaps you were a friend who'd come to mourn – though if you were, you'd be the only one. The result of being a tax collector, I suppose. No one but the undertaker's women to lament at all – and even they have given up and gone, saying they were only hired for one day, and to send for them again when the funeral begins.' He shook his head and seemed to recollect himself. 'But if you're the person we've been waiting for, come and see him for yourself – and then perhaps we can dispose of him, before his ghost decides we've shown him disrespect and starts to haunt the house.' He stood aside and gestured that I should walk ahead of him.

I glanced at Victor, who was still standing by the gig-mare, holding her, but he simply raised his hand as if to say farewell and motioned to Trinculus to climb up into my former seat. Then he got up himself and the gig drove briskly off. They had gone to fetch Loftus back – at my request, of course – but for the moment I was on my own.

'Straight on down the passage, citizen,' the soldier said, as though I might have been tempted to dive off to my right, into the little cell the doorkeeper would use, with its peephole out into the street and a tiny wooden stool the only furniture.

I walked into the house. Few candles had been lit and it was dark and shadowy. The entrance passage led into a waiting room (a sort of atrium, if this had been a normal dwelling) – a largish area, almost entirely occupied by benches round the walls. There was a small niche in the corner (for the household gods no doubt, though there was no statue or altar in the space), and provision for a brazier on the other side, but those were the only concessions to domesticity. Even the floor was covered with rushes from the stream – like any poor man's house – though that might have been to muffle noise in deference to the dead.

Nor did there appear to be more ornament elsewhere. Through the half-shuttered window opposite I could see that the room gave out onto a longish narrow yard, with what was clearly a stable and kitchen block beyond, but there was no sign of a fountain and only straggling bushes instead of garden beds.

'Left now, citizen,' the soldier said, indicating a chamber to that side, where a taper was burning in a holder on the wall.

I obeyed and found myself inside a spacious room. The shutters here were closed, but the candlelight revealed painted friezes and a patterned floor, and rows of shelves and niches for storing record scrolls. This was the tax collector's private office, unmistakeably. A huge carved desk-table, with ornamental metal strips on front and sides, was the only furniture. It clearly should have stood beneath the window-space – one could see the marks of it against the painted wall – but it was pushed aside into one corner now, to make space around the central object in the room – a bier, and on it the shrouded form of what had been Acacius Flauccus.

More candles were burning at his head and feet, and the air was full of the scent of funerary spices, oils and herbs – almost, but not quite, strong enough to mask the scent of death. Whoever the tesserarius had hired to prepare the corpse for the funeral had done it properly.

Having put down my parcels on the desk, I bent to move the cloth from round the head, but I was interrupted by a startled gasp. I turned. The guard was looking horrified.

'You are intending to unwrap the face?'

I was surprised to find him openly disturbed. Any Roman is accustomed to looking at the dead (a Roman soldier in particular!): the corpses of the wealthy are displayed to lie in state, precisely so that mourners can have a final view. Nor is suicide a special cause of fear: it is sometimes considered an honourable end, as when a defeated general falls upon his sword, or a man takes hemlock to preserve his family's legacy and prevent it being divided up among his creditors. So what was disturbing my companion so?

Perhaps the fact that this was no 'heroic' death? Hanging is not an honourable way to kill yourself – a woman's method, to the Roman mind (which is precisely why Druid rebels dangle dead victims from the trees – a final insult to the unhappy corpse). And this suicide was more cowardly than most – Acacius had stolen money from the state and was attempting to evade the punishment – so he could hardly expect a welcome into paradise. Was the guard afraid displeasure might leak out from the Shades and somehow attach itself to us? Soldiers are famously superstitious, where the Furies are concerned.

I was not long in doubt. 'Would you object, if I turned the
other way?' the man said, anxiously. 'The women have prepared
the corpse and I've kept due watch on him. I've even kept the
candles lit throughout. But unwrapping him again is showing
disrespect. And since there's been no funeral yet, his spirit's
still abroad. If it is offended, it might put a curse on me.'

And me, in that case, I thought wryly. But I simply said,
'Better still, why don't you go back to the front door and keep
watch for the gig when it returns? They're bringing the former
steward here. I want to question him. He'll know, for instance,
if anything's missing from the house.'

'Missing?' The guard had turned away, relieved, but now he
whirled back in alarm. 'What could be missing? I thought
Flauccus had gambled everything and lost?'

I thought quickly. This man was terrified of curses as it was.
If he realised that I thought this might yet be homicide, it would
trouble him still more. (A decent funeral can put even a suicide
to rest, but the ghosts of murdered men are said to walk the
earth eternally – unless and until their deaths are properly
avenged.) If the guard supposed that there might be an uneasy
spirit in this room, he would be unlikely ever to venture here
again. (Indeed, it was something I did not care to think about
myself!)

I temporised. 'Flauccus gambled with the tax money,
according to the note. But his furniture was sent to Glevum, I
believe.' I tried to sound as matter-of-fact as possible. 'Though
not quite all of it. That desk, for instance, seems to have
remained. So there may be other items, too, to be accounted
for.' I was thinking of that missing carriage in particular.

The guard was reassured by such practical concerns. 'I see,'
he said, and went off, visibly relieved.

But I had work to do. I took a deep breath, murmured an
apology to any phantoms that might be hovering nearby, then
knelt down by the corpse and pulled the covers back.

Acacius Flauccus had not been a handsome man in life. I
had never actually met him then, but it was obviously so. His
nose and eyebrows were too large, his eyes too close together
and his chin too small. Certainly he had recently been ill –
I had remembered that from Marcus's remarks – but he was

clearly short and weedy anyway, with thinning hair and warts, and was not improved by having been dead for several days. And hanging is never a pretty way to die.

Mercifully the face was no longer black and blue, since the congested blood had long since drained away, though a strange bruised duskiness remained and the piggy eyes still bulged beneath the lids that covered them. I moved the binding cloth from around the jaw and the mouth sagged open in a disgusting way, showing the ritual coin on the blackened, swollen tongue. I was momentarily startled, though I should not have been. The stiffness of the body had dissipated now: it was an effect that I have noticed in such circumstances before. At least, I told myself, that made it easier to move the shroud and get a better look.

He was dressed in a handsome dark-blue tunic, with silver embroidery at the neck and hems – suggesting that Acacius Flauccus had expensive tastes. That might accord with the accounts of gambling. Just above the neckline was what I was looking for, a deep red line which marked the ligature. Two lines in fact: one straight and low around the neck and the other cutting obliquely upwards with a bruise behind the ear, where the knot had obviously been. Exactly as one might expect if someone hanged himself. So why was I convinced that there was something not quite right?

Two lines, I told myself. But there was nothing particularly notable in that – a cord that passes twice around the neck can make a double mark. Except that the bottom one here was unnaturally low and deep – almost as though somebody had come up from behind and . . .? I took a closer look. The funeral women had done the best they could, but it was still possible to see the pattern of the ligature – not rope, but something woven, by the look of it. A strip of fabric – possibly a belt? The sort of thing that might make a garrotte?

I shook my head. It wasn't possible. The man had left that note. I was inventing things. I had come with the impression that this was not what it seemed, and I was finding reasons to convince myself.

For the sake of thoroughness, though – which Marcus would expect – I continued my examination of the corpse, gently turning it to get a better view. There were no wounds, no other injuries – apart from a few bruises on his arms and back, as if he'd fallen in attempting to tie up the noose. Or – my rebellious mind insisted – as if there'd been a struggle, possibly? Someone thrusting a knee into the victim's back to stop him fighting as the ligature was tightened round his neck? Flauccus was elderly and slight – and had been ill, besides. He would not have been difficult to overcome. And it would have been very easy to hang him afterwards, both to disguise the mark and to suggest a suicide.

I shook my head at my own imaginings, and turned the body gently onto its back again. It flopped grotesquely, but I tried to rearrange it as nearly as possible to the position that I had found it in. In doing so, I had to move the arms and realised that the bruises there would fit my theory too. In fact, when I looked closely, I could convince myself that I was not looking at one single bruise on each, but several smaller bruises in a line – like vicious fingermarks.

On impulse I picked up a flaccid hand and gazed at it. The funeral women had washed and cleaned it well, but surely there was something under the index nail? And that finger, and that? Little traces of something reddish-black, suspiciously like remnants of dried blood? I looked around with sudden interest, but there was nothing in the room that might account for it. No ink, no tinctures, pigments or even sealing wax. Presumably those essential items had gone to Glevum with the rest of Flauccus's effects.

Blood, then? That seemed distinctly probable (although, of course, impossible to prove – even if I could remove those traces from the fingernails, there was not enough for me to test by tasting it). But if so, then the blood was not his own. There was some evidence of blood-seep round the ligatures, but none of the clawing and scratching that one might expect, if the would-be suicide had changed his mind, too late, and tried to tear the noose away. Nor – although I checked most carefully again – were there grazes on any other portion of the corpse. Flauccus had dug his nails into someone else's flesh, almost certainly while attempting to defend himself.

I sat back on my heels and tried to think. I was convinced by this time that my hunch was right, and this was murder, not a suicide. But who would profit by the death? Only a robber, as far as I could see.

Acacius Flauccus was likely to have made a will of course: all Roman citizens of any rank did that (they often make a series, altering bequests depending on what favours or patronage they need – especially if, like Flauccus, they have no natural heirs). In the circumstances his was likely to be challenged in the courts and his possessions sold to help defray the missing tax – but it might help my understanding of the man if I could find a copy of the document, since creditors are often mentioned as major legatees, both as a way of repaying what is owed and also of persuading them to wait. Even gambling debts can sometimes be deflected in this way, and Flauccus was shrewd enough to have attempted that.

I rewrapped the corpse as neatly as I could (making sure to shut that gaping jaw again) and began to search the scroll-pots on the shelves. Most of them were empty. I turned my attention to the contents of the desk. There was a record of receipts, neatly written on a roll of bark-paper, a register of taxable properties within the area, and another careful list of those who had and had not paid. And that was all. No sign of any will.

I was still looking when the guard returned to say the gig had come.

THIRTEEN

I turned to welcome the steward as he was ushered in, but I was so shocked at the change in his appearance, that my words of greeting froze.

I scarcely recognised Loftus as the man I'd seen before. He was as tall as ever and his nose as hooked, but the blue eyes – once so piercing – looked tired and faded now, and the upright stance and air of effortless authority were gone. He was pale and dirty, clearly shaken from his sojourn in the cell and his wrists and ankles bore the evidence of chains. His dark hair had been shaved off to the scalp – and presumably sold to the nearest wig-makers – a humiliation usually reserved for female slaves or slave-youths so handsome that they awaken jealousy (though on some estates the land-slaves are annually sheared, to provide another cash-crop). For a high-ranking steward, though, it was calculatedly demeaning – a visible symbol of disgrace.

He still wore the pale-blue steward's tunic that he'd been wearing when we met in Glevum: a long-sleeved belted robe, adorned with embroidered bands of darker colour at the neck and hem, and reaching almost to his calves. Then it had been the height of elegance, but now it was crumpled, filthy, smirched with mud and grime, with wisps of mucky straw adhering to it here and there.

All the same he made an attempt at dignity. 'You wished to see me, citizen?' He sketched a little bow, moving stiffly as though it gave him pain. 'We met before in happier times, I think. But I owe you gratitude. I understand that I have you to thank for my temporary release.'

'I am sent to make enquiries about your master's death,' I said, sensing that business-like normality would be the best approach. 'I hoped that you could help me. You found him. I believe?'

He nodded. 'I did, and of course I'll help in any way I can.' He glanced at the shrouded figure on the bier. 'May I look on him a moment and offer my respects?'

'Later,' I assured him. 'First I want to hear your full account of things.' That sounded unfeeling so I added, with a nod towards the guard outside, 'The man on duty will expect no less. That's the only reason the army authorised your liberty.'

'But I fear there's nothing new that I can tell you, citizen. I came in from the slave market, suspecting nothing wrong, thinking he'd gone ahead to Glevum as arranged – and while I was making a last inspection of the place, I came in and found him hanging there.' He gestured to a high beam above our heads, the central one of three that supported the attic rooms above. There was a stout metal hook attached to it.

'And the stool?'

'Was lying on the floor, upended, under it.' He pointed to the spot.

'So what happened to that afterwards, do you suppose? I notice there's no sign of any stool here now.'

For the first time the phantom of a smile lit his gaunt features. 'There is not much mystery about that, citizen. The guard is using it. I saw it in his waiting cell, as I came in.'

'Of course!' I had noted it myself, without realising the part that it had played. But it prompted a question. 'I suppose, as loyal steward, you cut your master down at once?'

'I would have done so, citizen – though there clearly was no hope of saving him – but I could not reach the noose.'

'Not even with the desk?'

'That was in its proper place then, over by the window opposite and it's far too heavy for one man to move alone.' There was something shifty in his manner suddenly, as if he knew something that he wasn't telling me.

'And too expensive to transport?' I prompted, suddenly guessing the answer to another mystery. 'That's why it wasn't taken to Glevum with the rest?'

He gave me a sideways look but answered readily. 'I doubt that would even fit out through the door and passageway. My master had it constructed to his own design – the craftsmen, brought especially from Londinium, came and built it in the room. They were the ones who installed the hook in fact, to help them to manipulate the larger planks of wood – they had to bring them, from the court, in through the window-space

– but he always regretted afterwards that he'd had it made so big. Its size was inconvenient, but it was imposing, which was the intention, I suppose.'

I was still pressing for whatever was disturbing him. 'And the stool – I don't imagine that he usually sat on such a lowly thing?'

A shake of the shaven head. 'He kept that back, so there was somewhere he could sit to make the last adjustments here before he left. He said he wished to count the tax money again, to make sure that he was tendering the accurate amount – and the stool was adequate for that.'

'So – as far as you knew, he had the money, then?'

'He was concerned that several small sums were overdue, but otherwise I know for certain it was in the coffer-box, ready sorted and counted into bags. I helped him check through the accounts the night before. But my master was always one to double-check.' He looked at me a moment, then dropped his glance again. 'I assume that the man that he'd been gambling with, heard that he was leaving and demanded instant payment – with menaces, no doubt – so Acacius was forced to give him everything, including all the money from the tax. Always knowing that he would have to kill himself, because he could not live with the disgrace.'

I had my own opinions about that, but I wished to hear this story to the end. I judged that Loftus was telling me the truth, as he perceived it anyway, and though (for the reasons that I'd outlined to Marcus at the start) I was fairly certain he was not involved, I still had that feeling that I was missing something here. 'So he sat here on this unaccustomed stool . . .?'

'Exactly, citizen. It might fit in the carriage with him, if there was sufficient space, but it was not of any consequence if it were left behind. At least that's what he told me at the time – though I realise now he had a different use in mind. That stool was almost the only thing that wasn't sent ahead; when I went to cut him down I realised that I didn't have a knife – I don't carry one, of course – and even the kitchen goods were packed and gone.' He paused. I realised tears were brimming in his eyes, though whether for his master or himself, I could not tell.

'So . . .?' I prompted, more sympathetically.

'I ran into the street and found a man who lives close by –
someone my master had friendly dealings with – and brought
him in to show him what I'd found.' It may have been because
of the difference in my tone, but Loftus seemed to be talking
much more freely, suddenly.

I made another sympathetic noise.

'He had an attendant with him, naturally, and it was he who
saw the writing-tablet on the floor – I was so upset I hadn't
noticed it. Between us we managed to move the desk across to
underneath the hook, and bring the body down. It wasn't easy
because the corpse was getting stiff. Meanwhile the neighbour
sent a message to the tesserarius – and the rest I think you
know. The slave and I had hardly got my master to the floor,
before the army came and marched me off and locked me up.
They seemed sure that I knew where the money was, or at least
the names of those my master lost it to – but there was nothing
more I could tell them, however much they threatened to beat
it out of me.'

So Loftus had not, after all, been flogged. Marcus's message
had spared him that, at least. I was glad of it – for his sake of
course, but also (selfishly) for mine. He was not a young man
and under torture he might quickly have succumbed – if not to
death then to inventing things to satisfy his questioners – and
then I would never have been able to rely on his account.

'All the same, there may be aspects of all this that only you
can know. For instance, did your master make a formal will?'

I hoped to surprise him by the question, but Loftus answered
willingly enough. 'He did. A new one too. Not very long ago.
Though not because of any gambling debts. The previous one
had been in favour of the Emperor Commodus – in return for
the tax-collection licence, I believe – and when the Emperor
was assassinated . . .'

'It had to be revoked?'

'Exactly, citizen. My master drew up a new one when he
went to Glevum last, to render his half-year accounts. He was
anxious to have things properly arranged, as he was already
feeling ill – the first signs of that fever which seized him afterwards. So the will was duly registered before a magistrate,

sealed and witnessed by seven citizens, all of them members of the local curia.'

I nodded, calculating swiftly in my head. The old Roman calendar accounted the Kalends of Mars as New Year's Day – of course that altered centuries ago – but, bizarrely, for official finances that system still pertains. So September (as the name suggests) is the seventh fiscal month, when half-year tax falls due. That date made perfect sense. If Flauccus went to Glevum then, it would be the first time since the news from Rome had reached Britannia. And – in the absence of close acquaintances – members of the curia, who at least knew who he was, would satisfy the criteria for formal witnesses.

'Leaving everything to the Imperial Purse, this time, perhaps?' I enquired. 'If Flauccus had employed that well-tried formula, and not referred to the Emperor by name, his first version wouldn't have had to be annulled.'

But Loftus shook his head. 'He left it to the Glevum colonia instead,' he said, to my surprise. 'He had decided to retire there, as you know, and he hoped to leave his mark. Some to be used for memorial games and the rest for public works – except a small amount that he set aside for a new fountain, here. He financed the existing one, in fact, though it did not win him the public favour that he hoped. People simply grumbled that they'd paid for it themselves!'

'He confided the contents of the will to you?' I was surprised, again! A tax official is obviously required to read and write, so Flauccus hardly required an amanuensis to frame the document. And it's unusual for a servant – however senior – to be in his owner's confidence where money is concerned. Though it was conceivable: Loftus had been sent to negotiate with me, and to make a payment on that villa too – so he had been handling large quantities of his master's cash.

My question brought a wry smile to the steward's lips. 'He told me what was in it, citizen, because I was also a beneficiary. He had bequeathed me freedom – at least he said he had. Not that it makes the slightest difference now. Even if the will were found, it would be set aside – since he deliberately killed himself to avoid a debt to Rome.'

That was something I had not thought about – a suicide's

will is normally as good as anyone's. But a man who owes money directly to the state (rather than to a private creditor) is – like slaves and common soldiers – explicitly forbidden to destroy himself. (I remember Marcus remarking on it once, and privately wondering how that law could be enforced!) But, as Loftus was reminding me, if such a person does succeed in taking his own life, everything he owns is immediately forfeit to the Imperial Purse, regardless of what provisions might be laid down in his will.

So Glevum would not get its games or Uudum its waterspout. Nor Loftus his freedom. The opposite, in fact. A slave is one of his master's assets, naturally, so Loftus would now officially belong to Emperor Severus. But, by tradition, responsibility for the disposal of human chattels – too expensive to transport – falls to the highest-ranking local fiscal officer, who has the option of keeping the choicest for himself, in return for forwarding the proceeds of the rest. In this instance, with the tax collector dead, that was now the principalis at the bridge, so – as Loftus was the only asset left – the officer would be presumed to own him from now on, and was free to do with him exactly as he pleased.

I wondered if Loftus was aware of that. Almost certainly. As a tax-collector's steward, he obviously knew more about such laws than most. But I had news for Loftus that might change everything.

'Loftus,' I said, 'it must be proved, of course, but I don't believe that we've been right about the way your master died.' He was about to interrupt me, but I raised a hand. 'Answer me two questions, and I will explain. First, and this has exercised me from the start: what happened to your master's carriage, do you think? It was seen to leave the house.'

The steward stared at me. 'Of course. How foolish! I had not thought of that. It was not in the stable block when I came back, and neither was the horse – but at that time I simply thought that he'd set off in it. But then I found his body, and I thought of nothing else! I'm sorry, citizen. I have no explanation I can offer you.'

'I wondered if he might have sold it on and hired one for the trip? If he'd disposed of the slave that drove it, that might make good sense.'

Loftus shook his shaven head. 'There was no question of his hiring transport for himself, though I was to do so – with the slave money – and follow him as soon as possible. In fact I'd already made arrangements for the hire. But I did not take the coachman to the slave market. He was retained to drive my master one last time.' He brightened. 'Unless he and the carriage were taken in part-payment of the debt? Or – on reflection – perhaps my master sent the coach driver away, on some imaginary errand, in order to have no possible witnesses on the premises? That's seems the most likely explanation of events. But there was a second question?'

There was. 'What did you first think when you read that note?'

He was not expecting the enquiry and he thought before he spoke. 'I could not believe what I was seeing, citizen. I'd no idea my master had been gambling. He always said he disapproved of it. And as for using the money from the tax – he must have been quite desperate, though I don't know why.' He stopped and peered at me. 'You're looking sceptical. You don't think this was a gambling debt at all? Yet it involved a lot of money – I saw him counting it. Do you suppose that somebody was forcing him to pay for something else?' A look of sudden comprehension crossed his face. 'To ensure their silence? About some discrepancy in the accounts, perhaps? Now that, I could understand more easily. Master cared about his reputation very much – and if he'd made some terrible mistake . . .'

'Blackmail?' I exclaimed. The thought had not occurred to me, and I was tempted to wonder if the steward might be right. But only for a moment. 'An interesting theory,' I told him with a smile, 'and it shows you are a man of some intelligence. And loyalty, as well, since it does not occur to you that he had really been misappropriating funds?'

'My master?' Loftus looked appalled. 'I could not begin to imagine such a thing. But an error – possibly. He was very meticulous, of course, always used an abacus to double-check, but everyone is human. And if someone found it out and threatened to announce it publicly . . .' He tailed off again. 'He had private funds, of course, and I'm sure he would have called on these at first – but I hear these people keep on raising the amounts they ask. In that case I could even imagine him borrowing from the tax, or even gambling to accrue enough to pay. Then, since he could not produce the money when required, he took the only honourable route! You think that's what happened?'

'Not a bit of it. I think that we are dealing with a clever robbery. I don't believe he killed himself at all.'

Loftus was so incredulous he sank down on the corner of the desk. But after a moment he firmly shook his head. 'But of course he did – I found him hanging there. And he left that note. It was his writing-tablet, I'm quite sure of that – it was a special one he used for official purposes.' He scrambled to his feet. 'Forgive me citizen, I should not have sat while you are standing – but you startled me.'

I waved the apology aside. 'It's of no importance. But this question is. Was it his writing? You could swear to that? I saw the writing-tablet in my patron's house – and the words are scratched into the wax in an untidy scrawl. I would have expected Acacius Flauccus to write a standard military hand.'

Loftus stared at me a moment and then shook his hairless head. 'He did. Though I agree, you could hardly tell that from the note. I supposed that emotion had taken hold of him. It was most unlike my master to write untidily – but anything might happen if you're going to hang yourself! But now you make me question it . . .' He paused. 'You don't believe he wrote it?'

'I am becoming ever more certain of that fact.'

'But . . .?'

'Loftus,' I said gently. 'That is your master lying there. He was a little man, shorter than you are by a hand's breadth, if not two. Yet you tell me that, when you found him hanging from the beam, you could not reach the noose. Not even by standing on the stool?'

He nodded. 'Exactly, citizen. Nor from the desk, it was too far away.'

'But if you could not move the desk alone, he certainly could not – he was aging and had recently been ill. He couldn't have pushed it, single-handedly, to underneath the beam, let alone have shoved it back into its place again – using his feet presumably – once he had the rope attached. The stool, as I glimpsed it in the doorman's waiting cell, is simply far too low. And there is no other furniture. So can you tell me how he could have contrived to reach that beam at all – far less secure a cord to it and hang himself?'

FOURTEEN

There was a long, long silence, then Loftus raised his head. 'So you believe that someone put a noose around his neck, then lifted and suspended him by force?'

I shook my head. 'I don't believe that force would be required. I think your master was already dead – strangled from behind, with the same cord, I think. Something silken, judging by the mark around his neck. Do you know what became of the ligature, in fact?'

The steward made a face. 'I think the soldiers took it when they took the writing-block. They took the stylus and the coffer-box as well – and several other things. I think that they intend to use them as evidence. The tesserarius means to charge me with withholding information about illicit gambling, and assisting my master with evading debts and effecting an illegal death. That would have seen me sentenced to the mines. Now he will change the charge to murder, I suppose – so there's no longer any hope for so merciful a fate. But I didn't kill my master, citizen.' His voice was breaking with terror as he spoke.

'I am quite sure you didn't,' I assured him. 'And, since you have witnesses – both to your presence at the slave market and to the stiffening of the corpse when you returned – I think it can be proved. But someone did. Two people probably – since it's almost certain that the desk was moved to hoist him into place.' I saw that he was close to tears of relief and gratitude, so I added quickly, 'Now, you asked if you could see him – this is the time, perhaps. Lift the cloth and look closely at the marks around his neck. The lower one is not at the right angle for a noose. And I believe that there are vestiges of blood beneath his fingernails, but not from scratches inflicted on himself.'

Loftus said nothing more, but knelt beside his master on the floor and reverently moved the shrouding from the face. He shuddered for a moment at that discoloured skin, then bowed and muttered something to his gods. I left him for a moment to pay his last respects before I murmured gently, 'Do you see the marks I spoke of?'

He nodded but he did not turn to look at me. 'Did someone call his name aloud, as he would have wished, to ensure his spirit was entirely gone? And hasn't there been anyone to keep up a lament? Or does the tesserarius actually hope my master's spirit will return and haunt the place?'

'I'm sure the funeral women have done what is required,' I said, evading his question. 'The tesserarius himself arranged for them to come and I think he would insist on at least the minimum, for the sake of decency.'

'Then why have they left him in a tunic, like a common tradesman?' Loftus demanded, sitting back on his heels to look up at me. 'Why not his toga as befits his rank? He was no patrician, but he was a citizen.'

That was a sensible question. I should have thought of it myself. A corpse is always dressed in its best finery for the journey to its last resting place. Of course, all the arrangements here were most unusual, insofar as Flauccus's goods were forfeit, so he could not pay for the funerary rites himself, but you would expect the toga. There was to be a proper ceremony at public expense, because he'd been a government official, and anything else would be an affront to the state. (Though only a small cremation, like the humblest private one – so perhaps he was lucky he was dressed at all, and had not simply been thrown into the pit for common criminals. It may have been my patron's interest in the case which had prevented that.) I didn't say any of this to Loftus, naturally.

'Did he have a toga with him? He hadn't sent it on ahead?'

He shook his bizarrely shaven head. 'He had his best one waiting on the desk when I left to go and sell the slaves. I folded it and left it in readiness myself. He was on official business – he would have wanted it. I suppose the soldiers took it, with the other things.'

'I'll mention it to the tesserarius,' I said. I had plans to ask him about several things, in fact. 'I promised he could have the body later, to dispose of it. He has planned a funeral pyre. Do you wish me to ask him if you can attend?'

Loftus gave a mirthless laugh. 'He would not permit that for a moment, citizen. It is merely your warrant that has allowed me out at all. The man is simply waiting to lock me up again.'

'Then I fear that he'll be disappointed,' I replied. 'This is demonstrably a murder, so matters are entirely different now. For one thing, your master's legacies will stand, so you won't be automatically forfeit to the state. Indeed, when the will is found and proved before the witnesses you should have your freedom after all.'

He looked at me, hope springing in his eyes.

'And secondly,' I said, 'I have a task for you. I wish you to return to Glevum with the gig and report to my patron, Marcus Septimus – telling him what my conclusions are – after your master's funeral, of course. In the meantime, do you wish to start your own lament? I will try not to interrupt you, if you do, but I'd like to continue searching for the will.' I saw his startled look and added hastily, 'I'm sure your master's spirit will understand the need.'

Loftus sighed. He plucked a sprig of hyssop from the folds around the corpse and placed it carefully upon his master's breast, then gently covered up the body again. He rose, still painfully, and turned to look at me. 'To restart the lament, once it's been interrupted for so long, would be more likely to disturb his spirit than to flatter it. The mourners will beat their breasts and wail when they move the bier. I can lament him then. In the meantime, I will assist you in your search. But, citizen, I do not have much hope. I suspect my master left the will in Glevum with the authorities, for fear that he would not survive the journey back. I told you that he was already feeling ill. But if it is here, there is only one place it could be.' He gestured to the desk. The realisation that his master had not killed himself had altered everything – and now he was clearly anxious to assist. 'If you could help me move this further from the wall . . .?'

It was as heavy as he had suggested it would be, almost too heavy for the pair of us, and I almost shouted to the soldier to assist. Then I remembered that Victor was outside in the gig. I had almost forgotten that he was waiting there with Trinculus, but I sent the guard out for him and he soon came hurrying.

'You called me, citizen? I've left that young soldier outside to hold the horse.' He spoke with courtesy, trying to appear unworried by the corpse, but could not stop casting uneasy looks at it.

I explained why he was needed, and he gave a little nod. 'Would it be best to move the body, first?' he enquired, nervously. 'I should not like to treat the dead with disrespect, by knocking him or treading on him while we move the furniture.'

I glanced at Loftus who indicated that – although unwillingly – he accepted this. 'Then let us put the bier into the atrium before we start,' I said. 'It's the honourable place to leave a corpse.' And where he should have been in any case, since he did not kill himself, I thought, but did not voice the words. 'We'll slide him gently through, and strew him with the herbs and flowers again.'

Victor nodded and between them he and Loftus eased the bier into the atrium-cum-waiting room, moving it with care (so as not to deposit the contents on the floor, which would have been a dreadful augury!) and making sure that it was lying with its feet towards the door so that the spirit could escape – though Flauccus's had departed long ago.

This done, and with the three of us to help, it was the work of a few moments to move the desk from the corner and reveal the shelves behind. They were manifestly empty.

I was disappointed. 'Never mind. It was essential to look . . .' I saw the expression on the steward's face, and stopped. 'There is a hiding place? Concealed at the back?'

Loftus gave the vestige of a smile. 'Not in the desk, itself – my master would not have been able to move it out unaided, to reach the strongbox when he wanted to. But it has a part to play.' He ran his hand along the side of it, and removed a strip of bronze that I'd supposed was part of the design. Removed, it proved to be intricately shaped, tapered and finished with a foot-shaped end, set at an angle and with several slots in it. As we watched, the steward slipped the wider end into a gap between the shelves and moved it sharply downwards.

There was a scraping noise as though a bolt had been released, and half of the bookshelves swung outwards and away, revealing what looked like a large cupboard set into the wall. It was closed and obviously locked.

Loftus grinned at our astonishment. His nervous manner had now disappeared – this was clearly the information he'd been withholding earlier. 'Another of my master's personal designs, which he had completed when the desk was made,' he confided with a smile. 'Though only the carpenters were supposed to know and they were sworn to secrecy on pain of dreadful death. That's why he brought them here from far away, kept them in the room until the job was done, then packed them off again, though I believe he paid them very handsomely. It was some time before he confided this hiding place to me, but when he started to feel ill, he did, saying that if he died I was to see to everything and that he wanted me to know where this was, just in case. So if I can remember how to operate this key . . .'

This time it was the shaped end that he slid into the lock, which had clearly been made to accommodate the shaft. He wriggled it a moment and there was a distant click as the pins which held the inner bolt were raised out of the way, permitting him to move it sideways and so unlock the door. I have heard of clever Roman keys like this, but never seen one used, and was intrigued to find that the mortice piece – held in its new place by springs and pins – became a handle by which Loftus pulled the door ajar.

'Just as I thought,' he murmured. 'No will here, I fear. Though there are still these other things . . .' He opened the compartment fully as he spoke.

There were 'other things' indeed. Several gold statues, piles of silver plates, more items wrapped in linen and stored in narrow crates, and at least a dozen bulging leather bags which rattled with the chink of coins at his touch. A little fortune neatly packed to take away. I stared at Loftus.

'My master's private treasure,' he told me, with some pride. 'Enough to complete the purchase of the villa that he'd contracted for – and to pay for the bathhouse I spoke to you about. Obviously he was going to take it when he left.'

This explained why there might not have been sufficient room, even for a tiny little stool, I realised – and more than sufficient to repay the missing tax! And it would all be left to Glevum, when the will was read – so no doubt the curia could find a legal ambiguity which would allow them to use it to make up the deficit. Marcus would be relieved and – though the thieves, at this distance, were unlikely to be found – would regard himself as justified in having sent me here. A relief to me, as well – since I could now decently relax, move on to Abonae and enjoy a wedding feast.

I turned to Victor. 'You'd better relieve young Trinculus, and have him fetch the tesserarius from the bridge. He ought to witness this. Tell him we have proof that Flauccus was not a suicide – no one hangs himself, despairing of a debt, when he has a treasure hidden twenty paces from the spot. And there are other signs besides, which I will show him when he comes.' Victor nodded, and hurried out while I turned to the steward with a smile. 'Meantime, Loftus, I would like to see the stable block.'

Loftus looked astonished. 'But there's nothing there. I explained that, citizen.'

'All the same,' I said. 'I'd like to see the place. It's central to another puzzle which I'd like to solve, though it is not of great importance any more. Your master clearly did not sell the travelling carriage and the horse in part payment of a debt – as I was at first half-ready to believe – so someone must have taken it and driven it away. And he had not sold the slave who usually drove, you say?'

Loftus shook his head. 'He was intending to buy a different driver when he got to Glevum, I believe. He even made an offer, but heard nothing more. But it was always planned that Aureax would drive him there.'

'So what became of him?'

Loftus looked at me, alarmed. 'You are not suggesting that Aureax killed our master – or was involved in robbing him?' He shook his head. 'I can't believe that, citizen. He had not been with Acacius Flauccus very long but he was happy here.'

'Happy?' I echoed, wondering if the recency was significant.

'Pleased with the prestige. I heard him only recently in the servant's hall – when some visiting page was bragging of his horse – boasting that he drove the finest equipage for miles and was treated with respect by all the army guards, even at the toll posts where he was recognised. Not that he could have been involved in this – he was very slight, even shorter than my master, and hardly built for struggle and exertion, beyond what's called for in dealing with the horse. Though Aureax knew exactly how to handle her – it did not call for strength.'

'Just the one horse?' I enquired.

Loftus nodded. 'Just one nowadays, though it was very strong. My master used to keep another he could ride, but since he had that fever he got rid of that and used the coach to take him everywhere. He kept it single-rigged and did not mind that it was slow. Aureux was very proud of that, in fact. Used to say that it was a tribute to his skill, to manage a big coach with just a single horse.'

'You're talking of him in the past,' I pointed out. 'Almost as though you think that he is dead.'

Loftus shook his head. 'I hope not, citizen – when I thought this was a matter of a gambling debt, I assumed he was simply sent off on a false errand to get him out of town. Let's pray that's still the case. Otherwise . . .' But he was already leading me out of the atrium, and through the inner door into the narrow court.

It was not a decorative area. There were a few sorry fruit trees and spindly herb bushes fringing the walkway either side, but apart from that the area was simply paved, with what were clearly storage pots set along the further edge. There was even a faint smell of putrefaction in the air – presumably the funerary herbs were not sufficient to disguise it here: though I did wonder if it was emanating from something overlooked and left to fester in the kitchen block, which I took to be one of the separate buildings at the rear.

I enquired of Loftus, who took this as invitation to point out the salient features of the whole house as we passed.

'That is the master's bedroom over there, with a spare room next to it, which would have been for guests, if any ever came,' he told me with pride. 'While on this side—' he indicated a row of narrow doors – 'are places for storage and for slaves to wait till they were called. And here's the staircase to our sleeping spaces in the attic room upstairs. I had a central cubicle, so I could keep a watch on all the rest, though we kept no female servants my master had no interest in such things – so there was not the trouble that some households have. And over there's the kitchen.' He pointed in exactly the direction I'd supposed. 'It's built across a channel from the stream, to provide fresh water and run under the latrine. And here—' he gestured to a larger building on the left – 'is what used to be the stable, where the horse and travelling coach was kept, and where the groom and driver used to sleep.' He pushed open the heavy wooden door and stood aside to let me in. 'Entirely empty now, as you can see.'

FIFTEEN

Not entirely empty. There was still a little pile of bedding straw in what had been the stall, and even the remains of what looked like oats half-eaten in the manger at the back. And above us, on a sort of gallery, a lumpy palliasse – with a folded blanket still on top of it – showed where the missing Aureax had once slept (with one eye half-open to watch the horse, no doubt). Of the carriage and animal there was no sign at all.

Loftus looked enquiringly at me. 'Is that all, citizen?'

'Not quite,' I told him. 'I take it that the large door opposite was designed to let the vehicle directly out onto the street?'

'Onto the rear alley,' he corrected. 'Though we're only a few paces from the market square – and so to the main road that you came on earlier, which leads down to the bridge. There is not much the other way.'

I stared at him as the implication dawned on me. 'There is another way? An east gate to the town?' Surely the solution to the missing carriage could not be so simple? I shook my head at my own stupidity.

Even Loftus was regarding me with undisguised surprise. 'Certainly, citizen. Forgive me, but don't most towns have at least two entranceways?'

Of course they did, though it was not altogether a ridiculous conclusion to have drawn. Celts didn't, in general, live in towns until the Romans came, but they did build defensive enclosure-fortresses, where whole tribes might repair in case of an attack, protected by palisades, of course, and sometimes walls and ditches much like the ones around this town – but always with a single gate because that is so much easier to defend. 'I was misinformed,' I said, with what dignity I could. 'A woman told me Uudum was the last place on the road.'

Loftus nodded. 'The military road, no doubt she meant. And that's true, of course.'

On reflection, that was exactly what she'd said. But I had no
time to acknowledge this before the steward added, with a
smile, 'But there's another ancient trackway leading through
the hills, still passable by ox-carts, pedestrians and mules.
I travelled to Corinium and back that way, the day I took the
other servants to be sold.'

'Corinium is reachable from here?' I was surprised again.
It is not far from Glevum, half a day at most, but we seemed
to have travelled many miles to reach this lonely place. It was
hard to credit that we were still so close to home.

But it seemed that was the case. 'Fourteen or fifteen thousand
paces, possibly? The old road is difficult but not impossible.
Too far to walk, of course. My master arranged for us to travel
on a pair of mule-carts which set off before dawn – a farmer
and his brother who were going to Corinium market to buy
geese in any case. It took three or four hours to get there,
I suppose, with so much weight up on the carts – and winter
hours are shorter anyway, of course – but we arrived in time
to meet the auctioneer who runs the slave market before the
trumpet sounded noon.'

'And you had time to sell two cartloads full of slaves? And
still get back before the day was out?' That sounded so implaus-
ible that I began to wonder if Loftus was lying after all.

But he shook his head. 'I was selling them directly to the
auctioneer, and that was all arranged. My master had written
to him earlier and the trader had agreed to take them, "provided
they were reasonably healthy", as he said. He just wanted to
inspect them before we fixed a final price – to look at their
teeth and make sure they weren't diseased. Of course they were
exactly as described, so that did not take long. I had to haggle,
as you might expect, but he paid a reasonable sum. I kept a
record for my master's sake.'

'And came back with the farmers afterwards?'

'Of course not, citizen.' He sounded half-amused. 'That would
have taken hours. Flauccus had pre-arranged for another
customer to bring me back here riding pillion on his horse,
which took half the time. I don't know exactly what hour it
would have been when I arrived, about the eighth perhaps?
It cannot have been more – there were hours of daylight left.'

I nodded, satisfied. Two hours past noon. That gave four more till dusk – just time enough to get a message to the Glevum curia that day. A break-neck ride, of course, even for an official courier, and even then the rider turned up at the villa after dark and must have exchanged horses more than once. But it was possible. I turned my mind to another line of thought. 'I suppose there is a guard post at that exit, too?'

'Of course. No toll point that way because there's no official upkeep on the road – which, of course, is really what the toll is for – but there is a man on guard. Usually just a single soldier, or a watchman from the town, but the gate is always manned.'

'So if your master's carriage went out by that gate it might not be observed?' I was pleased to have found a simple answer to the puzzle now – though it brought me no closer to bringing the criminals to trial. Corinium is a thriving market town with dozens of travellers passing through each day – and no Roman garrison, merely the town watch to man the gates. Our killers could lose themselves among the crowds there, easily – and dispose of a coach and horses, with few questions asked.

Loftus was staring at me as though I were insane. 'But, citizen, naturally it would be observed. Everyone knows my master's coach. It's quite conspicuous – all red paint and gilding on the upper-works and crimson curtains at the window-space. If it went out towards the ancient track, it would have been the gossip of the town – there's a bawdy house that way and not a great deal else, at least within this tax authority. The administrative boundary ceases at the stream.'

'All the same!' I was impatient with details of fiscal areas and disappointed that my promising theory was in ruins. 'Surely it's likely that the carriage went that way? No one remembers seeing it pass the western gate!'

He looked mildly at me. 'No one remembers, citizen – but that does not prove it did not happen. Going that way was not remarkable. The carriage went across that bridge a dozen times a moon.'

'But the guards were to escort it to Glevum later in the day!' I was recalling what Marcus had told me at the start. 'They were simply waiting for Flauccus to confirm the time – though he was intending to collect some outstanding revenue first.'

He raised a brow at me. 'I had forgotten that. My master did not care for escorts, as a rule, even in his current . . . even in his weakened state of health. But, even so, if the guards believed that he was merely calling on a defaulter to collect, they would have let him pass without a further thought. Though I had not heard that, citizen. I thought he was awaiting payments at the house. I wonder who took the message to the guards?' He frowned. 'It must have been Aureax. There was no one else.'

'It's not impossible.' I did not want to state the obvious, that – since he'd disappeared – it was likely that Aureax had been party to the plot. 'And presumably he also drove the coach, since surely the soldiers would have noticed, otherwise? He boasted that they knew him, so you said.'

Loftus looked doubtful. 'That's true. Do you think the killers forced him into it? Holding a dagger to his back or something of the kind?' He sounded horrified.

'Was he a person of distinctive looks? A small man, I think you said? That might be hard to feign.'

'With red hair too – though he might have covered that. There was a heavy travelling cloak he used to wear.' He glanced around the stable. 'I can't see it here. But why would Aureax disguise himself at all?' Clearly Loftus did not wish to think unkindly of his friend. 'Perhaps the killer put it on to drive the carriage through, hoping the guards would wave him past? Though it would take some expertise to manage that, perhaps, especially with an unfamiliar horse.'

'Taking Aureax? Since he is not here?'

'Perhaps he was their prisoner.' Loftus looked sharply at me. 'But you think the killers stole my master's coach and used it to escape?'

I was still inclined to think that Aureax was involved, but I didn't tell him that. 'I'm almost sure of it. It's fairly certain now that Flauccus didn't send it on an errand, as you hoped.'

'But, citizen, these people must have had transport of their own. They got here somehow.'

That was true of course. 'Unless they hid that outside of the town – or lived locally themselves.' I was thinking fast. Anyone contributing to tax was a potential suspect here, especially those with grievances at being overcharged – not merely cash tax but the *annona* too. (That dreaded Imperial corn tax is so unpopular that there have been riots, and not merely in Britannia.)

Some local farmers would have motive, then. They should be identified and questioned, one by one. I sighed. All that would take at least a half a moon – and I was instructed to be at this wedding feast.

Well, the tesserarius would have to deal with it, I thought. He was better placed than I was to do so anyway. Not only did he know the chief inhabitants and who was therefore liable for tax, his men might know if any of them came to town that day. Perhaps, if he asked the proper questions, he might discover if the dead man's coach had been noticed anywhere else in the vicinity.

The little officer would not be very pleased at the implication that he'd not investigated properly before – though admitted he'd believed then that the death was suicide. Perhaps he would enjoy this opportunity to flaunt his authority by interrogating half the town.

Either way, he would be arriving very soon, and we must be there to greet him when he came. I nodded to Loftus.

'Time that we went back to the house. Thank you, though, for showing me the stable area.' Not that it had helped much – rather the reverse.

Loftus gave a deprecating little bow and stood back to let me out into the court, where I was instantly aware of that vague unpleasant smell again. It must be the height of the adjacent buildings, I thought, trapping vapours on the ground: it did seem stronger here than in the stable block. And – quite clearly – it was not from the latrine. I stopped and glanced towards the kitchen area. 'Is it possible that food was left behind? There's a peculiar odour in the court. Faint, but obvious once you've noticed it . . .'

Loftus looked surprised. 'I don't think so, citizen. I'd taken all the kitchen slaves to sell, and what we had not eaten had been sent ahead. My master would not have thought of preparing food himself – that's what slaves are for – if he'd wanted anything he would have bought it from the stall. Anyway he was proposing to leave here shortly afterwards, so he could have stopped at an official inn . . .' He broke off. 'But you're quite right, citizen, there is a smell out here.'

'Could there be something in the storage pots?' I asked.

He shook his head. 'A little flour or olive oil, perhaps – it's difficult to clean amphorae out completely when they're set into the ground. But nothing that would make that sweetish putrifying smell. You don't think it's coming from the corpse . . .?' He tailed off and turned to stare at me wide-eyed. 'Or . . .?'

The same thought had occurred to both of us at once. I nodded. 'There is only one way to find out.' And without another word we bent in unison, and began to lift the lids and peer inside the pots. It was not an easy task, given my aged joints and the steward's recent ordeal in the cells: the covers were heavy, and overlapped the apertures, and each had a flange that was close-fitting at the neck – necessary for storage vessels out of doors. Our first attempts revealed no result, but nearer the ground the scent was more pronounced and it did not take us long to locate the source of it. With a glance at each other we stood on either side and between us raised the lid.

We had hardly lifted it a thumb's-breath when we let it fall again. The stench which emerged was overpowering and I was almost forced to join the steward as he turned away and retched into the shrubs. But when he came back to join me a moment afterwards – apologetic, shaken and white-faced – I realised that it was not the stink alone which had affected him.

'Did you see what was in there?'

I shook my head. I had jerked my head back, half-instinctively, screwing up my eyes, and in the gloom I had not glimpsed anything.

'It's Aureax – or at least it was,' he said. 'I'm almost sure of it. I saw the red hair and the uniform. What is he doing in the storage pot?' But, of course, he did not really need to ask. It was hardly likely the fellow had climbed in willingly.

We raised the lid again, more cautiously this time and – holding my cloak before my nose to help suppress the smell – I gazed into the aperture myself. It was a large amphora and

Aureux was a smallish man, but storage pots are not designed for human occupants. He was crammed stern-first into the space, his bare legs folded to his shoulders in a way which only a Nubian dancer could have naturally achieved, and would have torn the sinews and dislocated bones. Not that he would have felt it: the cause of death was clear – the throttling tunic-belt was still tight around his neck, so his eyes and tongue bulged from a black contorted face, which was upturned at a dreadful angle and staring straight at us.

But someone had beaten him very savagely before he died. The flesh on his back and shoulders had been whipped into a bloody mass – that much was evident from the little we could see – and he would most certainly have been alive for that.

'Aureax?' I murmured, though it obviously was.

Loftus nodded speechlessly then – after a moment – managed, 'Poor man, this isn't fitting. Can we get him out of there?'

It wasn't easy. He was firmly wedged and – unlike his killers – we were careful with the corpse. And there was little that we could lay hold of decently. I was beginning to think of sending for Victor to assist. But Loftus managed (with a struggle) to insert his hands and grasp the body underneath the arms while I pulled up the feet, and slowly we began to inch the lifeless form out of the hiding place. If it had not been for the presence of a trace of olive oil, which served to grease the sides a little as we worked, I doubt we could have freed him, even then. But finally, with a lurch we hauled the body free and laid it face-upward on the courtyard floor, both of us panting with exhaustion from the task.

And that was how the tesserarius found us when he came swaggering from the atrium a moment afterwards, with a flushed and nervous Trinculus at his side.

SIXTEEN

The principalis began in his usual bustling tone. 'I hear that you have something to show me, citiz—' He broke off in dismay, staring at the dishevelled body on the ground. 'Is this all you wanted me to see? A slave? Whose is it, anyway?'

'This is Flauccus's missing coachman,' I explained. 'Killed by the same hands that murdered his master, I suspect, and which subsequently stole the coach in which to flee.'

'Murdered . . .?' The tesserarius looked genuinely shocked. 'But surely . . .?' He glanced at Loftus. 'Is this the result of what the steward has been telling you?'

I shook my head. 'Obviously you have not seen what we have found,' I replied. 'You would have come to the same conclusions as myself. Come into the house and I will show you, too. Though someone had better make arrangements for disposal of this dead servant, as soon as possible.'

'With your permission, citizen, he will be a member of the local slave guild,' Loftus put in, deferentially. 'Our master saw that all our dues were paid. It's not a large association, in a town this size, but there are obviously more slaves than free inhabitants so there was an arrangement with the funeral house.'

'The same one that was called in for your master?' I enquired, surprised. I was accustomed to Glevum, where the slave guild had funeral directors of its own.

I glanced at the tesserarius, who nodded. 'I imagine that's the case. To my knowledge there is only one such business in the area.' He seemed to feel the need to exert authority, and began to snap out orders. 'Trinculus, go to the place that arranges funerals, explain that this concerns a member of the guild, and fetch the women with herbs back here to deal with him.'

'And you may tell them that they can recommence the inter-rupted funeral for Acacius Flauccus, too,' I put in. 'I think I have completed my enquiries here.'

Trinculus looked doubtfully at his superior.

'Well! You heard the citizen! Do as he suggests!' the tesserarius muttered. And then, lest he should seem to have deferred too much, he raised his voice again. 'Snap to it, soldier! Say that I have sent you and be quick about it too.'

'As you command, sir!' Trinculus, who had taken his helmet off (presumably in deference to the dead) now jammed it over his dormouse ears again, raised a stiff arm in salute, then scuttled off as if the ghost of the dead coachman might haunt him for ever if he wasted any time – as perhaps he feared it would.

I turned to lead the others back into the house, but Loftus seemed reluctant to accompany me. He did not actually refuse, of course, but he was clearly unwilling, even when I gestured him to come – which puzzled me, until I guessed the cause. 'You wish to keep a watch upon your friend?'

The steward gave me a grateful glance and dropped to his knees beside the corpse. 'Citizen, permission to close the eyes for him at least?'

'And call his name three times, no doubt, while you are there, to make quite sure the ghost has flown?' the tesserarius suggested mockingly – as though there were any possibility that life might linger in that anguished corpse.

Loftus ignored the taunt, and addressed himself exclusively to me, 'And I may remove the cord around the neck?'

The principalis looked outraged and drew in a deep breath, clearly intending to protest, but I said, 'Granted,' before he framed the words. 'But steward,' I went on, 'once you have done that, join us in the house. The funeral women will do the rest of what is needed here – wash the corpse and prepare it for the pyre. And we'll leave them to provide the mourners, too – since you will want to join the lamentations for your owner, I presume?' I turned to the still-bristling army officer. 'Now, if you'd like to come this way.'

The soldier puffed his chest out like a fattened hen. 'You intend to leave that slave here quite unsupervised? I presume there is a rear entrance to this place – what is to prevent him making an escape? And what is this about attending his master's funeral? He should be in custody. I released him, temporarily, at your express request . . .'

'Into my custody, I think. And I take full responsibility. Although, now he's answered all the questions that I put to him, he will not be returning to the cells.'

The little officer looked ready to explode. 'He is to be freed? On whose authority?'

'That of the warrant that I showed you earlier,' I said. 'Which requests that you assist me in all respects and allows me to take decisions, I believe.'

'Then I dispute your decision in the strongest terms! I'll tell your patron so. I cannot accept your claim that someone murdered Flauccus and he did not kill himself – but even if true, it does not alter the steward's case at all. The law says clearly that a slave who is so much as present in the building where his master's killed, is guilty of criminal negligence for which the penalty is death.'

'But Loftus was not present in the house, and there is proof of that: he was at the slave market,' I said. 'You imprisoned him simply to question him about his master's suicide and secret gambling. Reasonable enough, and I would have done the same. But it is clear now that there was neither suicide or gambling, so Loftus is not forfeit property but remains a part of Flauccus's estate. So – as he had no hand in what occurred and has told us everything he knew – I shall send him to my master, aboard the gig when it returns to Glevum, with a letter explaining that he was arrested by mistake.'

He saw the implication that the error had been his. 'Mistake!' It was an expostulation. 'The steward was party to everything his master did – by his own confession, freely made!'

'But he did not collude in plans for any crime – because there was no such plan. As I hope to prove to you. I take it you did not stop to view the corpse as you came by?' I led the way into the atrium as I spoke and the tesserarius was more or less obliged to follow me, muttering that he'd already accorded the tax collector more than due respect and was not attracted to viewing him again.

So he was not happy when I partially unwrapped the corpse once more, and he stood impassive, clearly unimpressed, while I explained my reasoning – pointing out the shortness of the corpse, the angle of the lower mark around the neck and the remnants of dried blood beneath the fingernails. When I had

concluded, he made no response at all. Even an attempt at flattery – 'I am asking you to observe these things, because I need
an independent man of rank to witness them' – scarcely
produced more than a reluctant grunt.

But when I ushered him into the inner office, and showed
him the open cupboard which had been revealed and the shelves
packed with more riches than a booty-cart, his manner thawed
at once.

'Citizen Libertus! I confess that I have doubted you, till now.
But I see you are deserving of all the praise your patron heaps
on you.' The clipped efficiency had gone and he was fawning
'like an emissary to the Emperor' as the saying goes. 'You have
found the missing treasure.'

I shook my head. 'On the contrary, worthiness. You misun-
derstand. This is not the money from the tax accounts. This is
the private fortune of Acacius Flauccus – which the murderers
clearly did not know about. But proof enough that he was robbed
and killed, I think. No one hangs himself for debt with all this
hidden in the house.'

The soldier frowned. 'But can it be used to make up the deficit?
Or will the curia in Glevum have to do that, still? Suppose, for
instance that Flauccus made a will?' He shot me a malicious
little glance. 'If his estate is not forfeit, as everybody thought, it
would be valid now. In that case your patron may not be so happy
after all. I know he was hoping you could retrieve the tax.'

I smiled. 'Indeed, there is a will – already lodged in Glevum, I
believe, and witnessed by members of the curia itself. But
fortunately, it seems that Flauccus has bequeathed his wealth
to the colonia,' I said, aware of a certain malicious pleasure of
my own at seeing the triumph fading from his eyes. Behind
him, I saw Loftus come into the room as I added airily, 'I am
sure it will be more than adequate to pay the sum involved.
Besides, this isn't all the money Flauccus left behind, I think?'

The tesserarius looked bewildered and even Loftus frowned.

'There is the little question of the money from the slaves,' I
urged. 'Loftus brought it here and you confiscated it, together
with his careful record of the sales. No doubt the neighbour-
witness can corroborate that fact. He should be informed, in
any case, about the truth of things.'

'Ah . . .!' The tesserarius flushed and looked suddenly more anxious than young Trinculus had done. There was a little pause before he added, silkily. 'I fear I used that money to defray the funeral costs. I assumed, of course, that it was forfeit to the state. Was that not in order, citizen?'

'Perfectly in order,' I assured him with a smile. 'Though there must have been enough for several funerals. But no doubt you kept a record, as the steward did, so it will be easy to calculate how much of it remains.'

The tesserarius had turned ashen now, and I realised that – as I'd guessed – he had not expected to be called on to account for this and was going to find it difficult to produce the residue.

'Of course,' I went on relentlessly, 'one would not expect you to recollect precisely the proceeds of the sale of someone else's slaves – but perhaps the steward can enlighten us? Then he can take that money with him too, back to Glevum for when the will is read. Loftus, can you recall the sum involved? Though if not, we can find it from your record by and by.'

The steward stepped forward with such eagerness that it was clear that he remembered the exact amount, but before he had the chance to tell us anything, the soldier murmured, 'Citizen . . . a word!' And Loftus – like the well-trained slave he was – ceded precedence at once.

'Estimable citizen,' the tesserarius took me by the arm and led me over to the window-space, dropping his voice so Loftus could not hear. 'The records will be found, of course they will. Though it may take a day or two. I am not altogether sure what I have done with them.' He spoke as if they might be anywhere in town, instead of almost certainly in his office at the guard-house by the bridge. 'And until I find them I cannot be sure how much I should repay, that is, how much is owed to the estate, after the expenses of the funeral.'

He was so obsequious and his tone so unctuous now that I began to feel that I preferred his self-important mode. I detached my arm discreetly from his grasp and told him sweetly that I understood, and that instead of sending the money back in the care of Victor and Loftus, as I'd planned, I would return this way myself and take it back with me, after I'd attended the famous wedding feast. After all, I would have to return the ox-cart, wouldn't I?

But the ox-cart, it appeared, was no longer good enough. A military gig could be provided, suddenly – if I took his advice and went back the way I came, to take the military road from Aquae Sulis to the port. And, if I preferred not to venture to the inn – 'which was in the wrong direction anyway, and on reflection might not be entirely suitable' – he could offer me his private hospitality tonight.

So the place he had arranged for me was clearly primitive. However, I did not relish the idea of spending the evening in his company, or of sleeping in a draughty tower on a military cot (though possibly the army had requisitioned more comfortable accommodation in the town). So I thanked him gravely but indicated that I preferred the *hospitalis*.

'I understand it's on the ancient track. I want to make a few enquiries, to make sure that Flauccus's coach was not seen to go that way. In the meantime, perhaps you would be good enough to ask your men again? And interview several of the townspeople, as well – though after the funeral will be good enough for that.' I outlined the questions that I wanted him to ask, both about the carriage and the corn tax too.

The tesserarius was flattered, as I'd hoped. 'You can safely leave that questioning to me. I know all the major landowners and businesses round here – I can guess who paid their taxes, and who resented it. Though . . .' He glanced at Loftus.

'I think you'll find the information that you need, sir, in my master's record scrolls. I believe you took most of them away as evidence,' the steward said. 'Together with his toga and his documents.'

'I have the documents. I will investigate. But . . .' he broke off. 'But now, I think, I hear noises at the door. Female voices – the funeral women, perhaps?'

In fact it was Trinculus who came into the room. 'I have brought the herb-women, as you commanded, sir. Where would you like them to prepare and wash the body of the slave? Out in the stable, perhaps? It's obviously not fitting for them to do it in the house, with the master still lying in the atrium.' He nodded in the direction of the door. 'Speaking of the tax

collector, sir, the undertaker has come to talk to you in person
– to find out what you want to do about that funeral. The pyre
is ready and it could be done today, especially since you wanted
no procession or musicians to attend.'

I looked at the principalis in surprise. 'No music and no
mourners?' Even the average slave would hope for that.

The tesserarius was turning pink again. 'In the interests
of discretion, citizen. I think I told you that I feared unrest, if
the people of Uudum discovered what had happened here . . .'
He tailed off, in dismay, as Trinculus gestured to the door,
where the sounds of an excited crowd could be distinctly heard.
'Though it seems that news has reached the gossips now.'

'You told me to be quick, sir, not discreet.' The young soldier's
dormouse ears had turned distinctly pink. 'Somebody asked me
what the hurry was, and I answered them. I did not think it was
a secret any more.'

The tesserarius scowled. 'That was foolish, soldier. No wonder
that the news has spread all over town. After all the trouble that
we took, to have the funeral women come in through the back.'

'But then you thought that Flauccus had committed suicide
and gambled all the tax,' I said smoothly. 'And that's why no
musicians were planned. But now you have discovered otherwise. I'm sure that something of the sort could be arranged,
even at short notice. I should like to tell my patron that an
officer of the state was laid to rest with proper dignity – he'll
expect a full account, since of course I intend to attend the
rites myself. But the funeral houses always have lamenters and
pipers they can hire – and there will be time enough, presuming
they're not intending to light the pyre till dusk.' (It is still usual,
in Britannia, to hold important funerals after darkness falls,
though Marcus tells me that the custom has died out in Rome.)
'And you have sufficient funds,' I added wickedly.

The tesserarius nodded, rather wearily. He turned to Trinculus.
'Have the undertaker in and we will see what we can do. And
tell the soldier at the door to disperse the crowd, at once.'

I grinned, not displeased with what I had contrived.

So everything that happened afterwards was my own fault,
perhaps.

SEVENTEEN

It began with me spending a wholly wretched night. The funeral, for one thing, lasted several hours. Far from it being a private and restrained affair as the tesserarius had hoped, rumour of the death had now spread like a flood tide through the town. So, though the usual invitation was not publicly proclaimed, most of the inhabitants of Uudum seemed to have joined the procession to the pyre – though drawn more by curiosity than respect, I guessed, since the night was cold and damp.

Then, the place prepared was in a field some distance outside the walls and of course everyone attending had to say a word or two in praise of the deceased – so by the time the final eulogies were said, the ashes cooled by pouring on of wine, the ritual piece of bone was buried in the ground and the pig was sacrificed – it was very late indeed. And there was no escape – as Marcus's representative I was in the place of honour at the front, standing by the tesserarius throughout.

Even when it was over I could not get away at once. The undertaker came across to find me, purposely ushering Loftus back into my care and asking if I was satisfied with the pipes and mourners he'd managed to provide. In fact, I was heartily wishing by this time that I'd never shamed the tesserarius into arranging them, because although they'd howled and tootled most impressively, they had done so often and at enormous length.

However, I forced a smile and murmured that things had all gone splendidly, but I was now anxious to go and find my bed, whereupon – instead of bowing himself politely off – the fellow seized my arm. 'Citizen, if you wish I could arrange the cleansing of the house when the nine days are up – make sure that all the proper rituals are observed.' He glanced at the tesserarius, who – with one eye on me – agreed to the arrangement instantly, but left me to fix the price.

This was followed by still more delay as the tesserarius made one last impassioned plea for me to accept his offer of hospitality. 'Forgive me, citizen. I have been preoccupied. One of my new recruits deserted recently, and of course the garrison will hold me to account for that. And the tax collector died when he was under my protection, officially. I am already in disfavour with my superiors. Allow me at least to offer you a bed.'

Perhaps that should have warned me what might lie in store, but I had left Victor to await me in the town (where he was overseeing an official inventory of the treasure we'd discovered in the house, and incidentally guarding my personal luggage too) so I declined the offer, shook off the officer and walked back with the remnants of the crowd.

I had insisted that Loftus should remain with me – someone had lent him a clean tunic and a cloak against the rain – so together we plodded to the gate where Victor, together with Trinculus and the horse, was waiting with torches to escort me to the inn. 'The treasure's all listed and packed into the gig, and your things as well. It's under guard tonight, I'm to collect it in the morning, though I wouldn't leave the horse – she's highly-strung and now she's used to me, I fear she'll be restive if I'm not somewhere near. Now, if you're ready, citizen? I've already made enquiries as to where to find the inn. It's quite a step, I hear. You might be wise to take your toga off and leave it in the guard post overnight. The duty soldiers will take care of it for you – I have your warrant here, and that will vouch for you.'

It was a good suggestion and I was glad to follow it. I'd redraped my toga before the funeral, but it was a sorry sight – sodden round the hems and stained from travelling – and would be nothing but an encumbrance if we were walking 'quite a step'.

We had to walk, of course. If the road was too difficult for lightweight gigs by day, it was almost impossible to ride a horse by night – and in the rain – without risk of damaging a valuable animal. So I was glad when we saw glimmering lights ahead and our torch-brands showed a bunch of tattered holly nailed above the door, a sign that accommodation was available within. Victor assured me that this was the place, though Loftus seemed uneasy from the start.

'If this is the house I think it is, it's certainly an inn, but I am surprised that the tesserarius selected it for you. It's . . . the kind of establishment that lets its rooms out by the hour.'

'You've visited before?'

It was a jest but it did not raise a smile. Loftus was serious. 'I came out last year to interview the landlord of the place, a scoundrel who had been evading the register for tax. But they must have seen me coming, or had word of me. When I arrived there was no one but an ancient crone in evidence, crouching over the remnants of a fire, claiming that she'd found the place abandoned a day or two before and moved into it for shelter.'

'Which you did not believe?' I said.

'A ploy to account for the ashes being warm, if I am any judge, while the owner and his staff took cover in the woods beyond the stream. In his absence there was nothing I could do, as no doubt he was aware, but it didn't strike me as a wholesome place to stay. Though if the army have arranged it, it will no doubt be all right,' he said, adding with pretended cheerfulness, 'anything would be an improvement on where I spent last night.'

'I am so tired, I could sleep anywhere,' I replied. 'It should be dry at least and they have promised me a meal.' I'd had nothing since breakfast, shortly after dawn, except a sip or two of milk – though Victor had apparently been rather luckier. He'd been offered some of Trinculus's evening pottage earlier, he said, while they were waiting for the funeral to end. 'We thought you'd have at least a bit of sacrificial pig.'

I'd harboured hopes of that myself – they generally hand it round to the mourners afterwards – but it was stringy and well-nigh inedible, and one symbolic mouthful was enough. 'Let's go in.'

It was well that I was tired. The inn was terrible – a rundown hovel with a leaking roof run by a swarthy, one-eyed innkeeper and his fat and toothless wife. Victor and Trinculus went to the stable block, to get what sleep they could while taking turns to guard the mare – and it's possible that they had the best of it.

The 'room' that I was shown to was a curtained cubicle, with filthy bedding and a straw mattress of such antiquity that I immediately kicked it over against the outer wall, resolving to wrap myself up in my cloak, however damp, and sleep directly on the floor rather than brave the bedbugs and the itch. However, the sack was rotten and the stuff cascaded out, so Loftus stuck his torch up on a spike and came to help. We cleared it in the end, but it left a nasty damp patch on the floor, and I tried not to look too hard at what came scuttling out of it.

We had scarcely finished when the landlord reappeared, accompanied by a pair of sulky half-clad girls, tousle-haired and not especially clean, who were, he said, 'My daughters – virgins both of them!' but manifestly weren't either of those things. One was dusky and the other olive-skinned, and each bared a shoulder and assumed a practised sultry smile, but there was no attempt to mask the boredom in their eyes. 'Choose one to keep you company, or have them both,' the innkeeper went on. 'One each if you like.'

The girls smirked hopefully, surprised when I did not require their services, and more so when I refused their 'private dance'. They flounced off, offended, and clattered down the stairs.

The landlord looked aggrieved and said to Loftus, loudly enough to ensure that I could hear, 'I don't know what your master thinks he's looking for. I was told he wanted the best we had to offer! And he's destroyed the bed. I hope that he has gold enough to pay for it.'

'Now look here, my good fellow,' I began, in a tone that would have suited the tesserarius, 'what I wanted . . .'

But Loftus shook his shaven head to silence me. 'This is not my master, innkeeper. Nor one of your common towns-folk, as you seem to think. This is a Roman citizen, the personal representative of one of the most important magistrates in all Britannia.'

I produced my warrant from underneath my cloak.

The landlord did not look especially impressed. 'Citizen, is he? Well how was I to know? In any case, he's not the only one. Forced to leave the legions when I lost this eye and bought this place with my retirement pay, so I don't owe anything to anyone. And as for his patron, I don't care who he is – my girls are not diseased. The Emperor himself would not find better anywhere round here.'

'He isn't looking for a girl, he's looking for a bed. A decent bed, clean water for a wash, and something hot to eat. And you'll provide it too, if you know what's good for you. And as for your not owing anything, I was the steward of the tax collector here, and know that – as a citizen – you're liable to tax.' He spoke with an authority which made me realise what an excellent assistant to Flauccus he had been. 'Meals, accommodation and stabling, I believe you offer here. Making you liable for your basic census charge, door tax on your property and sales tax on your wine. Not to mention the levy on exotic slaves – I imagine yours would qualify for that? – or offering special dance performances, which I presume would come at extra cost?'

The innkeeper was looking flustered now. 'The steward of Acacius Flauccus? Why did you not say as much before? I would have made arrangements—'

'To be somewhere else?' The steward was so scathing I was surprised, myself.

The landlord's single eye refused to look at us. 'I was simply told a stranger was to come, at the invitation of the guard post here – and naturally I assumed he'd have a soldier's tastes . . .' He tailed off, helplessly. 'But a meal, of course, I'll see what I can do.' He gave a nod, which might have been a bow, in my direction now. 'Give me a moment, citizens' – Loftus had been promoted, suddenly! – 'I'll have to go and discuss this with my wife.' He moved towards the curtain which acted as a screen.

'And while you are about it,' Loftus called after him, 'find us somewhere more salubrious to sleep. Where, for example, we're unlikely to be woken every hour by noisy occupants in the cubicle next door!'

The landlord paused and gave us an ingratiating smile. 'No offence intended, gentlemen,' he said and hurried down the stairs. A long, long wait ensued. I was so weary that I sat down on the floor – a decision I regretted almost instantly, when a sensation on my skin told me that I had managed to pick up a flea or two. I scrambled to my feet, and with the help of Loftus and the guttering torch was attempting to find and dislodge my visitor when the landlady came toiling up the stairs and pulled the curtain back.

'I'm sent to tell you that we're heating up some stew. It is nothing fancy, I meant it for ourselves, but I'm told that you must have it and I do as I'm told. You'd better come and have it while it's warm.' It was hardly gracious, especially when she added with a scowl, 'I suppose you'll want some sent out to the stable too?'

I was about to murmur something, but Loftus said, 'Of course!'

'I hope that you can pay for all this special treatment,' she exclaimed. 'I don't know what you threatened my husband with, I'm sure. Most guests are happy to get cheese and bread.' She held up her taper to survey the room. 'And what's happened to my bedding? There'll be a charge for that.'

'It disintegrated with old age and decay,' the steward said, using that authoritative tone again. 'It was so full of rot and creatures that I'm surprised it did not do so long ago. Discuss it with the army if you want recompense – though it hardly warrants it. No doubt your pleasure-slaves can stuff a sack with straw before another customer arrives – and be glad to do it, too, if it means that they escape the bugs themselves.'

'There are to be no other customers tonight, by order of the tesserarius,' the woman said, frowning more than ever and completely unaware that she had just confirmed what role the girls fulfilled. 'Now do you want this stew, or not?' And without another word she waddled off again, leaving us to follow with our torch as best we could.

The room in which we finally arrived was smoky, dark and small, with a number of tables surrounded by small stools and no sign of benches or couches anywhere. A brazier in one corner gave off a feeble heat, and we made towards it, grateful for the glow. I even ventured to take off my sodden cloak and spread it on a neighbouring tabletop with some vain idea of helping it to dry, but the air was scarcely warm enough to have the least effect. This did however have the positive result of shaking out the flea and I had the satisfaction of squashing it, though queasily aware that the blood that stained my thumbnail was my own.

The stew, when it arrived, was barely passable – a glutinous concoction of who-knows-what bits of meat – but it was warm and filling and I shut my eyes and ate. Loftus did the same, though the innkeeper hovered round, anxious to offer another seat elsewhere, if I proved unhappy at eating with a slave.

I shooed him off and he disappeared again, to return a moment afterwards with a flagon of the cheapest Roman wine – so watered that it was hardly wine at all. I did not mind it – I do not greatly care for wine in any case – and drank the proffered beakerful in one, simply grateful for the faint warmth it engendered as it went. Loftus followed my example, though I saw him wince – no doubt Flauccus kept a better class of drink.

The landlord was back again now, with a pair of battered cushions and the sort of blanket that you might throw across a horse, though unused and therefore clean. 'Best that I can offer at short notice, citizen. I'll push the tables up together and you can sleep on them – it will keep you from the draught, and any rats – and it's fairly warm in here. No one will be wanting to use the room tonight.'

I nodded. It was at least a good deal more inviting than the cubicle upstairs. 'And my driver, the soldier and the horse?'

'They've been taken care of, citizen. Unless you think the soldier might, perhaps . . .?' He sketched the outline of a woman in the air and gave what might have been a wink – though with one eye it was difficult to tell.

'On no account,' I told him. 'He's riding guard for me. I don't want him afflicted with the pox!'

The landlord shook his head dejectedly. 'Well, in that case, citizen, if there is nothing else . . .'

I was about to say, 'Nothing,' but a thought occurred to me. 'There is one thing, perhaps. In the daytime, what happens to the girls?'

He was calculating what I meant by this and wondering if he ought to name a price or lie – I read it in his face. So I said, bluntly, 'I just want information, not a sample of your wares. Your dancing whores – where do they spend the day?'

He shrugged. 'It all depends,' he muttered. 'If they've been entertaining customers, they sometimes sleep. Otherwise they sit outside beside the door, or in the window if it's raining, looking out to watch for trade. There's always one, at least, available.' Flaunting themselves to passers-by, he meant, but that was exactly what I'd hoped to learn.

'Then ask them – every one of them – if anybody saw a fancy coach go by a day or two ago. A covered travelling carriage, carved, ornate and painted red and gilt. If so, can they recall the driver? Any description at all would be of help. And of the occupant, if possible – though it's very likely that the curtains would be shut.'

The innkeeper's one eye looked piercingly at me. 'That would be the tax collector's coach?' he said.

'You know it?'

He gave a shrug. 'Everybody does. It's a distinctive thing. But it would not come down here. And if it had, the girls would let me know at once so I could . . .' He broke off, aware that he was likely to incriminate himself. 'But he went to Glevum, didn't he? Moving up there to retire. Everybody knows that, too. So he'd go the other way.' He frowned. 'Surely this steward could have told you that, if he's really the taxman's servant as he claims.'

'Oh, he's the taxman's servant,' I replied. 'Or was. But Flauccus didn't go to Glevum after all. He didn't go anywhere – someone murdered him. Then, it appears, they made off in his coach. So I repeat again, ask your girls if they saw it go this way.'

He was about to protest, but gave a nod instead. 'With pleasure, citizen. But – murdered?' He glanced at Loftus. 'And his steward did not die in his defence? I'm surprised you were content to purchase him.'

'His steward had gone to market selling slaves,' I said. 'No suspicion can attach to him. He's under the protection of my patron and myself, until such time as the murderer is found. In the meantime, he is not my slave.'

'Citizen, I don't care whose slave he is – as long he isn't telling the taxman about me,' the landlord said, with something of his earlier swagger evident. 'And, it seems, he won't be doing that.'

'He can't tell Acacius Flauccus,' I said. 'But my patron has a particular interest in local tax affairs. That's why he sent me here. And I am myself a candidate for the Glevum curia, which deals with the collation of Imperial revenue from here.' I had never expected to find myself boasting about that, but I'd learned from Loftus what impressed the man.

I had succeeded – insofar as it was possible. The innkeeper

became a model of helpful industry. Tables were pushed together to form the promised bed (though they were rocky and of slightly different heights, which did not make for a relaxing night). He placed another coal upon the brazier, lit a taper to replace the torch and produced another pitcher of questionable wine. Then: 'I hope you will be comfortable, gentlemen,' he mumbled, and withdrew.

Loftus assisted me to take my sandals off and climb onto the makeshift bed. He placed a pillow underneath my head, and wrapped me in the blanket, which at least was dry, insisting on keeping the damp cloaks for himself. 'Loftus, you are not my slave,' I said.

'Without you, citizen, I would be in a cell,' he answered, as he lay down at my feet.

'Flauccus must have had a travel warrant too. I wonder what became of that,' I murmured, but there was no reply. Loftus, exhausted by his recent ordeal and not withstanding the uncomfortable bed, had blown the candle out and fallen instantly asleep.

I turned over and tried, without success, to do the same.

EIGHTEEN

I must, in fact, have dozed a little in the end, because I woke to find Loftus standing by the bed, holding a candle and proffering a bowl of dubious-looking curds with a hunk of loaf in it.

'Citizen, I'm sorry to rouse you, but it is long past dawn,' he said. 'The landlord has sent in this homemade cheese and bread. The others have already breakfasted and have set off with the horse. I said we'd meet them at the guard post when they've harnessed up the gig. Your transport should be waiting by the time we get there, too. We all have long journeys ahead of us today, so I felt I had to waken you.'

'Waken me!' I grumbled as I struggled to sit up, realising that the night's discomfort had left me stiff and sore. 'What makes you think I've slept? Here, never mind the food – help me with this blanket and assist me to get down.' He put down the bowl and taper and hurried to my aid.

It took a moment to disentangle me – the blanket had succeeded in entrapping both my feet – but with the steward's help I scrambled from my unforgiving perch. I ached in every limb.

The curd cheese looked uninviting – and tasted rather worse – while the homemade bread was so coarse I almost broke a tooth (cheap flour from the miller is always full of grit) but I forced myself to swallow some of each. As Loftus said, the day was likely to be long, and it might be many hours before I ate again and – this not being a military inn – I would no doubt be expected to pay for this repast. (That sparked a train of thought and I quickly checked my purse, but was reassured to find that I had not been robbed – always a possibility in a place like this.) So Loftus helped me lace my sandals and put on my cloak and we ventured, blinking, out into the daylight of the court.

The rain of yesterday had given way to frost, but the landlord and his lady were there outside awaiting us. 'I asked my . . . the girls, as you requested, citizen,' he said, bustling across to greet us instantly. 'My wife and I both questioned them – and rigorously too – but I am persuaded that it is exactly as I thought. None of them saw the taxman's coach go by.'

I wondered if he'd really beaten them to make them talk, or was simply posturing – after all they were his merchandise – but I was persuaded that he was right about the coach. I thanked him curtly and enquired what I owed, expecting to be asked for an outrageous sum, but the amount he named was so modest I could not believe my ears.

'A special rate for curial candidates,' he said, and did that one-eyed wink again. 'Please tell the tesserarius that you were treated well – though perhaps you need not mention me to anybody else?'

To the tax authorities, he obviously meant. They left me in something of a quandary. The size of the bill was clearly a sort of bribery-in-reverse, but it was hard to know how to avoid appearing to accept. In the end I gave him twice what he'd demanded, which was probably too much.

Loftus thought so and he said as much, as we set off on our way, the crisp ground now crackling beneath our feet. 'I fear, sir, that he managed to outwit you there! Now he'll doubtless boast of how you left a hefty tip.'

'I wanted to make it clear that I would not collude with him,' I said.

Loftus grunted. 'Citizen, that was doubtless wise of you. Though – despite my threats last night – his tax commitment will not be very great. He may incur a fine for evasion of his dues but I doubt that anybody will take the trouble to pursue him now – at least until the new publicanus is installed – when the rogue will doubtless temporarily disappear again.'

I laughed. 'He has amazing impudence. Asking me to mention my treatment to the tesserarius! Well, I shall be doing that all right – although not the way he meant. Though it's really not his fault. The army must know what kind of place it sent us to!' But Loftus, like the respectful steward that he was, and despite what I'd supposed was a mutual friendliness, seemed uneasy at continuing conversation beyond immediate concerns.

Besides he was setting such a pace that I had no breath for
casual talk until we reached the town.

There, at the guard post, two gigs were standing by: Victor
with Marcus's vehicle, now piled with bags and parcels of
treasure from the house, and the other a swift-looking military
cart with an enormous driver in a military cloak already on the
seat, dwarfing young Trinculus who was beside him with my
luggage at his feet. I thought the tesserarius might be avoiding
me, after the night that he had put me through, but he strutted
out as soon as we appeared.

He gestured to the orderly, who trotted after him bearing
my toga which had obviously been dried. 'Citizen, your toga.
We have—'

I interrupted him. 'Never mind the toga. I'm minded to report
you to Marcus Septimus!' I fumed. 'An insult to his representative shows disrespect to him. What made you suppose that place
was suitable?'

The tesserarius looked disconcerted, momentarily, but his
self-conceit was as impervious as his shield, and he had
his answer – no doubt carefully prepared. 'My orders were to
find you accommodation at a local inn – and genuinely, citizen,
it is the only one. If it displeased you, I planned to offer you
hospitality myself. Which indeed, I did, not once but several
times.'

He had a point, which made me more inflamed. 'By which
time it was far too late to change my mind!' I stormed. 'It must
have been the fifth hour of night before I saw the place!'

'But, citizen, when I heard you were to come here and conduct
enquiries, I could not guess how swiftly you'd succeed. I thought
the funeral would be delayed for several days. I never intended
you should arrive there in the dark.'

'Simply that I should have a long and fruitless walk, because
you were affronted that I was called at all? Yet putting me
under an obligation to yourself, because you were personally
entertaining me?'

He dropped his eyes and I realised this was more or less the
truth. He'd resented the presence of an inquisitor, especially a
civilian one from miles away, and had deliberately set out to
disoblige. However he was too self-important to be easily

abashed. 'But you were given what special treatment could be offered, so Trinculus declares, so I hope that you are reasonably rested and ready for the day. You still wish me to question the Uudum populace?'

'And your own soldiers, too!' I said sternly. 'Especially the men on duty at the guard post on the day the death took place. I'm anxious to discover what has happened to that coach – especially now we know that the taxman's murderers killed Aureax as well and almost certainly used it to escape.'

The man thrust out his chest again, like a prize partridge ready for the pot. 'I have already done so, citizen, and they are adamant. No one recalls seeing it after we received the message to stand the escort down. And – lest you should wonder if that message was a trick – I can tell you that not only were we half-expecting it, from past experience, but that Flauccus wrote it under seal and sent it by a messenger who had dealt with him before and would have recognised an imposter instantly. So at that time he was obviously alive. That would have been about an hour before midday.'

I was disappointed. Obviously this information was useful in its way – it gave us a better indication of the earliest the killers could have struck – but it did not answer my immediate concern. I said, 'Ask everyone to search their memories again – if there is any way it could have passed here unobserved.'

He shrugged. 'Naturally, citizen, I'll do as you request, though I can't see how such a thing is possible. The bridge is always guarded – I'm exacting about that.'

'Always?' I said, sharply. 'My own experience suggests that one man is on guard, and if – for instance, someone comes and asks for you, the sentry would have to go inside and summon you. Or if someone asks directions, he might desert his post long enough to point out where to go. Not a long absence, in either case, of course but, with careful planning, either might give time for a vehicle to pass.'

'I suppose that is remotely possible. I'll make enquiries.' The tesserarius had turned very pink indeed. 'Though the vehicle in question would need to be extremely quick. Speaking of which, your vehicle awaits. I have detailed Trinculus to ride with you, and guard you – as you see. Though your way lies the same way as the other gig until you reach the main road south, I'm sending a full escort to accompany that – the one that would have gone with Flauccus, if he'd lived – to guard the treasure hoard. You may wish to travel in their company at first.'

It was tempting, but the escort meant that Victor and his gig could only travel at a marching pace. 'Best if I press on to Portus Abonae,' I said. 'I am in danger of missing the wedding feast.' And being away from home at Saturnalia, I thought, though I did not mention that. 'If you discover any information, send it after me.'

The tesserarius ignored this last request. 'A wise choice, citizen. The gig is very fast. You should pass Aquae Sulis easily today. And – following your unfortunate experience last night, and since I have messages to send that way myself – I've taken the liberty of sending my courier on ahead to warn all mansiones on the route that you will be calling on one of them tonight, under special warrant . . . I presume you still have that?'

I produced it from beneath my cloak and flourished it.

'Then they'll take good care of you. I've given your driver directions where to go, and which mansio to aim for, if the road permits. Orderly, give the citizen his toga now. We've managed to dry it and sponge off the muddy hems – though it will require a fuller to clean it properly.'

All this was clearly an attempt to compensate for the choice of last night's inn, and I managed to accept it with a modicum of grace, though I decided not to put my toga on to travel in. Experience had taught me how muddy it became, and the presence of my warrant – to say nothing of Trinculus and the military cart – was proof enough of entitlement and rank. But the certainty of finding a proper mansio tonight (and one which had been warned to ensure I had a bed) relieved me of much of the anxiety which always accompanies travelling long distances on unfamiliar roads. So I thanked him cordially, said farewell to Victor and the steward – both of whom, though slaves, I'd come to value and respect – and climbed up in the gig.

The driver, a lugubrious-looking brawny giant of a man, did not even glance around to check, but the moment I was in my seat he flicked the reins and urged the gig forward at an alarming pace. Poor Trinculus, crammed up against the edge in very little space, almost pitched forward and fell onto the floor – where he would have been safer, as far as I could see.

I said so to the driver, who was sitting next to me, but he did not turn his head. 'Citizen, arrange yourselves however you see fit. I'm simply required to get you to your meeting point as fast as possible – and the sooner I do so, the sooner I can get back to my farm.' And he relapsed into silence.

A civilian then, despite the military cloak! Obviously he had some skill as a driver and the army had commandeered him for a day or two – they were entitled to co-opt non-citizens, and doubtless the Glevum escort required all the spare manpower available. He was probably lucky that they hadn't requisitioned his horse and cart as well, but he clearly resented his predicament and me, in particular, for causing it.

Nor was Trinculus any more inclined to talk. He had settled himself into the cramped gap at the edge, and was now wholly occupied with balancing himself and preventing his helmet from flying off his head, so I abandoned all attempts at conversation, held on tightly to the seat and simply endured the constant bouncing and juddering of the gig, and the mud that was constantly thrown up to spatter me.

After all, I told myself, I'd come this way before, and this gig was just as fast. This painful journey could not last longer than our journey yesterday. All I had to do was close my eyes and wait.

NINETEEN

I was wrong in all respects. This time the journey seemed twice as long. My jaw was stiff from the clenching of my teeth, my bones were aching and my face flayed by the coldness of the air, but at last we reached the junction where we'd turned off yesterday. There was no sign of the woman with the goat's milk but our new driver seemed in no need of directions, let alone anything so human as a drink. Without hesitation he turned the gig and swept off towards Aquae Sulis as if the cavalry were after us.

I had expected that our progress would be faster now, but in fact it seemed the next few miles might be extremely slow. True, the road had wider verges here – but it was more frequented, too, and the crisp crust of frost had melted or been churned away so those margins were a mire of trampled mud. We had not gone a hundred paces before we had to slow behind a heavy wagon carting baulks of wood, which was clearly unwilling to pull across and let us through. Our taciturn driver was moved to speech at last.

He turned to me and gestured with his thumb. 'Get that soldier stood up in the cart – this is army business, and other travellers will have to let us pass.'

I was frankly doubtful whether this would have much effect. Trinculus was not an imposing figure – especially rocking on unsteady feet in insufficient space – but our driver was correct. The sight of Roman armour seemed to be enough. The wagon moved across.

Our driver gave a grunt, which clearly meant, 'I told you so!'

Nor was it an isolated incident. People moved their oxen obligingly aside, and pedestrians trudged uncomplainingly off the road into the muddy margins as we passed. The presence of a soldier – even a skinny one with dormouse ears – seemed to have produced this instant deference. Or perhaps, I thought, watching our driver sweep past without the least acknowledgement, it was his presence which occasioned such respect – the fact that he wore a military cloak and must have been a full four cubits tall: not the sort of man with whom to pick an argument. Whatever the reason, it had the right effect: our pace was as brisk as it had been before, except that the horse had now begun to tire.

It was now that the value of my warrant proved itself. Our driver drew up without a word at the first army relay-station that we passed (not a mansio, but one of the mutationes that the mansionarius had been so dismissive of) and I produced my document, and experienced for myself what services such places could produce. In what must have been no longer than an hour, my party had been provided with a drink, a hunk of bread and proper Roman cheese, a welcome rest and a fresh horse to see us on our way – all paid for by the state (or at least the local population who are required to maintain this system for the Imperial Post). The same thing at any civilian establishment would have incurred a hefty bill – and not included any change of animal.

I was beginning to appreciate the advantages of being a member of officialdom – and to wonder if I should reconsider the idea of joining it.

I had more cause to do so, much later in the day, when – having passed through Aquae Sulis without a pause (to my regret, I had been there once before and much admired the place) – we turned off onto the road towards the coast and, just when I was thinking I could bear no more, we drew up at a proper mansio.

At first our welcome was a cautious one, till I got down painfully and produced my document, whereupon the man in charge was summoned instantly, and hurried out to greet us with a smile.

He even seized my forearm, in the way that Romans do when meeting friends. 'Citizen Libertus, a thousand welcomes. We were told that you might come. I'm delighted that you've chosen our mansio tonight.'

In truth I had not chosen anything: it was entirely the decision of the driver – or perhaps, on reflection, the tesserarius. I would have favoured stopping long ago, but I smiled and murmured a few felicities. By this time the gig and driver were already being led away towards the stable block, leaving Trinculus beside me, standing awkwardly with all my parcels in his arms.

The mansionarius ignored him and addressed himself to me. 'Would you care to come inside? We have several other visitors tonight – including a councillor from Glevum who knows your patron and is keen to talk to you – but says the morning will be time enough for that. In the meantime there is a private room for you, together with your orderly of course. And a bathhouse, if you'd care to visit it – very soothing after hours of travelling.' He glanced at Trinculus. 'And your orderly, of course, if you permit.'

I'm not a very enthusiastic user of the baths in Glevum, usually – one is in danger of having one's garments stolen while one bathes, and returning to find inferior ones or none at all, even if one pays an attendant to watch one's locker-niche. But after hours of painful jiggling the notion of a steamroom and a plunge seemed irresistible – even if Trinculus had not been looking pleadingly at me.

I nodded, and was duly shown the separate bath-suite at the back. It wasn't large, but it was well-equipped: a changing area, a small heated pool, a steamroom and a plunge, and a final anteroom, warmed from the furnaces next door, and complete with a massage slab where one could lie down and be rubbed with oils and strigilled afterwards. It looked inviting, and after leaving our cloaks in our pleasant sleeping-room – not a special chamber of the kind I'd had before, just army palliasses, some blankets and a stool, but as clean and neat as last night's inn had been the opposite – Trinculus and I set off to try the baths.

I had judged it safer not to leave things unattended, even here, so I left him in the changing room to guard my garments and the precious parcels while I bathed, promising that he could have his turn when I came back and then help me put on my toga for the evening meal. (There is no rank distinction in the baths, of course: men are generally equal when they bathe, but I am never comfortable wrapped in just a drying-cloth and was not sorry to have these few moments to myself.)

It was as pleasant an experience as I could have hoped, and

I felt the stiffness ebbing out of me as I went from room to room, though as I moved into the massage area and lay down on the slab, I was surprised to hear the voice of Trinculus. He seemed to be talking to somebody nearby – possibly the army slave who wielded the oil – but I heard him say, 'Thank you. I'll go in straight away' and then heard footsteps behind me where I lay.

'Trinculus? What are you doing here?' I half-raised myself on one elbow and peered round as I spoke, but could see nothing but a pair of naked legs. 'I thought I told you to remain there with our things?'

'Citizen, this isn't Trinculus,' replied an unfamiliar voice. 'Although, I have invited him to start his bath, as well.' I rolled over, to see a young man whom I had not seen before, an athletic looking fellow in a tunic and bare feet, whose ink-black hair was cut short in an untidy style which clearly showed that he was not an army slave.

He smiled at my perplexity. 'Do not concern yourself, your property is safe, a guard has been arranged. I've come to offer you my services. You'd like a massage and a strigil afterwards? The army attendant is not especially skilled. My master thought you might be glad of greater expertise.'

I sat up, surprised and absurdly flattered too – though reflection told me that this must be the slave of the Glevum councillor and the compliment was not to me at all, but to my patron. 'Do I know your master?' It was possible of course. 'He must be the Glevum magistrate I heard about.'

The young man laughed. 'Exactly, citizen. I don't believe you've met. Though he knows your patron well – and yourself, by reputation – as does nearly everyone. You are the citizen Libertus, I believe?'

'And your master?' I was still slightly on my guard.

'Crassus Posthumous. Perhaps you know the name? A relative and friend of Titus Flavius.'

I nodded, feeling any anxiety subside. Crassus Posthumous. I had heard him spoken of – an aging fellow in indifferent health. But any friend of Titus was a friend of mine. 'He's staying at the inn, I understand?'

'And anxious to meet you, as I'm sure you have been told.

To thank you for your services and endorse your nomination to the curia. It seems you will have saved them from needing to contribute to the missing tax . . .' He saw my face and laughed. 'Don't look so startled, citizen – not only does your young attendant praise you to the skies, the news reached here this morning, anyway.'

'This morning?' I was puzzled, but then it occurred to me. 'A messenger from the army-post at Uudum, I suppose?' Obviously he had not felt the need to be discreet – and a courier has more ways of spreading news than delivering a sealed despatch.

'Exactly, citizen. He told us you were travelling this way – though it was not entirely certain which mansio you'd choose – and that you'd caused a sensation in Uudum, by proving that Flauccus was not a suicide! My master spoke to the courier himself, and was amazed to learn what you'd achieved within so short a time. He's delayed on purpose to talk to you himself, and is happy to convey news to your patron, if you wish. So if you'd care to have this massage, with his compliments?'

I nodded gratefully and lay back on the slab. The slave began to work the oil across my back with soothing hands and I abandoned myself to the pleasure of his touch. 'I am only sorry that I cannot meet with him tonight,' I said. 'I would be glad to have the recent news – whether, for instance, the legate has arrived.'

'There, I'm afraid we cannot help you, citizen. We have not come from there. And my master has already eaten early and retired. He is elderly and we have a lot of journeying ahead of us – it is many miles to Glevum.'

'Indeed it is,' I said, with feeling. 'And yet more to Portus Abonae! I suppose the road is good?'

'Kept in good repair, to speed the flow of trade.' The firm hands worked my muscles as he spoke. 'Though naturally better when there's less cold and rain. My master has business interests at the port, which necessitated this wretchedly unseasonable trip, but could you not have avoided it yourself? It's a time of year when few boats venture out to sea.'

'I'm on my patron's business,' I replied. It is an axiom that everybody talks to massage-slaves and – since it is always

pleasing to have the chance to brag of influence – I found myself
explaining about the wedding feast. 'His Excellence would have
come himself, but he is expecting an important visitor – that
Imperial legate that I mentioned earlier. He has sent me as his
private representative.'

I was hoping for some exclamation of impressed surprise,
but perhaps such things are commonplace to the slaves of
magistrates. Or perhaps he was not really listening to my words,
because the massage did not pause and there was no reply. So
I said nothing more and let him do his work.

All too quickly it was over and I was strigilled clean. The
young man handed me my drying-cloth. 'One moment, citizen,
I'll have them fetch your clothes – they were taken into safety,'
he said, and disappeared.

Suddenly, I felt a clutch of fear. Had I let myself be lulled
into a false security? Here was I with nothing but a towel, and
my young companion was no doubt similarly attired – had I
been tricked and robbed?

I was contemplating how I could maintain my dignity while
running out to call on the mansionarius for aid, but at that
instant the massage-slave came in again, accompanied by an
army orderly, bearing the garments I had taken off – now dried
and neatly brushed. Even my purse was there and – when I
discreetly peeked – the contents all complete.

'Citizen, your tunics – and your cloak. I'm instructed to tell
you that the rest is in your sleeping-room, awaiting you,' the
orderly saluted briefly, and hurried off again. I was so relieved
my knees had turned to cheese.

The slave-boy turned to me. 'Now, with your permission,
citizen, I'll do the same for your young orderly? Or would you
prefer me to help you to get dressed?'

I hoped he hadn't realised my moment of mistrust – it might
be construed as an insult to the kindly councillor. I tried to offer
a gratuity (sometimes expected for a borrowed slave) but he
wouldn't accept, so I tiptoed off shamefaced and left him rubbing
oils into young Trinculus.

At the sleeping-room, I found the promised soldier at the
door, and a brief inspection told me that all my things were
there: the present, the toga-parcel, and the precious warrant

safely in its bag. So when Trinculus returned, glowing and grateful for his bath, I did not even chide him for gossiping and disobeying me.

We had a simple meal accompanied by wine – which the guard sent in to us – then lay down on our respective mattresses and fell gratefully to sleep.

TWENTY

I woke next morning to find the sun already up, and Trinculus still snoring gently at my feet. I grunted. I should not have permitted him to drink my share of last night's wine, but after our long journey, even a few sips had made me sleepy, so – with painful recollections of the feast at Marcus's – I had left the rest for him. With no immediate alternative (such as my favoured honeyed mead) I had risked drinking the water from the jug, which looked reasonably clear and was (allegedly) from a nearby spring. And luckily, there'd been no ill effects – in fact, I'd slept much more than usually well.

I sat up now and prodded the soldier gently with my foot. His response astonished me. He leapt up and was on his feet at once, babbling apologies and pulling on his clothes. It took a moment before he realised where he was and sank down on the mattress saying piteously, 'I thought I'd missed the trumpet . . .'

'As no doubt you have,' I said, remembering the wake-up bugle at the other mansio. 'In which case, so have I. So let us move as soon as possible and see if it's too late to find a meal, and whether our driver is still waiting with the gig. I'm sure he'll be resentful because we are so late. Crassus Posthumous will no doubt be awaiting me, as well – I hope we've not delayed him overmuch. I'd like to thank him for his kindness yesterday, though it may have been the massage which encouraged us to sleep.'

A few enquiries did produce a plate of fruit and nuts, and the assurance that our driver was awaiting us. I urged on Trinculus, who seemed to be having trouble with his sword-belt, suddenly, and we hurried out into the inner court.

The councillor, however, had already left. 'Sends his greetings, citizen, but regrets he cannot stay – he has many miles to travel before dark. Though he says no doubt you will encounter him again – you are standing for the Glevum curia, I hear?' This was the mansionarius who had come again, in person, to escort us to the gig.

I waved aside this attempt at social flattery. 'I'm sorry to have missed him, all the same. I would have liked to thank him for lending me his slave and arranging guards for my possessions yesterday – though no doubt I should thank you for providing them.'

'I was pleased to accommodate him, citizen. He was anxious to assist, and to provide you with that rather better wine. I'm glad that you were pleased. But perhaps you will have a chance to tell him so yourself. His coach is heavier – it's possible that you will overtake him on the road.'

I laughed. 'Ah, but we are going towards the coast,' I said. 'I have an important function to attend. Our driver is returning to Uudum – possibly today – but Trinculus and I are staying for a day or two, guests at a wedding feast.'

The mansionarius had sensed a potential customer. 'So will your driver require accommodation and stabling during his return? If so, direct him here. It would be covered by your warrant, and I'm sure we could oblige. I know he's a civilian with no licence of his own, but he's working for the army and it's their vehicle – if he would like to stop.'

I shook my head. 'I doubt it very much.' If I judged correctly the man would drive home as fast as possible, not pausing anywhere. 'Besides, the gig will be considerably lighter without its passengers, and faster on the road.'

The mansio-keeper smiled. 'Of course. But if we can be of service . . .? A change of horse, perhaps . . .?'

I was about to tell him that I would suggest as much, but I was interrupted.

'Citizen?' Trinculus was plucking at my sleeve. 'The driver – he is asking if you wish to go. Otherwise, he says, he won't have time to get you where you're going and drive back to Uudum before tomorrow noon. After that he is liable to punishment, for being absent with a military gig and animal.'

I nodded. Typical of the tesserarius, I thought, to compel someone to drive us many miles, against his will, and then fine him if he dares to be delayed. 'Tell him I'm already on my way,' I grasped the mansionarius's elbow and gave his arm a parting shake – I was becoming accustomed to such Roman tokens of esteem – and left him smiling as I joined the vehicle.

I muttered apologies to the driver as, with the help of Trinculus, I climbed up and assumed my seat again, but the only answer I received was a disgruntled snort. I sighed. The fellow had been requisitioned for his driving, not his charm and I settled for another long, uncomfortable ride, in the disaffected silence that we'd suffered yesterday.

There was not even pleasant countryside to occupy my thoughts. The land we passed through here was dismal, flat and dull – the more so, the further that we moved towards the coast. Land which doubtless dried in summer to verdant pastureland, was now awash with rain and stretched in mournful puddles for miles on either side, interrupted every now and then by little 'islands' of high ground, where miserable homesteads cowered under stunted trees, surrounded by a few limp crops and huddled animals. The lanes that led away to them were either submerged in water or buried in thick sludge, only a few paces from the major road. No wonder that Darturius – with salt flats even nearer to the sea – had to send a guide to lead us safe across the marshy ground.

And judging from the sky it was about to rain again! I pulled my birrus up around my ears and closed my eyes, bracing myself for hours and more hours of this bouncing misery and wondering if Imperial torturers had ever thought of using travel as an interrogation tool. A day or two of this and I – for one – would have confessed to almost anything! I rebuked myself (such matters are not a subject for even mental jests) and allowed my thoughts to turn to home and Gwellia, and picturing how she was faring with the wool.

So I was startled when I heard the driver's grumpy voice. 'Well, here you are then, citizen – this is the mansio. Last one before Portus Abonae, if I've counted them aright. This is where I am to leave you, I believe – though you had better check that with the man on duty, I suppose.'

I nodded, almost too relieved to speak, so it was Trinculus who said, 'It clearly is the place. Here's the keeper of the mansio! They have clearly been expecting us.'

I looked and saw that Trinculus was right – the mansionarius, a portly fellow with a hook nose and protruding eyes, was hurrying towards us with a worried frown. He was accompanied on one side by a burly guard and on the other by a skinny inn-slave, perhaps eight or nine years old, both of whom looked equally concerned. Evidently our lateness had been causing some anxiety.

'You get the parcels. I'll get the warrant out,' I murmured to Trinculus, sliding rather gracelessly to earth and fumbling in the leather pouch to find the writing-block. I passed it to the keeper of the establishment, who glanced at it briefly and passed it to the guard. 'Very much what we'd been alerted to expect?'

The soldier was reading it more thoroughly, then turned to me with a peculiar smile. 'It seems to be in order, but we will need to keep it temporarily, in case authority is needed later on.' He thrust it back into its leather pouch and gave it to the little serving-lad, who clutched it as though it were a polecat and might bite.

'Apologies, mansionarius,' I murmured with a smile, offering an arm-shake in the way I'd learned to do. 'We've discommoded you. I fear that we were treated so well at last night's mansio, that we were very late to rise.'

Perhaps it was a mistake to mention another military inn – it implied comparisons, which I had not meant at all, and seemed to cause offence. The arm was as cold and flaccid as a fish, and the tone was not much warmer as the mansio-keeper said, 'Can you confirm your full name, traveller?' He spoke as though he had not seen my travel document at all. 'And your business here?'

I gave him the advantage of a full account. 'Longinus Flavius Libertus,' I replied. 'Here representing His Excellence, Marcus Aurelius Septimus, chief magistrate in this part of Britannia. I am on my way to visit the Celt Darturius, who owns the salt mines on the marsh, to mark the wedding of his daughter. He is expecting me, as you no doubt are aware. I believe there is a signal that you are to give, to let him know I'm here, so he can send a guide for me.'

The mansionarius was using those protruding eyes to look most curiously at me, and at my young companion who had collected our possessions from the gig by now and – having placed them at my feet, had come to stand beside me, rear-ranging his ill-assorted armour round his skinny form and ramming his large helmet down on his dormouse ears. 'And this . . .?'

'Is Trinculus – from Uudum. My escort,' I explained. 'Is there some problem with accommodating him? I realise that you were expecting me to be alone.'

The mansionarius did not answer that. 'And the coach?' he enquired, watching that vehicle make half-circles in the dust as the driver urged it round and down the road again.

'Also on loan from Uudum,' I said, pleasantly. 'And anxious to return there to avoid a fine. I'll hire another when it's time for me to leave. In the meantime, you are expecting me? You have your instructions?' It occurred to me that perhaps he'd not been fully briefed.

The large eyes swivelled back to me again. 'Oh, we have indeed. I'll send a signal just as soon as it is dark and they will send for you tomorrow when it is possible to cross. You have missed the tide today. In the meantime, follow me – I have a room prepared.'

The advantages of rank again, I thought contently, as I followed him through the inner court with Trinculus trailing slowly after me with all the baggage. The inn-slave, who was still clutching my warrant, made no attempt to help him with his load, but did seize a lighted taper from a stand and hold it up to light the way – not into the wider corridor beyond, but up an open wooden staircase to the upper floor.

It is not uncommon for inns, of any kind, to offer upstairs rooms and a glimpse of the scene from a window-space we passed suggested that there was at least a view of sorts – of the river and the marshy wetlands either side. The river was enormous – making the Sabrina, where it flowed through Glevum, seem a tiny brook; I could imagine I was looking at the sea, as I had done from my tribal lands when I was young. My last glimpse of freedom had been a glimpse of it, shimmering as far as human eye could see, before my kidnappers had forced me down into the stinking blackness of the slave ship hold – and in all my travels I'd never seen it since. (Glevum, where they sold me, is of course a river port.)

That memory – combined with my weariness, no doubt – brought unexpected tears to mist my eyes, and at first I hardly paid attention to the room into which the guard was now escorting me. The inn-slave thrust the feeble taper into a holder on the wall and I vaguely saw the shape of a mattress on the floor, and a narrow window-space set high up in the wall. But that was all that I had time to recognise, before the guard and slave retired, the door was shut behind them and I found myself alone.

I had expected to share my quarters with Trinculus, as before – he was acting as my attendant now, and I'd almost come to think of him as such – but as a member of the army he was obviously entitled to accommodation of his own, so on reflection I was not entirely surprised. Perhaps they had no private room here to accommodate us both. Facilities in this mansio were clearly minimal. The mattress, on inspection, was small and comfortless for one – with two it would have been extremely difficult to sleep. And there was nowhere else, not even a small rug. Otherwise the narrow room was bare, beyond a water jug and basin on a stool and a larger jug, clearly for other purposes, beside the door.

Doubtless they had separate arrangements for the ranks, I thought – probably a communal sleeping-room with shared amenities. I did not envy Trinculus his bed.

On the other hand, he had my baggage and I was keen to wash my feet and legs and put my toga on before I went to find a meal – to say nothing of ensuring the wedding gift was safe. So I picked up the taper and went over to the door. I would simply have to find him. I could ask a guard, perhaps.

I put my hand upon the latch, and found – to my dismay – that I could not open it.

'Trinculus?' I called, but there was no reply. Somewhere in the distance another door banged shut. 'Trinculus!' I rattled at the lock, to no avail.

So this lack of comfort was no accident – not the result, as I'd supposed, of being miles from larger towns! There was to be no wash and toga and warm evening meal. They had thrown me into this upstairs room and locked me in.

I was a prisoner.

TWENTY-ONE

I could not believe it. Surely this was just an accident? Some unfortunate mis-function of the lock? I rattled it again. 'Trinculus!' This time my shouting brought a swift response. The door flew open, but it was not my big-eared friend, it was the bulky guard.

'What is the meaning of this noise?' he growled, more like a bear than ever.

'The door,' I muttered, voiceless with relief. 'I think it locked itself.'

He laughed. It was not a pleasant sound. 'Hardly that, my friend. It's bolted shut – by special order of the commandant.'

I frowned. 'But you've seen my documents.' I tried to sound appropriately affronted. It is an offence to deprive a citizen of his liberty without due cause, and the penalties are harsh. 'You must know who I am.'

That laugh again. 'Oh, indeed we do. We've been expecting you. And we wouldn't like anything to happen to you, would we, now you've come this far? So it's for your safety, in a way. Try to be grateful, that is my advice and be glad that things have not gone worse. As they may do, yet – if I hear another squeak from here!' And he slammed the door again and disappeared. This time I distinctly heard the bolt slide to.

And that was that! I squatted on the lumpy mattress-sack (there being nowhere more convenient to sit) and tried to think.

In some ways, of course, the guard was right. As a prisoner, I was fortunate. Conditions were far better here than those I had endured at that civilian inn. The mattress was merely a sack of grass and reeds but it was clean and – by contrast – almost welcoming. There was no blanket but I had my cloak and though the place was chilly at least it was not damp.

Nor was it windowless. By moving the water bowl and jug and standing on the stool, I found that I could even see out into the world – though there was not much to look at, simply the river and the swampy marsh. No habitation was visible from here. And though I could not look directly down, I could distinctly hear voices from the court below – a connection with normal life beyond, even if I could not make out what the speakers said.

However, by this time dusk was drawing in and a draught was coming through the open window-space, so I climbed down and gazed around, aware of how hungry and thirsty I'd become.

There was a little water in the water jug, I realised, as I put it back onto the stool, but no cup of any kind. I tried sipping directly from the jug but the contents were so brackish that I spat it out. No drink for me tonight – nor any food, it seemed. There was nothing whatever provided in the bowl, not even the driest crust of mouldy bread. And very soon I would be wholly in the dark – that candle was already guttering and I could not conserve it as I had no method of relighting it. So with a sigh I lay down on the bed, wrapping my birrus round me for a little warmth, and closed my eyes – though there was no chance of sleep.

My brain was buzzing with my predicament. This had all happened so unexpectedly. But now I was alone in this unfamiliar place. Trinculus, and all my luggage, had been removed from me. More unsettling still, I had let them take my travel document. What use was that to anybody else? And why, for that matter, did that warrant – which had earned me such splendid treatment hitherto – suddenly seem to produce the opposite effect? Or more precisely, why had they locked me up? 'For my own safety'? It made no sense at all.

There was only one explanation which occurred to me – though I must have been weary because it took some little time for me to think of it.

Something had befallen my patron since I left. That would account for everything of course, especially with the Emperor's legate visiting from Rome! Emperors are always unpredictable. One stroke of the Imperial pen and Marcus would be instantly 'proscribed' – not merely exiled from the Empire for life, but denied the essential elements of water and fire within its bounds, on pain of death for anyone providing them.

An unenviable fate, and those who suffered it often expired

in hungry misery, alone and unattended on some cheerless rock. Marcus would try to protect his family from that (as one sometimes could) by leaving immediately himself – though his property and wealth would automatically be forfeit to the state. Fortunately Julia had brought a dowry with her when she wed, of which he only had the usufruct, so the house in Corinium should revert to her and she and the children would be provided for. The villa, however, was likely to be sold, together with the contents, including all the slaves.

But that left me with a problem. My roundhouse, and Junio's too, had been built on part of what was once the grounds – granted by Marcus as a favour years ago, but there were no formal witnesses to that. What would be my legal status now?

Worse, if Marcus had experienced a sudden fall from grace then not only would his seal carry no authority, it marked the holder as his protégée. And I knew what that could mean: any of his associates might find themselves arraigned – guilty by connection – and exiled in turn.

In which case my welcome here was no surprise at all. My best course – indeed the only one available – was to cease to draw attention to myself and try to be grateful, as the guard had said, that I'd not been treated worse. As yet, anyway! I hardly liked to think of what the dawn might bring. For the moment I was glad enough to settle down again, waiting for the feeble taper-light to fail and plunge me into total darkness for the night. In the end I must have drifted into troubled sleep.

So I was astonished a little afterwards to be wakened by a rattle at the door. I did not even have the time to sit upright before the guard came in again, accompanied by the inn-slave, who was carrying a tray. And not an empty one! To my astonishment I saw a bowl of food and a metal cup of something that looked very much like watered wine.

'Put that down beside him!' barked the bear. 'And change that taper so that he can see.' The inn-slave hurried to do as he was told.

I blinked up at my captors in surprise. 'Food? For me?' I was beginning to consider if this might be a trap.

'For you, indeed! Who else do you suppose? But if you do not want it, we can take it back again.'

'Oh, I want it,' I said, struggling to sit up and snatching for the tray before it disappeared. 'But I have no implement to eat it with.'

Too late I realised that this might be a trap – the food might be poisoned – but I really had no spoon. If I had been a normal civilian traveller, I would have a combination spoon-and-dining-knife – they are readily available at market-stalls, and the only kind of blade that non-soldiers are permitted to carry on the road. But I had not felt the need for carrying eating implements – a wedding host is likely to provide them for his guests and they are generally supplied at any mansio.

Even at this one, it appeared. The guard slapped down a spoon that he'd been carrying. He showed no signs of departing and leaving me to eat, so – trap or not – I took a morsel of the food. It was a sort of oatmeal stew with tripe and beans thrown in – so it was uniformly white, and did not taste of much. On the other hand, I seemed to take no harm from it. Besides, the slave, I noticed, had just licked his hand where he'd accidentally splashed it with the food. And I was hungry. I took another bite.

I was convinced by now. This was standard army fare – wholesome and sustaining, but not designed to titivate. (Though it did occur to me to wonder if Trinculus had been served the same, and whether – since presumably he ate this all the time – he might even be enjoying his.)

'Army gruel?' I said, approvingly. For someone who'd expected to receive no food at all, even army porridge is a privilege, and I was anxious to sound grateful. 'I'm very glad of it.'

The bear-guard nodded. 'But the wine's your own.'

'Mine?' Of all the inexplicable events today, this was the oddest. 'I possess no wine.'

'Your so-called attendant had it in the cart. Left over from last night – or so he says – the inn-keeper put it into a little amphora for you to take away. Rhenish, apparently, and highest quality. I don't know how you came by such a thing, but the mansionarius insisted that it should be served to you, in case it had been poisoned and was meant for someone else. So you drink it at your peril, and don't say you've not be warned.' He favoured me with an unpleasant grin, displaying a range of pointed yellow teeth. 'Though if you refuse it, we shall know what to think.'

It was so exactly the reverse of what I'd previously feared myself that it was almost comical – once my befuddled brain had worked out the provenance of the wine. 'Ah, the gift of Crassus Posthumous! Of course! That was kindly of the innkeeper,' I said.

After my experience at Marcus's dinner-feast, I was not really anxious to drink any wine at all – especially not 'best Rhenish' which had been my downfall there – but this was clearly no moment to decline. Besides there was just a single cup of it, no doubt watered in the accepted style. (No self-respecting Roman drinks undiluted wine, except for anaesthetic purposes, such as having teeth extracted or wounds and boils lanced!) And I was very thirsty.

'To all the gods,' I said, swirling it in the cup to shed a drop or two as a small libation. 'With thanks to Crassus Posthumous.' I raised it to my lips.

After the brackish water it tasted marvellous, and I had to force myself to put the cup aside and save the rest until after I had eaten all the stew. Some instinct told me that it was important to continue to behave in ways expected of a Roman citizen, though my claims to be entitled to the rank appeared to be ignored.

The guard, however, did not look impressed. 'Not poisoned then? We thought it might have been. Well, if you've finished that, the slave will fetch a blanket and you can get some sleep. In the morning they will come and get you, as arranged.'

'So you will send the signal?' I had not expected that. In fact I was not sure that I believed it, now.

That yellow smile again. 'And we shall deliver you unharmed and in good health – and that will be the end of our responsibility. And frankly we shall be glad to be relieved of you. Now, if there are no more questions . . .'

There were a thousand things, of course, that I would have liked to ask, but I knew better. I simply shook my head.

'Then give him that blanket, slave, and leave him to his bed.'

The inn-slave tiptoed out and came back with the cloth

– which must have been waiting just outside the door. It was coarse and brownish-coloured, but it was clean and dry and made a better cover than my cloak. Why was I being favoured with these things? Another mystery.

But I was suddenly too weary to think any more tonight. The moment that the door had closed again, I wrapped myself in this unexpected luxury and lay down on my sack.

I must have fallen instantly asleep, because when I opened my eyes again, what seemed like only moments afterwards, I found that the night had now completely fallen in the room. The second taper had burned out and I was in the dark.

Almost total darkness – but not quite. Through the open window-space there was a sullen glow, a reddish glow that flickered, and a strong smell of smoke. And there was frenzied shouting from below – that was clearly what had awakened me.

I felt my way over to the window-wall, but as I moved I overturned the rocky stool – knocking the metal bowl onto the floor and splashing my bare feet with the contents of the jug. The shock of the cold water seemed to rouse me, though, and I was less clumsy as I set the stool upright and stood on it to look outside and so confirm my fears.

Fire. There could be no doubt of that. And I was a prisoner on an upper floor. For certain no one was about to come and rescue me. I was already considering if there might be some way to escape. How could I hoist myself up onto the sill? Could I succeed in sliding through the narrow gap? And what were my chances of breaking just a leg – and not my neck – if I let go and slithered down into the dark, paved court below?

Well, it was a risk that I would simply have to take. Anything was preferable to being burned alive. Panic lends one an un-natural strength, and after a number of strenuous attempts I succeeded in hauling myself upwards by my arms, so that I was half-lying chest-down across the sill. I wedged my elbows firmly in the gap and was trying to imagine how I could raise my feet, when the shouting below me was suddenly renewed.

'There, look! The fire's been noticed.'

I pulled back a little, thinking that my effort to escape had been observed.

Another shout. This time I recognised the voice. It was the

bear-guard bellowing, 'They've seen it. See, they're answering! You can begin to dowse the flames.'

I edged a little further on my arms. Now, from my strange vantage-point I could see the ground below – and confirmed what the shouting had been telling me. How could I be so stupid? This was not an accidental fire. Various of the inn-staff were dancing round the blaze – which seemed to be a pile of broken furniture and straw – and were now attacking it with flails. As I watched, another soldier hurried up bringing a pail of water which he threw into the flames raising an acrid smoke which filled my lungs.

Instinctively, I leaned away from it, coughing and spluttering, and slithered to the floor, losing my precarious grip upon the window-space. But not before I'd glimpsed, what seemed like miles away, the answering glow the voice had spoken of. Someone had lit a bonfire in reply.

This must be the signal they had promised me.

It should have been a reassurance, but somehow it was not. Was I still expected to attend this wedding then? Of course it was a comfort and relief to know the inn was not on fire and I was not about to roast, and perhaps it suggested that Marcus's disgrace – whatever it consisted of – did not extend entirely to me.

In fact, when I considered, I should have guessed as much. I was being treated, if not with courtesy, at least no worse than any common soldier might expect, who happened to be visiting the inn. Except for losing my possessions and being locked into the room!

'For your safety', according to the guard. Safety from what? Were there local rebels who'd become so bold they would dare attack a military inn? Someone with a personal grudge against my patron perhaps, who saw this as an opportunity to wreak revenge – by killing me, knowing that Marcus was now power-less to respond? I could see why that might frighten the mansionarius: the death of a citizen at his mansio would mean disgrace for him, loss of his rank and privilege at least, if not indeed his life. So perhaps that did make sense?

I shook my head. It was impossible. Granted that the fall of an important man is always the subject of gossip which spreads faster than the plague – how could rebels have come to hear of it so soon? Indeed, how could news have travelled to this mansio and not have reached us yesterday before we left? The mansionarius there had been helpfulness itself – as witness the provision of wine. He was clearly unaware of anything amiss. Yet a messenger would bring the news to each mansio in turn – and we'd not been overtaken by a courier on the road.

So was there something that I had overlooked? Or was my theory simply incorrect? It was only my conjecture, after all. I shook my head. It was inexplicable. Tonight, however, I could think no more. I groped my way across the room – even the dim glow had disappeared by now. I felt the mattress with my feet and lay down gratefully.

Whether it was the strain of travelling, the panic of the fire, or my scrambled half-escape I did not know, but I was exhausted. I closed my drooping eyes.

I did not stir again until I heard a voice. 'Get up then, sluggard! It is almost noon. Your guide has come for you.'

TWENTY-TWO

I did not have to look to know it was the guard. I forced my eyes to open – which they seemed disinclined to do – and blinked up at him. He was standing at my side, holding out my sandals.

'Get these on your feet. And if you want to break your fast at all today you'd better do it soon. The inn-slave brought this to you hours ago.' He gestured to a tray beside me on the floor, containing a crust of bread, some crumbs of cheese, and a beaker of water. 'The guide is waiting at the gate and your companion too. I'll tell them that you're finally awake. Back in five minutes.' He went out and I heard him lock the door again.

I sat up, astonished to discover that I had slept so late. I must have been exhausted by the events of yesterday and the panics of the night. No doubt the days of jolting travel had played their part as well, but even now I did not feel entirely refreshed.

But hungry! I picked up the bread, which was no longer fresh. I dunked it in the water pot to soften it, and used the sop to eat the cheese fragments, then gulped down the water, which was clear and cool. The brackish contents of the jug, I realised, were meant for washing with, so – feeling a little foolish – I made use of them, dipping my head and dusty beard into the bowl. My tunic, though, was hopelessly bedraggled by this stage. I was just wondering where my other garments were, and whether I could expect them to be given back to me, when the bolt flew open and the guard was back again.

'Ready or not, it's time for you to leave. Downstairs, double quick – and don't try any tricks, or I'll have the greatest pleasure in persuading you.' He pulled his dagger out. It was wickedly sharp and he looked as if he meant exactly what he said.

I pulled my cloak and sandals on as fast as possible, not even pausing to fully fasten them, and hobbled to the door – aware that the weapon was inches from my ribs. I would have liked to ask him what 'tricks' he was expecting me to play, but my first attempt to turn my head earned me a dagger-prick, and I resigned myself to simply scuffling along. The passageway was dark and shadowy and I was glad when the little slave appeared with a lighted taper to show us to the stairs.

When we reached the doorway that gave out onto the court, the sudden morning light was so sharp it blinded me, though the day was cloudy and the sun no more than peeping through. The wind was cold, besides, and I shivered as I shuffled down the steps.

Now my eyes had adjusted to the glare I looked round for Trinculus, but I couldn't see him anywhere, only an inn-slave drawing water from the well. I was about to risk the dagger-point and enquire of the guard, when I was interrupted by a timid voice behind me.

'Citizen?' It was Trinculus himself. I whirled around and caught my breath. Without the dormouse ears I would not have known the lad. They had stripped him of the armour of which he was so proud, and left him skinny and insignificant, dressed only in his faded tunic and a pair of hobnailed sandals which looked incongruous on his scrawny legs. They had deprived him even of his military cloak.

But that was not the worst. His shoulders were a mass of yellowing bruises, fresh weals could be glimpsed around his arms and legs, while his face was red and swollen and one eye half-closed. Someone had clearly beaten him, most efficiently.

'Trinculus, what happened?' I was ready to protest on his behalf, though it would do little good, I knew. This was a military inn: the army manned and ran it, and he was subject to their discipline – which is often harsh. Even minor misdemeanours can be brutally chastised. Though I could not imagine what he might have done to deserve so severe a punishment.

But he shook his head and simply darted his undamaged eye in the direction of the guard, obviously fearing that he might be struck again. 'Nothing,' he managed, through split and swollen lips, though it came out as a croak.

I was furious and whirled to face the guard. Foolish of me, as I immediately realised – he was quite capable of stabbing me – but he simply raised his dagger and pointed to the gate. 'Your host has sent his servant as a guide,' he said, laconically, 'and he's welcome to you both!' He made a gesture for the fellow to come in.

The man who entered was a tall, athletic youth, wind-tanned and muscular, and strikingly handsome in a non-Roman way. He was dressed in a brightly-coloured tunic with long tube-like sleeves which would have marked him as a Celt, even without the plaid breeches, and his long, combed, blonded tresses and moustache. He was barefoot and apparently impervious to chill – the trousers had been folded to above his knees. As a slave, he did not wear a long cloak like my own – which in Celtic circles suggests a man of status – only a short hooded cape which hardly reached his waist, and even that he had pushed back so that his head was bare. A bulging bag, made from a cured sheep's stomach by the look of it, was slung across his back and held in place with cords.

All this I took in at a single glance, but as he approached I found that I was staring at his belt – a heavy leather one with an enormous clasp, which would have made a useful weapon in itself – and thrust through it, for good measure, were a bludgeon and a knife. Perhaps he was expecting trouble from us on the way, because he also held a three-pronged fishing spear, a wicked-looking object with long sharpened prongs, which he was spinning between the fingers of one hand as if to display his careless expertise. I was in no doubt that he could use any of his equipment with the same efficiency.

'These is prisoner?' His voice was silky but his Latin poor. 'Then we go before come too much quick the tide.'

His words added to my increasing unease. So we were 'prisoners' after all? Or was that simply his misuse of Latin words? I turned, in one last desperate attempt to ask the guard. But now it was the fish-spear that was pointing at my chest.

'Quickest, quickest or you death by swim!' the youth said urgently.

The bear-guard laughed. 'You heard the slave!' he said, triumphantly. 'If you don't hurry there'll be "death by swim". So if you have further questions, ask Darturius. We have delivered you as we were asked to do.'

'But my baggage?' I persisted. Panic made me brave. 'My own bedraggled toga is of no account, perhaps, but a friend

entrusted me with the finer woollen one, and my patron sent a
wedding present made of solid gold.'

Another grin. 'We'll keep the "borrowed" garments here—'
he stressed the word 'borrowed' with heavy irony – 'and the
golden plate as well. When the tide is more convenient your
host can send for them. This, on the other hand, will be needed
straight away.'

And to my surprise he produced my warrant, in its pouch. I
risked a glance at the writing-block within, but it was the one
I'd brought: Marcus's distinctive symbol was etched into the
front and his seal was still adhering to the tie.

'On second thoughts, perhaps I'd better give that to your
guide. I should not like to see it disappear into the marsh.' He
snatched it from me and gave it to the youth, who placed it in
his shoulder-pouch without a word. The bear-grin reappeared.
'No doubt there would have been a little accident, but I'm too
clever to allow that, as you see.'

And that was all. The guard had turned his back and was
now ignoring us, conspicuously talking to the inn-slave with
the pail. I took a step towards him, but was tugged urgently
away by the young Celt who had propped his spear against the
wall and produced from his knapsack a length of hempen rope.
As I watched he tied one end of it securely round his waist and
was making signals that I should raise my arms.

I shook my head.

'Must, must,' he urged, impatiently.

'I am a free man and I will not be bound,' I answered,
using my native tongue. 'I am not a prisoner, I am a citizen
and your master – I assume Darturius is your master? – is
expecting me.'

He looked at me a moment, with a puzzled look, then his
face relaxed and he replied in the same tongue, 'As to your
being a Roman citizen, that's none of my affair. You look and
sound exactly like a Celt. But certainly my master is expecting
you. Though you need fear no harm from me. This rope is to
guide you and keep you on the path. The route is dangerous at
this time of day. If you should slip or lose your footing and be
overtaken by the waves, I have a means to pull you safely back
before the mud can suck you down. And believe me, traveller,

you might well be glad of it. Two or three strangers are drowned here every year.'

'I see,' I said, humbly. I raised my arms obediently and allowed him to affix a loop around my waist. The action required him to pull back my cloak, and my tunic slipped from my shoulder.

'You had a slave brand here?' he said, as he replaced my cloak. The tone was casual, but I thought I detected a hint of fellow-feeling in his eyes.

'Once!' I saw an opportunity to gain – if not a friend – at least a sympathetic listener, so I gave him a quick outline of my life, stressing that I was a chieftain in my tribe, before I was captured and sold to slavery. 'I was freed by my last master who had me taught a trade and also bequeathed me the rank of citizen – so I had the brand removed.' I hazarded a smile. 'But I heard the guard describe you as a slave – so I assume that you were a victim of something of the kind yourself. Though you seem to bear no brand?'

I phrased this carefully, in an attempt at tact. Celts have slaves, of course, especially nowadays – but rarely fellow Celts. Unless the status was inherited (and the lack of a slave brand here suggested otherwise) traditionally such slaves were captives, spoils of war, but the guide was far too young for that. There's not been tribal conflict of that kind for many years – not since the Pax Romana was enforced.

The youth was not offended. 'I'm not a slave by birth. I am bound to Darturius in payment of a debt. He even calls me Paigh.' The last word was bitter. 'Paigh' – meaning payment – bore a grudge. That might be a useful thing to know if things did not go smoothly when we reached the house.

'What is he saying?' Trinculus enquired, piteous with fright. 'And why is he tying you?'

I hurried to explain the dangers (though not translating the rest of what was said) and Trinculus, once he understood, was positively anxious to be secured himself.

'It is as well that my patron did not come himself,' I said, speaking in Latin for Trinculus's sake, as Paigh expertly knotted the rope around his frame, avoiding the weals and bruises where he could. 'He would not have willingly submitted to this indignity.'

Paigh shot me a look as he tugged his knot to test it would not slip. 'Like yesterday. Two other visitors – they want to take their coach. No good tell them it would down in mud. But in the end . . .' He gestured at his club. 'I make them understand.' He gave a final tug and stood up, satisfied. 'Now we ready, go.' He shouted this in the direction of the guard, who came across at once.

'Before come quick the tide!' the soldier hooted, laughing immoderately at his own wit. He used his spear to shepherd us outside onto the road and turned to me. 'Farewell, my so-called citizen. And your famous soldier-slave!' He raised a horizontal arm in mock salute. 'Quickest, quickest so no death by swim!' And, still laughing heartily, he closed the gate on us.

I looked apprehensively towards our guide. Where was he taking us? There seemed to be nothing but the empty road and the lonely salt marsh stretching out towards the sea.

But Paigh was smiling cheerfully. He turned to Trinculus who, under the bruising, was pale with pain and fright. 'Come quick, while dry the way!'

With that he marched straight across the road, and began to lead us firmly out towards the marsh.

TWENTY-THREE

There was a clear track – though it had not been visible from the road – a causeway of baulks of timber driven down into the mud, leading through the reeds and swamp across the inlet to the headland opposite.

Paigh looked at me, and said in Celtic, 'Don't you wish to take your shoes off first?'

I glanced at the slimy causeway, on which weed was flourishing, and decided that wet leather would be a wiser choice. I shook my head, and we moved on again. But we had not gone a hundred paces before the reason for the question, and the need for haste, became alarmingly – and abruptly – obvious.

Ahead the way was being lapped by water either side, where a moment earlier there was only glistening mud, and further on again the causeway was disappearing as we watched. With each incoming wavelet (and every ongoing step) the visible track was getting narrower, until very soon there was no dry ground at all and we were wading ankle-deep between little muddy islands of seagrass and tall reeds. I glanced uncertainly at Paigh.

'The river – or the tide, I suppose – is running very fast. And it's carrying so much salt and sludge with it, that soon it won't be possible to see which way the causeway lies,' I said, implying that I was ready to retreat and concede that our crossing would have to be delayed, but our guide continued to stride confidently on, only pausing now and then to sound the water with his spear.

'Don't worry, traveller. I can take my bearings from those rocks—' he indicated some which were only half-submerged – 'and from the buildings on the headland opposite.' He gestured vaguely, but I could not make out what he was pointing out.

But a moment later I had other things to think about. I lost my footing on the slippery timbers – which I could no longer see – and found myself treading into sucking mud which tried to hold me fast. I could not withdraw my leg, and my panicked efforts to free it only made it worse, until I toppled entirely from the track. For a moment I had a vision of a dreadful death – sinking to my neck and drowning slowly as the waters rose, aware but totally unable to extricate myself. But the swift reaction of our guide, shouting to me to spread my weight onto the line allowed me to haul myself forward while he reeled me in. I was sincerely grateful for the rope, as my foot came free and I scrambled back to solid ground again.

I did, however, lose my sandal in the mire, and was obliged to hobble from there forwards with my right foot bare. I contemplated – too late – pulling off the other shoe to match, but for one thing I did not have Paigh's hardy, hardened soles (treading on sharp shells was bad enough, but sinking into slimy weed was truly horrible) and for another he would not let me pause.

'Too dangerous. People who linger can be taken by the tide and if I lose the markers we may wander from the path – and you've already witnessed how the mud can suck you down. And here the rising water is deeper than it looks.' To illustrate he raised his sounding-spear and brought it down a little to one side, changing his grip to hold it near the prongs: it went so deep it almost disappeared. Paigh turned and grinned at me. 'So let us press on quickly, there is not much time.'

I needed no persuasion after that and nor did Trinculus, who had understood even without my having to translate. He was clearly terrified. He was in any case at greatest risk, since he was the smallest of us all – barely the four cubits which is the army minimum – and the water, which had almost reached my knees, was in danger of lapping to his thighs.

I was becoming concerned for him, in fact. The tide was moving even quicker now, and – though in general he had surprising strength for such a skinny frame – his recent beating had clearly weakened him and the surge seemed likely to pull him off his feet. Paigh noticed too and made urgent signs to him to shorten the length of rope that connected him to me, but the boy seemed incapable of understanding what to do, so in the end I did it: winding the slack around my hand and binding him so close that I could hold his arm. After that he clung desperately to me.

His weight against me made my clumsy stumbling worse and I was really anxious now. Only Paigh seemed unconcerned. He went on ploughing doggedly ahead, and I suddenly realised that by degrees we were gaining on the flow and the water was down around my calves again. For the first time since my sandal-loss I dared to raise my head and look about to find that we had almost reached a beach and the headland was rising just ahead of us. And on it there was evidence of life. A smudge of smoke was rising to the sky and a range of buildings was clearly visible – centred around a handsome villa in the Roman style, though the huts and outbuildings surrounding it were of the Celtic type, being mostly round and thatched. Clearly this was the Darturius estate.

I was about to say so, when I trod on something very sharp. I glanced down, automatically, to find that I had trodden on a shell – which I could see, because the water was only reaching to my ankles now. Relieved, I loosed the loop of line that I held in my hand, whereupon Trinculus promptly slipped off the causeway and sat down in the mud, almost pulling me over with him as he fell.

As we pulled him, dripping to his feet, I said quietly to Paigh, 'Surely there are other ways of getting to the house? I can't believe all visitors are forced to wade like this. And how, for instance, do you manage for supplies?'

The young Celt grinned, as he led us to dry land and loosened us from the rope. 'Well, it is largely a question of when you choose to come. When the tide is at a stand we sometimes use a boat – though a coracle is not generally suitable for transporting passengers. Especially more than one!'

I nodded. I had once been forced to travel in a coracle and it was not an experience I was eager to repeat. The thing was flimsy and unstable and threatened to capsize if I so much as stirred. I've never been so certain that I was going to drown – until today, that is. 'So it's easier to walk?'

'You can drive a cart across, if you choose your time with care. That, of course, is how we move the salt.' I must have looked astonished because he laughed aloud. 'At the lowest tide it's possible to walk across, dry-shod. Or one can ride a horse, if one possesses such a thing, like our visitors of yesterday.

At some seasons one can even cross and have an hour or more
to spare, but not, I fear, at this time of the year or this phase
of the moon.'

'But in between the household is marooned?'

'Not quite. If need arises, or the weather's terrible, we can
go inland. There are other properties the far side of the rise.
Both of them have better tracks than ours – though these are
prone to flooding in the winter months. Unhappily for you, they
do not lead this way – they are ancient ways that wind for miles
and do not meet the military road. But they converge at Portus
Abonae and the owners permit us to use them, sometimes, in
return for salt.'

'For salt? They don't produce their own?' I'd forgotten for
the moment the need for licences.

Paigh clearly hadn't; he gave me a wicked look. 'Not
officially, in any case. But we can refine it properly and they
cannot. Besides, my master's lands are closest to the sea, so
we get the best results. As you can see.'

He gestured with the hand that held the fishing-spear and I
realised that fringing the track ahead of us, on either side, were
areas enclosed within a series of stone banks. From a distance
I had taken them for fields, but on inspection I could see that
the area was full of shallow pools, clearly the 'salt ponds'
Marcus had spoken of.

I stopped, interested to deduce how it was done. The ponds
were clay-lined, by the look of it, constructed to allow the
flood to enter them through sluices in the banks. Presumably
this would slowly filter down, or else evaporate, leaving brine
behind – I could see where that was drained off into a lower
pit behind and the whole process was repeated several times.

I'd never seen a saltern, though I'd heard of them. I called
to my bruised and dripping friend. 'See, Trinculus. This is where
they make the salt.'

It was an attempt to distract him from his woes, but to my
surprise he seemed as interested as I had been, even standing
on a projecting stone to get a better look. 'Salt pans,' he
announced, as he got down again. 'They have these things in
Dacia, near where I was born. But here it must be difficult
to do. In Britannia there's not a lot of sun – it must be hard

to get the salt completely dry.' He had babbled this last in
eager Latin – addressing it to Paigh.

I translated and the Celtic servant laughed. 'Tell the lad we
do not even try. When the brine is really strong we scoop it
out, strain it into metal vats – we call them salt pans, too,
confusingly – put them in a kiln and light the fire. That dries
it beautifully. And refines it too.' He sounded half-amused. 'You
could not sell the product if you simply dried what's here –
there's too much sediment and broken shell in it.'

I explained all this in Latin, rather glad that Trinculus had
asked, so I had not accidentally betrayed my own (much greater)
ignorance. 'But it's a living for your master?'

Paigh nodded. He had taken a pair of soft shoes from his
pack and was now perching on the bank to put them on, having
dried his legs a little with his tunic-hems. 'And a good one too.'
The shoes were of a Celtic kind I recognised, cut from a single
piece of leather, rounded at the toe and pulled tight by leather
thongs. He rolled his trousers down, and secured the laces round
his legs. 'With sufficient profit to provide him a new kiln. And
just look at the fine new villa he has built.'

'Expensive,' I agreed.

Paigh laughed sourly as he coiled the rope into the bag.
'Folly, I would call it, but Darturius is ambitious socially. He
always wanted to have a Roman house, even if that meant he
had to borrow heavily. He put up half the saltern as surety, but
he's not a total fool. When his partner dies it will revert entirely
to him.' He stood up and, grasping his fishing spear again,
indicated that we should start walking up the hill. 'This marriage
of his daughter Aigneis seals that beyond a doubt.' He sounded
almost bitter, suddenly.

'Meaning that's she's marrying the man who owns the debt?'
I said. I signalled to Trinculus to walk ahead of us, sensing that
Paigh was quite content to talk.

'Exactly so, my friend. And since she is his only marriage-
able child (he has another daughter but she is only six) both
parties hope there will be issue very soon.'

So that explained the strange alliance which had puzzled me.
Not a love-match, as I had correctly guessed, but a way of
securing the business for the family. 'I hear the bridegroom is

no longer young,' I ventured, hoping for a smile. 'It is to be hoped that he can still oblige.'

The slave shot me a look. 'He's old enough to be her grand-father. But he's a widower and lonely and has no living heirs. His wife and children died in Aquae Sulis of the plague. And he's a Roman citizen, of course, so on her marriage Aigneis will take that rank, and any children will be born to it – some-thing her father wanted, but could never have achieved. And if she's left a widow – as one might expect, provided she survives the birth of any heir . . .' He tailed off, with a shrug.

I nodded. As a widow with the rank of citizen and a hand-some dowry to her name, next time she might have the liberty to choose. 'She is handsome?'

He raised laconic brows at me. 'Young and shapely, and that counts for much. But she is too clever for a woman, so her father says, a little too determined and indulged and, having no mother to instruct her, insufficiently adept at the spindle and the loom.'

Wilful, plain and spoiled, by the sound of it. No doubt her family had despaired of finding her a husband nearer her own age. 'So this wedding is probably a splendid thing all round?'

'You can judge that for yourself. You'll see her very soon.' His tone was suddenly business-like and brisk. 'Tell the boy to hurry, we are almost at the house and my instructions are to take you to my master straight away.'

I gazed at him in horror. 'But I have lost a shoe. My tunic's dirty and my cloak is wet. I can't greet my host like this. Give me a chance at least to have a wash and . . .' I was about to say 'and change' but I realised that was now impossible. I shook my head. 'I had a parcel of clean clothes back at the inn, but they would not let me bring it – thought it would be a hindrance while we crossed, perhaps. In the meantime perhaps a garment could be found for me? And even shoes, perhaps?' I was almost doubtful about asking this. Celtic hospitality would demand that any need was met, even if Marcus's name no longer earned respect.

Paigh gave a mocking bow. 'Indeed! And is there anything further you require?'

I nodded at my little fellow traveller, who was trailing

wretchedly along ahead. 'Well, perhaps the same for Trinculus, too? I am prepared to pay for that. I have a little gold.' I rattled the purse which I still carried at my belt. 'And there would be a small reward for you.'

Trinculus had recognised his name and glanced round hopefully, though he'd been excluded from the conversation until now. But Paigh's whole attitude had changed and he was looking grim. Perhaps I'd insulted him by mentioning the gold, though I had meant it kindly. I assumed that he was saving to repay his father's debt and secure his freedom as soon as possible.

He was eyeing Trinculus rather doubtfully, as if considering what could be found to fit. 'Something could be managed for him, I expect. It would look respectful, and it could do no harm, I suppose. Though it will be a servant's tunic, that is all.'

I tried a friendly smile. 'Of course. I'm not expecting that you'll have a spare military tunic in the house. But in the meantime, anything is better than what he's wearing now. The poor boy's wet and frozen – they took his cloak and armour and they beat him savagely. I don't know what he did to anger them, but he can hardly go and meet Darturius as he is.'

Paigh gave a bitter laugh. 'I doubt that he'll be meeting Darturius at all. It's you that I'm instructed to bring in for an audience.' He stopped and looked me shrewdly in the eye. 'Look, fellow Celt, there's one thing I must make clear. We have much in common and in any other circumstances I might have called you friend. But whatever game you're playing here, I can't be part of it. I'll do what's rational – I'll send you washing water and a change of clothes – but that is all the help you can expect from me. Is that understood?'

I stared at him. 'Not understood at all. What do you—'

He cut me off abruptly and aimed his spear at me. 'Enough! There's nothing to discuss. Another word and I will change my mind. Now, we're nearly at the gate. There's no guard needed when the tide is in, so you can go straight in.' I believe he would have prodded us with the barbed prongs if we had not complied.

It was strange to walk in through a Celtic palisade, so very like my own, and find oneself confronting a Roman country house – and a handsome one, though clearly very new. Even stranger to find that, instead of formal gardens or an open court, there was nothing around it but a patch of scrubby grass, full of ducks and geese and little round huts in the native style. Paigh gestured to the nearest one of these.

'Make for that dye-house and wait for me inside. And don't consider trying to escape – the front gates are guarded so there's no way through there, and no way back unless you want to drown.'

'Escape . . .?' I echoed, mystified.

But he had already set off at a run towards the house.

TWENTY-FOUR

'What was he saying, citizen? You look alarmed?' A frightened Trinculus was plucking at my arm.

I did not want to disquiet him still more, so I simply explained that Paigh had gone to find us clothes and we were told to wait. I gestured to the hut. 'In there. The door is open,' I finished, cheerfully. 'And it will be warm inside.'

It was. The place was bigger than my dye-house, but very similar and – though there was no dying actually in progress now – there were signs that there had been, fairly recently. There were still warm embers on the central fire and a now empty vat that was hanging over it gave off a vague heat too – though there was no sign of what it had contained. Perhaps there was a separate drying-room somewhere. But I no longer cared. I was simply glad to sit down on the floor, remove my single sodden sandal, and allow my old chilled legs and feet to find comfort near the hearth, while Trinculus huddled as close as possible.

As he did, I realised that he was shivering. Shivering so much that I took off my own cloak, and – despite his protests – wrapped it round his skinny form. 'It's damp but it is wool. It will still warm you,' I said, and then, in answer to his grateful smile, I said, 'What happened to your own?'

The shy grin faded instantly and he shook his head. But he did not reply.

'You can tell me, Trinculus,' I urged. 'The last few hours have been frightening, but now we're safely here.'

He turned his bruised and purpling face to me. 'Safe for you, citizen, perhaps.' I was distressed to see teardrops running down his cheeks, and that one eye was now so swollen that it was just a slit. 'You have your warrant, but how does that help me? I was assigned to guard you on the road, and I was proud to come. But then, last night . . .' He trailed off into silence again.

'Last night . . .?' I urged gently.

It came out in a rush. 'Last night they threw me into a dismal room, stripped me of my armour by brute force and said I was a thief. And when I attempted to protest, that soldier knocked me down – and kicked my teeth loose, by the feel of it. I tried to maintain a soldier's dignity – said that I was entitled to military respect – but that just made him beat me savagely.' He shook his battered head. 'It is an insult to our regiment!'

'We'll send a message to the tesserarius,' I soothed. 'Though I think I can explain why we were harshly entertained. I suspect events in Glevum may have overtaken us – we're probably fortunate that they allowed us to come here.' I outlined my theory about my patron's fall from grace. 'Though as a soldier-escort – rather than a slave – that should not strictly have affected you. But I'll make sure that your principalis is informed at once.'

But Trinculus was not comforted. 'Let's hope that you succeed. I'm sorry, citizen, if that sounds impolite, but I tried to send a message from that mansio myself. I asked them most politely to include it in the military post, with the day's despatches, but they would not hear of it. Said that I was suffi-cient trouble as it was – impersonating soldiers was a capital offence, and I would be lucky if the tribune did not feed me to the beasts.'

I frowned. 'But you *are* a Roman soldier! That cannot be in doubt. You arrived in armour, on a military gig, and I told them who you were.'

He hunched his thin-cloaked shoulders round his dormouse ears. 'But they did not believe it. Jove alone knows why. And when I referred them to your warrant all they did was laugh and say it did not mention me. I pointed out that I was sent to escort you on the road, but that infuriated that brutal soldier more. I knew the truth and I was hiding it, he said, and if I did not tell them everything he would beat it out of me.'

I shook my head, bewildered and appalled. No part of the last few hours had been what I hoped, but this was simply inexplicable. I began to wonder if this was all a dreadful dream and I was going to wake up any minute safely in my bed. 'But you were hiding nothing!' I exclaimed. 'Though they did not believe that, either, I suppose?'

Trinculus said nothing, merely rubbed his upper arms and looked away, as though he were embarrassed.

'Well?' I demanded.

'Well . . .' His voice was trembling. 'There was something, I suppose. But when I told the guard, he thrashed me even more. I think he would have beaten me to death, if that old mansionarius had not come in just then, saying that they must be careful, just in case.'

'In case of what?' I wondered.

'In case I turned out to be, not an imposter, but a deserter after all – they'd been warned that there was one in the area – in which event the local commander would want to deal with me.'

'But they still allowed you to accompany me here?'

'Only because I could not easily escape from here, they said – which would mean they were relieved of responsibility, but could send and arrest me at any time. I was not supposed to hear all that, of course, and when they realised that I had, the guard grabbed me by the tunic-front and shook me till the blood sang in my ears. I was not to tell you any part of this, he said, otherwise – even if I was not a deserter, and therefore to be stoned – he would see that I was sentenced to the mines as a civilian disobeying a military command.' The voice was tremulous, more with fear than cold.

'But you told me anyway?' I was oddly touched, although his tormentor's attitude made very little sense. 'Perhaps they really think that you are not what you claim. There was a deserter, as we know. But never fear. As soon as I see Darturius I'll ensure that a message is sent back at once, and then they'll be in trouble for mistreating you. You're a soldier obeying orders and did nothing wrong. Your tesserarius will be furious.'

There was a silence. I was rather expecting relief and gratitude, but after a little the boy said doubtfully, 'Will he have to be told that I confessed? He'd probably decide that I earned my punishment.' He had been staring at the embers until now, but all at once he turned and looked at me.

'Confessed?' I gave him a sympathetic smile. 'But you've done nothing to confess about – have you? Or is there something that I don't know about?'

He shook his head. 'It's nothing that I did. It's what I didn't do.' He paused, and then went on in a rush: 'I was going to tell you yesterday, once that driver had left us at the inn – I didn't want him telling tales when he got back. But at the mansio they dragged us apart, and I never got the opportunity. And it did not occur to me before. It was that coach, you see.'

'The coach? What coach? You mean the gig that brought us here?'

Trinculus shook his head. 'The one belonging to that other citizen – Posthumous or whatever he was called. I saw it at the inn. It reminded me of something and I could not think what, but as we drove along, the answer came to me. It was rather like the one that Acacius Flauccus used to have – though without the fancy paint. And that is when I realised what I'd done, or failed to do . . . Perhaps I should have thought of it before.' He hunched himself up by the embers as before.

'Trinculus,' I said, impatiently. 'What are you telling me?'

'I might have let the carriage past,' he said. 'You know, at Uudum. The tax-collector's coach.'

'You were on duty at the gate that day?' I could hardly believe it. 'And you never mentioned it?'

He shook his head, defensively. 'There was nothing to report. I hadn't seen the tax collector go past in his coach. But I would not have paid the least attention even if I had, because we'd just received the message that he still had money to collect. I was just pointing the messenger the way—'

I cut him off. 'The messenger!' I was an idiot. 'Of course! It wasn't Aureax after all. So how did Flauccus find a messenger? All of his servants had been taken off for sale. And he would hardly use an urchin from the street.'

Trinculus looked puzzled. 'Of course not, citizen. But there is no mystery about the messenger – he was an official courier who was known to us. He'd taken a message to Flauccus a little while before, and naturally he reported to the guard-post on the way. He'd been to Uudum several times before. I recognised him by his horse and by his uniform.'

I frowned. 'Yet he needed directions? An Imperial courier? And one who'd been before? Surely he must have known the route?'

'Not an Imperial rider, citizen, just an official one. From the Glevum curia, in fact – with a message from your own patron, I believe. And of course he knew the way. But first he wanted directions to a farmstead locally – one of the properties that had not paid their tax. Flauccus had commissioned him to take a message there, to warn them that they would be fined if they did not pay before he left the town. He said the curia was anxious to collect all missing tax.'

Indeed they were, I thought – because they'd have to make up any deficit. But a sad and dreadful image had come back to me: a young curial courier beheaded in a ditch. 'Dear gods,' I muttered. 'Perhaps he saw the killers without knowing it.' Not attacked by rebels after all, but killed because he knew too much and mutilated to make it look like Druid work?

Not that he would have seen the corpse, of course. If Flauccus's killers were already in the house what would they do if a messenger arrived? Pretend to be townsmen waiting to pay outstanding tax, perhaps, and wait politely till he went away? Or suppose they'd already murdered Flauccus by that time? Did they affect to be attendant friends, perhaps? Saying that Flauccus was busy and couldn't be disturbed, but offering to pass on the courier's message when convenient?

Quick thinking on their part, if that was the case – but it must have been something of the kind. The messenger would be questioned by the authorities, once the death was known – even if it was thought to be a suicide – and would innocently testify as to whom he had seen and what they'd said. And as a courier he'd be skilled at recalling word for word – dangerous, since most of it was evidently lies – and at giving exact descriptions of the people he had seen.

So he must be disposed of, but not there in the house – that would prove that there were murderers about. What could be easier than inventing another message for him to take away – saying it was very urgent, naturally? To some isolated farmstead up a lonely road – perhaps one they had noticed on their way, or one which was genuinely listed as being in arrears? That would not only conveniently get rid of the witness instantly, it also meant that they knew where he was going – where they could catch up with him, away from prying eyes, and silence him for good. And giving him a message to the guardhouse on the way was a final masterstroke – it not only made certain that he was seen to leave unharmed, it also ensured that the escort was stood down, so no one was looking for Flauccus – or his coach – till long after the killers, and the tax, were gone.

'Great Jupiter! I do believe that I have stumbled on the truth.' I turned to Trinculus. 'Was that carriage secretly following the courier, do you think – from a distance?' I enquired.

Trinculus looked doubtfully at me. 'I don't know, citizen. I suppose it might have been. I saw it when I was pointing out the farm to him. That's what I remembered yesterday. The carriage was in the background coming down the street – in the town, where it had every right to be, since Flauccus was supposed to be collecting debts – and I thought no more of it. I just went in and dealt with the travel documents, which had to be countersigned to prove the man had been there. But it occurred to me last night that I did not see the carriage again when we came out – and that perhaps it had been waiting an opportunity and crossed the bridge while I was in the guardhouse with the messenger.'

Meaning it was ahead of the courier, I thought. And waiting out of sight. Poor lad! Aloud I said, 'And meanwhile, there was nobody on watch? You left your post – for several minutes by the sound of it – and did not tell the tesserarius so, when he was questioning the troops?'

'I suppose so, citizen. Though he did not ask us that. In fact he did not ask me anything. I took your message to him, asking him to make enquiries, but I was on detachment and came straight back to you. Although I'm sure that he will blame me, when he gets to hear of it – and punish me again. Especially if I contributed to letting them escape.' He looked timidly at me. 'Unless you could tell him that I was otherwise of help?'

I tried to comfort him. 'You are not entirely to blame. If I am right there is a clever mind at work. But I think that you are right about the coach. It went past while you were in the guard-post with the messenger, and the killers went ahead and lay in wait for him. They left the body miles away where no one would connect it with the taxman's death – which they'd arranged to look like suicide. Easy enough to move the dead courier in the coach and leave it where Druids are known to be at large. Even easier to sell a handsome horse.'

'Body?' Trinculus gave an unhappy little moan. 'You think they killed him?'

'I'm certain that they did. I believe I saw the corpse.' I'd forgotten for a moment that he wouldn't know. I began to tell him, but I'd only just begun when the dye-hut door flew open and Paigh came striding in. In one hand he carried a pile of clothing and a pair of ancient shoes – in the Celtic style he wore himself. It had not occurred to me that a household of this kind would not have Roman garments, and to spare.

He threw them on the ground beside the fire. 'Here, citizen, this is the best that I can do. The tunics have been washed. The shoes were once my own. If you want to clean your legs, there's water in the pail.' He gestured to a wooden bucket in the corner of the hut.

The water was even colder than the sea had been, but I was glad to wash the salt and mud crust from my limbs and rub them dry with my discarded clothes. The tunic he had brought me was very short, and had abbreviated sleeves, but it was clean and decent and I was glad of it. I had forgotten too, how flexible soft Celtic shoes can be; the pair that were provided looked far too big for me, but tightening the cord around my foot pulled in the leather and made them wearable.

Thus washed and clothed I felt myself again and Trinculus was clearly grateful to be warmly clad, though none of the tunics really fitted us and my servant's garb was hardly flattering to Marcus, whose representative I was. However, a promise is a promise. I fastened my belt around my tunic of coloured homespun plaid and opened the drawstring of my hanging purse.

'What price are you demanding?' It would no doubt be high and I was in no position to protest.

He shook his head. 'I should have been obliged to clothe you anyway – and if you are to stay here in the house, I do not wish to make an enemy. A tip, however, would be acceptable.'

I gave him one – so handsome that he tested the coin with his teeth, before he slipped it in an arm-purse and thanked me with a bow. 'And now, I think, my master is awaiting you.

Though he is not alone – he is entertaining the wedding guests who got here yesterday. Not you,' he added quickly, as my young companion made as if to rise. 'I am told to leave you here.'

Trinculus sank down beside the hearth again – clearly torn between disappointment and relief – and Paigh turned to me. 'Follow me, I will present you in the house – together with that document that I was asked to bring.' He waved my patron's writing-tablet at me with a smile.

I nodded, doubtfully. I did not need my travel warrant here – it was merely authority to use the mansios – and if Marcus had fallen from favour, I was not sure it would help. But it was Marcus who had been invited to the feast, and perhaps his seal was still of some account.

'Lead on,' I said, and we set off towards the house.

The villa was even stranger as one got close to it. It was large and lofty, with pillars at the door and even a small flight of steps approaching it, but the effect was not harmonious. The pediment, for instance, was grand and finely carved, but the entranceway itself was flanked on either side by too many statues in too many styles – and not especially handsome ones at that. And all of this incongruously set in a Celtic enclosure among round Celtic huts, with not a formal garden, fountain or court-yard anywhere in sight.

Yet my host had borrowed heavily to build this residence – in an attempt to seem more Romanised. I shook my head.

Paigh misinterpreted. 'I'm afraid there is no possibility of retreating now.' He ushered me swiftly up the steps and through the vestibule, nodded at the suave-looking steward in the hall, and led me straight into the 'atrium'. It was a proper atrium – just as Marcus tells me that they have in Rome – built with the centre open to the skies, and a small impluvium collecting water from the rain and the gutters on the roof. Doubtless in Rome, where I understand that it is warm, such a feature is an appealing one, but here in Britannia it was simply dank and wet, especially at this season of the year. More statues stood around on every side. I don't pretend to be an expert about art, but as a pavement-maker I know a little about stone, and most of this was marble, fairly crudely worked, as if quantity, rather than the quality of work, had been the preoccupation of the purchaser.

But we did not linger there. Paigh hastened me into the triclinium beyond, where an early *prandium* had obviously been served, but now the dining tables had been moved away and three men were reclining on the couches, at their ease.

They were a strange assortment – very different in age and rank: two aging men in togas – the small and wizened one I took to be the groom; the other, tall and sallow, in a garment of a whiteness to rival Titus's, had a bandaged hand and an air of discontent. The third and youngest, an impressive-looking man of middle years, was obviously my host. He was not dressed in plaid, as I'd expected, but in an exquisite full length tunic dyed a vibrant green. However he did wear the traditional gold torc around his neck, and with his height, fair hair and long moustache he looked magnificent.

I moved towards him, conscious of my lowly dress, ready to bow, but Paigh hissed 'Kneel!' at me.

I did as I was bidden. 'My Lord Darturius.'

He held out a hand, weighed down with heavy rings. 'Ah, so you come at last! I hear you bring a document from Marcus Septimus?'

It was not the greeting I had been hoping for, but I gestured to Paigh and he presented his master with the writing-tablet, expressly exhibiting the seal on the tie. Darturius held it rather gingerly, as though unaccustomed to handling writing-blocks, whereupon the second diner – the tall, pinched fellow with a sallow face – came hurrying to his aid. He glanced at the contents but did not look at me.

He nodded as he returned the document. 'Merely confirmation that this is the man. I regret the slight delay. He was following us in a separate vehicle and must have missed the tide. I am glad to see that he has actually arrived.'

I gazed up at him, surprised. He spoke as if I ought to realise who he was, but to the best of my knowledge I'd never seen the citizen before. But then the explanation came to me. 'You must be the councillor, Crassus Posthumous,' I said, bowing my head in recognition of his rank. 'The mansionarius said that we might catch you on the road. I did not realise that you were coming here. But I am glad to see you. I have much to thank you for.'

He looked at me coolly, a flicker of cold amusement in his eyes. 'Fellow, the time for jest is past. Crassus Posthumous has been dead this half a moon. I am the citizen Libertus, pavement-maker of Glevum, and client of that same Marcus who dispatched you here – as you are well aware.'

TWENTY-FIVE

I f Jove had felled me with a lightening bolt I could not have
been more shaken. For a moment I was too shocked and
stupified to do more than gaze at this imposter, open-
mouthed – and when I collected myself sufficiently to try to
leap up and protest, Darturius's firm hand thrust me down again.

'How dare you rise till you're instructed to!'

'But my Lord Darturius, there is some mistake. I am not a
slave, I am a Roman citizen, and I have never seen this man—'
A savage slap across my face sent me sprawling backwards
on the floor.

It came from my so-called namesake. He had only used his
left, undamaged hand, but it was an expert blow. 'You heard
him, gentlemen. Exactly as I warned. His own words condemn
him.' He gave me a contemptuous little smile. 'The penalty
for trying to escape from slavery is forehead branding and a
flogging, at the least – but impersonating a citizen is a capital
offence. And this wretch is guilty of both crimes at once. I
submit that he is worthy of instant punishment – at the
discretion of his new master, naturally.' He bowed in pretended
deference to Darturius.

'Well, slave, have you anything to say? You have caused us
so much trouble with your antics on the way, that if I did not
hold your donor in such high regard, I would be tempted to
sell you straight to the galleys or the mines. But as you are
intended as a wedding gift, I suppose that I must accept you
with the best grace I can.' The Latin was fluent and grammatical,
but it was over-formal for talking to a slave, reminding me that
Darturius was a Celt at heart.

I took a gamble, and answered in my native tongue – a
strategy which (as you know) had served me well before. 'My
lord,' I told him, 'You are misinformed. This man is not Libertus,
as he claims to be. Do not trust what he pretends. If you cannot
read my travel warrant for yourself, have the other citizen

decipher it for you. That will explain my status, and it bears my patron's seal.'

To my amazement, he was furious. 'You try my patience, slave. Of course I am capable of reading messages. You wish to hear what Marcus has to say?'

He seized the writing block and read the Latin words aloud. 'Greetings, in haste, from Marcus Septimus. This is the steward that I promised you. He is astute and capable, but very devious. Keep him in submission and he will serve your daughter well, but keep good watch of him. If he offends, or is not suitable, do as you wish with him.'

I stared at him, wholly unable to believe my ears. I almost snatched the tablet from him, but some instinct held me back – fortunate, as I would certainly have earned another blow – and in any case the false 'Libertus' handed it to me, saying with a sneer, 'See it for yourself. If you can read, that is. As a steward, I presume that you have learned?'

I took it from him, still incredulous. But there it was, scratched firmly in the wax, exactly as Darturius had said – though not written in my patron's hand, of course. But underneath it was the imprint of his seal, repeated on the wax cartouche which still dangled insecurely from the ribbon-tie. For a moment I could not understand how this could be, though it explained my treatment of the night before – everything made sense if they had believed I was a slave, valuable but likely to escape, so not to be ill-treated but to be secured.

Then I realised how this had been done. Someone had heated up the wax – very carefully so as not to obliterate the imprint of the seal – erased the old message and inscribed the new. And there was only one moment when that could possibly have been – at the former mansio, when I was being massaged by that slave, while I believed my possessions were safely under guard. Presumably this false Libertus was to blame, claiming then to be Crassus Posthumous and sending me doped wine which ensured that I would sleep till he was gone – I should have guessed there was something unnatural in all that sleepiness – though I could not see what he hoped to gain by that. Or, even less, by claiming to be me.

But, I realised with a sinking heart, it was going to be very hard to prove the contrary. An Emperor may have his likeness on a coin, and rich men have images and statues made, but what evidence does a common tradesman have of his identity? Especially when he bears a letter actually saying that he's someone else? It is not a problem one often has to face.

In Glevum, surrounded by people that I knew, there would be no difficulty – one appeal to Marcus and the matter would be solved. He would disavow the letter and confirm my rank and name. But here were only strangers, who either now believed I was a slave or – in one case – claimed to know I was. The only people who might verify the truth were days away and anyway – given the so-called message I had brought myself – no such an appeal was likely to be made.

'I have a companion who could vouch for me,' I bleated, though I realised there was no hope of help from there. Trinculus had been compromised as well. All evidence of his rank and status had been stripped from him and his word was no more likely to be believed than mine. Moreover, I had just condemned him by my words. If I was supposed to be a would-be fugitive and he was my companion and associate, he was by that fact himself a criminal. And his predicament was even worse than mine, as the false Libertus instantly made clear.

'A deserter from the army, my Lord Darturius. He gives his name as Trinculus, I understand, though that is not the case. When discovered, he was posing as a guard, claiming to be travelling under orders from his superiors. But I think you'll find his sword-belt, which is being held with his effects, proves that he is nothing of the kind. The buckle reveals his true identity.'

I gasped. All this was just a lie. Trinculus had been introduced to me by the tesserarius himself. There could be no question of his being someone else. It is true that soldiers of a foreign unit, like his Dacian alia, all wear belts of a particular design, often with their name etched in the buckle-back. And certainly his armour was a piecemeal affair, so he might have bought a Dacian belt from someone else, but if the buckle bore a different name he would have been obliged to grind it out – and how could he have come by a deserter's belt? I shook my head. If Trinculus was really wearing one, then somebody had exchanged it while his back was turned – also during the massage at that mansio, no doubt. No wonder he'd had trouble yesterday with the buckle-hole.

I was about to say so, from my position on the floor (though at the risk of punishment) when the bridegroom, who had been listening to all this from his dining couch, interrupted with an irritated cough. 'A deserter, do you say? Then what's he doing here, Darturius, by all the gods? He should be handed to the authorities.' His voice was high and cracked with age but still imperious. He did not deign to rise.

It was the false Libertus who replied – a breach of etiquette, since he was of lower status and had not been the one addressed. (I would have known better, in his place, but he was apparently in mine, and seemed oblivious!) 'He was allowed to travel here at my request, on the understanding that we will hold him till they send for him. It was inconvenient to leave him at a mansio, where he could not be securely under guard.'

'Then I suggest that you lock him up, Darturius – I imagine you have facilities for that?' The older man addressed himself directly to his host, scrupulously treating my namesake with disdain. 'And perhaps this tiresome steward, too – he may be valuable, as everybody claims, but I'm not sure that I wish to have him working in my house. Though that might affront the donor, I suppose. A powerful magistrate, I think you said?'

Darturius nodded. 'One of the most important men in all Britannia. And personally involved in licensing the salt.'

I squeaked. I could not help it. 'Then he isn't in disgrace?' It was the only glimmer of good news that I had heard for days.

Darturius looked contemptuously at me. 'Disgraced! He's entertaining a personal legate from the Emperor as we speak, I understand.' He turned to the imposter with a smile. 'I sent a message to him yesterday, to tell him the good news that you'd arrived – and of course to thank him for his gift – and no doubt we shall have an answer very soon, with all the latest news. He's honoured me with several communications recently. I hear he was delighted that you'd solved that suicide – and saved the curia from needing to replace the tax.'

The eyes of the imposter flickered in my direction, momentarily, but he answered airily enough. 'Oh, the facts were evident enough, when one knew where to look.' I would have liked to bite his legs for his presumption – they were close beside my face – though I did not, of course.

'Don't be so modest, citizen,' Darturius replied. 'Your patron thinks most highly of your abilities. He will miss you sorely while you are in Gaul.'

'Gaul?' I was turning into Echo, the unhappy nymph doomed to repeat the last words she had heard. And like her, I'd spoken without intending to. In doing so I risked another blow – it was not my place to speak.

But my imposter simply turned a chilling smile on me. 'Gaul!' There was no mistaking the triumph in his voice. 'His Excellence has asked me to attend to some urgent business there, and citizen Gnaeus—' he gestured to the groom – 'has been good enough to promise to find a ship for me, and a captain who will brave the winter seas. It will be expensive, naturally – but Marcus is most generous in providing for such things.'

I looked at him with loathing – not least because I knew my patron to be extremely careful with his gold, but I was learning better than to speak. It was Gnaeus who interrupted with a sneer.

'Another good reason for not offending him, I suppose. Which means the steward stays. Or rather – since he is intended as a gift to Aigneis – perhaps she should decide? So if your slave could fetch her?'

Darturius said simply, 'Paigh!' and my guide, who had been standing behind me all this time, bowed himself out and hurried from the room. 'Stand up then, steward,' Darturius went on. 'Let your new owner have a look at you.' When I hesitated he aimed a kick at me. 'Quickly too, or I shall have you flogged.'

There was no help for it. I scrambled to my feet and closed my eyes, inwardly seething, but resigned to having my muscles felt, my teeth inspected and my body scrutinised. I have been subject to such indignities before, when I was offered at the slave market. This time, at least, I knew what lay in store.

It was not as humiliating as I feared. I was obliged to let the old man peer into my mouth, to ensure that there was no decay, and squeeze my arms to see how strong I was. But just as he seemed about to lift my tunic-hems (to check that I carried no disease) the inner door was opened and the girl came in, accompanied by Paigh – though not by any handmaiden, to my surprise.

She was not what I expected. For one thing she was older than the average bride – at least sixteen, I guessed. She was a big girl – taller than the groom – and more than 'young and shapely', she was very amply curved. Her face was striking – with intelligent blue eyes and dimples round the mouth – though too determined to be truly beautiful. Her long golden hair was already dressed in braids, as if in preparation for the wedding day, but there was no suggestion of a veil and none of the pretended modesty that Romans prize so much.

'You called me, gentlemen?' She held her head aloft and walked with dignity, unafraid to look directly at every person in the room – even at me – though all of us were males. Her dress was conventional enough – a floor-length tunic, made of finest wool and dyed a pinkish rose – but it was bound around her figure with gold silken cords, which (since she wore no covering stola as a married woman might) emphasised and drew attention to her buxom charms. Her bridegroom was a lucky man, I thought.

He seemed to think so, too. He was looking at her with unashamedly lascivious eyes, but for convention's sake he pretended a reproof. 'Aigneis! Have you no shoulder cloak, at least? There are strangers present. I shall expect more decorum after we are wed.'

She turned to smile at him. Her voice, when she spoke, was low and clear – an attractive trait, in women, I have always thought – and her Latin was impeccable. 'And you shall have it, Gnaeus, when I am your wife. But for the moment I am under my father's *potestas*, and my immediate duty is to him. So when he summons me to come, I do so instantly, regardless of my dress.'

Her groom looked disconcerted by this bold reply, which would have seemed impertinent on any other lips, but which she offered with a charming smile, as though simply stating facts. He looked at her father, but Darturius seemed more pleased than otherwise.

'Aigneis has always been obedient – in all important ways.' Despite the ambiguity, he spoke the words with pride. Clearly he doted on this wayward girl. And so, I realised with a shock, did Paigh – who had gone to stand behind his master now and, obviously thinking that he was unobserved, was gazing at Aigneis with adoring eyes. He saw me looking and coloured to his ears.

I must be getting old, I told myself. I should have realised how the matter stood, from the way he'd spoken of her earlier. How must he feel about this wedding then? And what did Aigneis think?

My thoughts were interrupted by the mention of my name. 'Citizen Libertus.' I glanced round instantly, ready to reply, but of course the lady was not addressing me. She was speaking to the sallow man. 'Citizen Libertus?' she repeated, with more emphasis. 'You have a slave to show me, as I understand.' She spoke as though she hated the idea.

This time the imposter seemed to recollect himself. 'Ah, forgive me, lady! My thoughts were otherwhere.' He waved a hand at me. 'This is the steward my patron promised you . . .' He went on, giving an account of my supposed abilities and flaws.

But for a moment he had betrayed himself. He had not responded to the name. And Paigh had noticed. I saw it in his face and in the almost imperceptible movement of the head with which he signalled something to the girl.

Darturius clearly had not noticed anything. 'I know that I had promised to lend you Paigh,' he said, placing a fond hand upon his daughter's arm. 'But that could not be for long – only until he's worked out his father's debt. While this slave is an outright wedding gift to you, quite an honour coming from his Excellence. A proper steward who is clearly skilled. However, there are disadvantages. He also has a history of being troublesome – perhaps the reason that Marcus chose to pass him on. Gnaeus felt that you should choose whether to accept the gift or not.'

My heart was sinking as I watched her face. She had been promised Paigh – who had doubtless schemed for weeks to ensure that this occurred – and it clearly was something she herself would much prefer. So I would be sold on as a nonentity, probably to labour in the mines, since I had been given a reputation as a liar and a would-be runaway, which would not endear me to a private purchaser.

But the girl surprised me. She did not even glance at Paigh again, but there was clearly communication between the two of them, because she raised her head and, without the slightest hesitation, murmured with a smile, 'Father, this gift was intended as a compliment to you. Of course, I shall be delighted to accept.'

TWENTY-SIX

I was enormously relieved, though it meant a return to slavery. The certainty of shelter, food and decent clothes is infinitely better than the galleys or the mines. And as a steward, I consoled myself, perhaps in time I could arrange to get a message home and let my wife and patron know my whereabouts. So it was with genuine gratitude that I embraced her feet and promised her my service 'as long as I'm your slave'.

I half-expected that the false Libertus would object again and try to have me punished for my alleged misdeeds or sold on to obscurity at once. But having won the battle of identity, he seemed to lose all interest in what became of me, and was more concerned to talk to Gnaeus about boats: what ships were in harbour at Portus Abonae, who the masters were, and who could most readily be bribed to go to sea. It was clear that he was really intent on going to Gaul as soon as possible.

Darturius was clearly happy at this resolution of my fate – because it avoided potential offence to Marcus, probably – and ordered that I should be taken out and cleaned, and put to work as soon as possible. 'Find him some decent clothing, Paigh. What he is wearing is not suitable for a senior slave, especially in a Roman household, such as Gnaeus's. My steward must have an old robe that he could use, and find him some proper sandals, if you can. My old ones, if you can find no others, though I doubt that they'd fit. And you'd better take him to the slave quarters and show him where to sleep. Then find a use for him. He won't have normal duties till my daughter's wed, but with the marriage imminent there is much to be prepared.'

Paigh bowed, nodded and led me from the room.

'You understand the language, though you do not speak it well,' I observed as he ushered me outside, into what would be a courtyard garden when it was complete. There were paths and seats and little flowerbeds, though there was little sign of plants, and statues of deities in half-constructed arbours either side. Most of all, there was a central hole – clearly intended to become a pool – where there was a statue of Neptune sitting on a rock, with an open mouth for a waterfall to spurt. Paigh saw me looking, and I spoke again. 'I wondered how you would have managed as a slave, in Gnaeus's house where Latin is spoken all the time.'

'I have been studying,' he answered. 'Aigneis teaches me.'

'And you would do a great deal to accompany her, I think. I am sorry if I have disturbed your plans. It was not my intention.'

He stopped and looked at me. 'Nor your patron's, if I read the situation right. I have come to wonder if you might be right, and you really are Libertus as you claim to be. I saw how you answered to the name – and he did not.'

I felt a swell of hope. 'So you believe me?'

He shook his head. 'It seems incredible. That man arrived with proper documents, a travel warrant and a letter – under seal – saying that he was also bringing you, to be a wedding gift. I was there when the document was read aloud, and it said that you were talented and quick, but anxious to obtain your freedom and willing to achieve it by almost any means – though adding that you were no longer young so it would be best to keep you for a time and then allow you to buy freedom when you were too old to work and would otherwise become a burden on the house. There was mention of a driver-slave as well, though he was not recommended – able, but lazy and headstrong and disinclined to work.' He looked at me and shrugged. 'How do you explain it?'

'I can't,' I said. 'It seems his claims are irrefutable. And yet I tell you that they are completely false. I am Libertus – and what's more, my little friend is genuinely called Trinculus and he is no deserter. He is a soldier on detachment from the Uudum guard. That, at least, should be easy to confirm.'

Paigh shook his head. 'But not by me, I fear. I have no influence with Darturius. Aigneis might persuade him, if she would agree to help.' He led the way out through the gateway as he spoke, and I found myself in a Celtic farm again, with animals and crops and a scattering of storage huts, and – further off – another larger building with a chimney hole, through which was issuing the smoke that I had noticed from the shore. Two slaves were feeding the furnace as I watched. Clearly this was the salt refinery.

Paigh, however, was still following the previous line of thought. 'Though I doubt that she could sway him even then. He is much impressed by Roman seals and official documents – such as the one you brought.'

'I have a theory about that,' I said, following him into the largest of the huts – clearly the sleeping-quarters for the slaves. I outlined my suspicions about the mansio and the part that the so-called Posthumous had played. 'There was a slave who did the massage,' I explained, 'a handsome-looking, very dark-haired boy.'

Paigh, who had been rearranging palliasses on the floor, straightened up at this and looked at me. 'Stranger, you convince me more and more. The fellow is at this moment in the waiting-room for slaves, where he has been allowed to sit idle half the day as the attendant of an honoured visitor. Later I will take you there, and you can see if he's the one. Though how Darturius is to be persuaded of the truth I cannot see.'

'Perhaps his daughter could suggest that if he doesn't hear me out, and give me the opportunity to try and prove my claim, then he runs the risk of offending Marcus very much – treating his representative as a common slave?'

'If your claim should turn out to be true?' Paigh said, but I knew that he could see the merits of the strategy. 'Very well. Best to leave this till tomorrow, probably – my master is too busy trying to impress the bridegroom now. But on the day before the wedding . . .'

I nodded. The marriage-eve is always a special day for brides, especially Roman ones, when her childhood is ritually laid aside – her toys and playthings offered on the fire – and she is bathed and perfumed and generally indulged. 'Gnaeus will not be here?' I enquired. It is usual for the bridegroom to stay well away, so she may have the last day with her family, but here – with the causeway – it might be different.

Paigh laughed. 'He is due to stay with one of the citizens nearby – who will come back with him to be a witness. You – or your namesake – will be another one, and the rest will be

composed of family. It is not to be a very grand affair. Darturius
is insisting on the plaits and veil, and is even demanding that
there be a wedding feast, but this is a *coemptio* marriage – where
Gnaeus ritually 'buys' her from her father – and all the rest is
simply show. And the feasting will be short – they'll have to
choose their moment to drive across the bay, though the tides
are improving slightly every day. But this was the only favour-
able day before the Saturnalia, all the others were ill-omened.
So it was then, or not until next year.'

I looked at him. 'Would that have been so very terrible? I
don't imagine you are pleased to see her wed.'

He shrugged his shoulders. 'It will be the saving of us all. There
are too few women in the family, and too many men. Even for
the marriage customs, as you'll see. She has no mother to escort
her through the rites – only a young sister and an ancient aunt.'

'But she has handmaidens, at least?'

'Not any more.' He gave another shrug. 'Aeignis had an
attendant maid, of course, but only recently the girl was sold.
For some misdemeanour.'

Something in his manner made me say, 'At your instigation,
I assume? So that the natural companion would be gone, and
you could accompany Aigneis in her stead?' Paigh did not
answer and I pressed the point. 'What was your intention,
anyway? It's clear that you love her – and she is fond of you.
Could you not have simply married her?'

He shook his head. 'Darturius would not hear of it – I'm not
a citizen – and anyway it would have led to ruin. I told you
earlier, there are too many men. My father had six brothers . . .
and all of them had boys. Except Darturius, my eldest uncle,
who as chance would have it, fathered the only girls.' He
made a little gesture of despair. 'You are a Celt, you know
how these things work.'

I did. It was the story of the goatboy, in a different guise. The
estate would be divided among all the heirs (meaning the males,
of course) with the eldest receiving the greater part each time
– and without daughters to ally to other families, how could
this be maintained? Women needed dowries, but – if they were
comely enough – these need not represent substantial capital.
Aigneis would bring hardly anything.

'So she marries Gnaeus, for her family's sake, and you accompany her as slave. What did you hope then? Presuming you did not intend to murder him!'

He gave a mirthless laugh. 'Nothing so dramatic. It is enough to wait. Gnaeus is old and cannot last for many years. And once she has produced an heir, the matter is resolved. The child will be a citizen for life and the saltern will remain within the family, even if Aigneis loses rank by marrying again. So either Darturius will no longer care, or she can defy him and run away with me. I shall be free by then. Within two years I shall have worked out father's debt.'

I smiled at this vision of domestic happiness. 'Always supposing that she does produce a child.'

'Oh, I think we can be certain about that,' Paigh said, too quickly.

I looked at him. 'Meaning that you already suspect she is with child?' Another moment, and realisation struck. 'Yours?'

He shrugged his shoulders, and did not reply, but I had my answer. This was urgent then. No wonder that the bride was so anxious to be wed, regardless of the tides and the dismal time of year. 'You will be very anxious to be with her afterwards?' I said.

'Let us say I have an interest in proving who you are,' the youth replied. 'In the meantime, this is where you'll sleep. I'll have the garden slaves prepare a palliasse. I've placed you next to me, and you can share my space tonight. There is talk of building a Roman servants' hall, but Jove alone knows when.'

'And little Trinculus?' I said.

'He will have been taken into master's custody. It won't be pleasant but he'll be clothed and fed. If you prove your case tomorrow you can plead on his behalf.' He was impatient, suddenly. 'Now, come, we have been talking far too long. We must not displease Darturius tonight, if tomorrow Aigneis is to plead your cause.' He was in the act of leading me outside, when he paused and looked at me. 'As a member of my master's household now, you'll have to serve at dinner, I suppose. Do you know what is required? You were a slave, I think? Marcus told us – and I saw the scar.'

I nodded. 'I'll manage, I am sure. Though it will irk me

greatly if I have to serve that fraud. He will be laughing at me behind his toga-folds.'

'He has a slave brand, too, were you aware of that?'

I shook my head. I'd hoped to use that mark in evidence, but if he had one too it was no proof of anything. I would have to find another way. In the meantime, there was work to do, and uniforms to find.

'Lead on,' I said to Paigh.

TWENTY-SEVEN

I had forgotten how hard it was to be a slave. Not that the work itself was very arduous – as a man of steward status I was given easy tasks – but even so I was exhausted long before it stopped. The endless standing and waiting by the wall, the kneeling and bowing as one passed the plates and cups, and the requirement for silence while keeping bright alert made me so tired that afterwards I could hardly eat my meal – though, in deference to my supposed rank, Paigh had contrived to have me offered the best leftover scraps.

He had also managed to have me serving on the master's right, meaning that I was dealing with Gnaeus rather than the presumptuous slave who had usurped my name. Somehow the knowledge of that slave brand – which usually created fellow feeling – filled me with additional indignity. It was horrible to watch him eating too – tearing at his food like a barbarian, and failing to rinse his fingers in the fingerbowls. Worse to know that the other diners thought that it was me!

I had hoped to get a glimpse of the dark-haired slave, to reassure myself that my theory was correct, but he was not in evidence. He had been given food and gone upstairs to 'prepare his master's bed' and doubtless sleep in comfort on a soft rug at his feet. Meantime, I had a prickly palliasse. It was hardly comfort but, because I was so worn and the hour now so late (dinner duties do not finish for the slaves just because the diners have retired to bed) as soon as I lay down I fell asleep at once and did not stir till Paigh awakened me.

'Come, fellow Celt,' he said, and I was pleased to see him smile. 'It is late and you are wanted in the house. Gnaeus has left and your namesake is asking where you are. Aigneis is preparing for the bridal sacrifice, and she's speaking to her father – but he'll soon be back, and if she succeeds you'll have your opportunity. I was sent to fetch you – you had best be quick.'

I groaned and rolled myself onto my aching knees, then heaved myself upright. Every joint was painful. I have never felt so old. I pulled on the sandals which Paigh had found for me – more in keeping with my status, but so tight they pinched my toes. I would have splashed my face and hands but Paigh clucked impatiently, so I abandoned my ablutions (and all hope of food) and followed him back through the half-completed garden to the house.

The false Libertus was awaiting me in the draughty atrium. He was sitting on a carved stool by the wall (under the protection of the roof) with a page attending him, and he raised a languid hand as I appeared. 'Ah, steward!' – he was gloating, it was unmistakable – 'I was enquiring for you. I see, from your performance yesterday, your serving skills have not deserted you.' He waved a cup at me. 'So fetch me another goblet of that watered wine.'

Helpless fury was pouring through my veins. I was supposed to be a servant and to disobey was death, but this was an insult that I would not endure. 'I will do nothing of the kind.'

I heard the shocked intake of breath from Paigh behind me and the little page.

'Then I'll tell your master and he'll have you scourged.' Triumph and satisfaction glittered in his eyes. 'Page, go and ask Darturius to come and witness this.'

The page looked frightened but he bowed and was in the act of hurrying away when the man in question came into the room, attended by the suave steward of the house (who looked much better in his robes than I did). Darturius bowed a greeting to the charlatan. 'I apologise for leaving you so long, but there are family rituals to perform.' He turned to me. 'Aigneis tells me that you have important claims to make and I must hear you out because they might be true – in which case I am in danger of offering offence to Marcus Septimus, whom I hold in high regard.'

The imposter leapt up to intervene – with no regard for proper courtesy. 'Pay no attention to what he says, Darturius. I was about to send for you. He has refused an order – in front of witnesses.'

Darturius raised enquiring eyebrows and I dared to speak. 'True, my Lord Darturius, because I am no slave and this man knows it. I am Libertus and should be your guest, not him – whatever his stolen documents appear to say.'

The big Celt looked appraisingly at me. 'You realise what a serious claim you're making against me? Depriving a Roman citizen of his liberty is a serious offence.'

I know how to grovel and I did it now. 'I know, my lord, but I am not accusing you. The fault is wholly his. You acted on the warrants which he gave to you. You could do no oth—'

The imposter interrupted with a sneer. 'Intelligent and devious, his master said. Obviously that describes him very well. If he has the slightest proof of what he says, let him produce it now.'

This was the opportunity that I'd been hoping for, but I had no concrete evidence at all. I hesitated.

'You see? He cannot,' the false Libertus sneered. 'You've seen my documents. What more could you require? You'd like me to describe the town of Glevum, possibly? Or my patron's country house?'

Both these things had occurred to me, of course, though as Darturius had not seen either, nothing could be proved – even if my namesake gave a false account. But it might help me to determine who he really was: it would tell me if he actually knew the town or not. I nodded, weakly. 'Let him try, my lord.'

Perhaps the invitation was a terrible mistake. The imposter launched at once into a full account. There could be no doubt that he knew Glevum very well.

Darturius turned to me. 'Well, are you satisfied? Or will you tell me now that he was bound to know, because he is the steward that Marcus promised me?'

I shook my head. 'I don't believe that Marcus sent a slave to you at all. I don't know who this person is – except he isn't me, and is very possibly a fugitive. And clearly he knows Glevum. Let us see if he can do so well with my patron's country house.'

There was momentary uncertainty in the fellow's eyes, but he was clever – cleverer than me. I did not anticipate his swift reply. 'But surely it is the steward who should speak first this time? Otherwise he can simply echo what I say – and what help is that to you? And I might add that Marcus has a large apartment in the town – I can describe that for you afterwards if you require.'

Darturius was losing patience, I could see. 'My lord,' I said, 'this is not proving anything at all.' I slipped into Celtic. 'I speak this tongue – I doubt he does the same.'

Darturius looked at the other man enquiringly, but there was no response. Clearly he had not understood a word. Darturius translated, but the scoundrel only smiled. 'It is quite true,' he said. 'I do not speak the native dialect. But you have only his word for it that Libertus does.'

It was a clumsy phrase and our host had realised it. I could see that he was wavering. I cast my winning dice. 'If he is a pavement-maker, let him show his skill. There are marble clips aplenty lying in the yard – let him set them to a pattern and show you how it's done.'

I had expected that this challenge would cause the man unease, but he simply gave that chilling smile again. 'I would be glad to do so, Lord Darturius,' he said. 'But I fear that I cannot. As you know, I have an injured hand.' He waved the bandaged appendage as he spoke.

I felt that surge of furious rage again. 'I don't believe him. He has wrapped his hand on purpose. It is too convenient.'

'You doubt me?' My name-thief startled me by looking smug. 'Then see it for yourself.' He began unwrapping the binding from his hand. He did it carefully, as though it caused him pain – although he had shown no signs of it before. I watched, dismayed, as he eased the cloth away. 'Convenient?' he sneered. 'Or are you going to claim that I did this purposely?' He held the hand aloft.

It was horrible to look – clearly badly burned.

Darturius looked at me uncertainly. 'Well? That seems genuine enough.'

I nodded, speechless with defeat. There was no more I could offer.

But the imposter had another trick in store. 'I fear I cannot meet your challenge, slave,' he said, with careful emphasis upon the final word. 'But if Darturius would like to see a sample of my work, I have one with me for business purposes. I hope to find commissions while I am in Gaul.' He gestured to the page still standing at his back. 'Rebind my hand for me.' And then, imperiously, to Paigh, 'Fetch my servant, have him bring the samples here.' The young Celt hurried off.

While the page was bandaging, Darturius turned to me saying, in Celtic, 'If he can produce mosaics, you have not proved your case. I confess that I would prefer your story to be true – the fellow is presumptuous and ill-bred, but he has the advantage of the documents, and official seals must be honoured . . .' He broke off as the dark-haired slave came hurrying in.

I was right in my suspicions, this was the massage-slave. I was now sure my warrant-tablet had been tampered with. But again, it was impossible to prove, and of course they would deny it. I simply said aloud, 'I've seen this man before.'

'Of course you have,' my namesake said at once. 'We were escorting you, until that final mansio, when your gig lagged behind us and so missed the tide. My Lord Darturius, how much longer must I endure this insolence? I am Libertus – and my servant has the proof. Show him, Maximus.'

Maximus! It was the name of a beloved slave of mine, now dead, and I was certain that the choice was quite deliberate – and new. I'd wager anything that his servant had not answered to it long. However a man is entitled to call his slave by any name he likes – and change it at a whim – and it is a common name for servants, anyway, so there could be no complaint. But the theft of my poor dead attendant's name made me more angry than the misuse of my own.

I was so busy fuming that I almost failed to see what the slave was taking from its leather packaging and holding out for Darturius to see. But when I realised, it made me cry aloud.

'Those are stolen. They belong to me . . .' I trailed off as I recognised where they'd been stolen from. They were the tiny hand-sized samples that I had prepared especially for Loftus to take back with him – all those days ago – so that Acacius Flauccus could select the pattern for his new bathhouse floor. And there was only one place where they could have been since then – among the items in the tax-collector's house. Proof positive that these two had been there recently – and once I had seen this, of course it all made sense. These were the murderers.

The courier would have told them that I was on the way, and that I was coming to the wedding afterwards. Perhaps they had begun by simply trying to escape, but when by chance – they learned that I was stopping overnight at the self-same mansio where they had already sought to hide, they saw an opportunity to evade the authorities – not briefly – but for life. My travel warrant would see them safe to Gaul, and once there they would simply disappear, living a life of luxury on the stolen tax money.

I frowned. Perhaps that did not quite explain things, after all. My travel warrant had been falsified, to say that I was this pretended slave. And then it dawned on me. Acacius Flauccus had a travel warrant too – of course he must have done. A proper warrant, given under seal – probably an impressive-looking scroll – identifying the bearer as a servant of the state, which would take the owner anywhere and make my prized wax version look insignificant.

'Well?' I realised that Darturius had been addressing me.

I shook my head and began to stumble out my tale, but the false Libertus interrupted me.

'My lord, these accusations are ridiculous. Of course we were in Uudum – I solved the suicide. But these samples came from Glevum; I am taking them to Gaul. Unhappily I am due to go there very soon, and during Saturnalia all the courts are closed, so I cannot bring a formal charge against this man, or hand him over to the authorities. I will have to ask you to do that in my stead. In the meantime, make an end to this. Either find for him – and decide that I am lying when I show your proofs – or find that he's the perjurer when he brings you none.'

'I have no choice . . .' Darturius began, but at that moment Paigh came in again and made a signal that he wished to speak. He approached his master and whispered in his ear.

Darturius nodded and looked round with a smile. 'Perhaps we can put this matter beyond doubt. My messenger has just arrived from Glevum now. He has waited on Marcus Septimus at his country house on several occasions very recently, and he agrees that the real Libertus was once there as well, though he can't – at this distance – describe what he was like. But we shall have him in. If he can identify either one of you, we shall have our answer. Will you fetch him, Paigh.'

'He's at the door,' Paigh said, in Latin, and he showed in the messenger.

I almost cried out with relief. It was the sulky boy.

Darturius beckoned him. 'Do not be afraid. We simply need

your help. These men both claim to be Libertus.' He gestured with his hand. 'If you recognise anyone as the man that you have seen, tell us and there may be a reward.'

The messenger looked doubtfully at me and then at the imposter, but he did not speak.

'You must remember me,' I urged him. 'I saw you at the villa, very recently. You were kept waiting in the atrium, while Marcus and his family were outside in the court. And a little later in the lane, you galloped past me when I was walking with my slave.'

To my dismay the courier shook his head. 'I'm sorry, master. What he says may well be true, but I was only interested in the task I had to do. I was anxious lest I get benighted on the road – I didn't pay attention to anybody else. I cannot pretend I recollect the face. Or that man either,' he indicated the pretender as he spoke. 'But this one,' he pointed at the dark-haired slave, 'I have seen before. In the slave room at His Excellence's villa, I believe, although I can't be sure of that. But certainly I've seen him – or someone very like. I hope that helps you, master?'

And of course it did. Darturius shook his head and turned to me. 'A clever story, steward, and a bold attempt. You almost had me duped. But now, I fear, there is no help for it. You've made false accusations in front of witnesses and that is something which I can't ignore. Despite the insult to his Excellence, I cannot permit my daughter to accept you as a gift. As soon as she is wed, I shall take you to the slave market myself.'

'But there are other crimes, as well,' the false Libertus said. 'Being a runaway, impersonating a citizen, and refusing an order from a guest. All of which is proved. More than enough to call the torturers and have him flogged to death.'

Darturius looked at him with ill-disguised contempt. 'I have said that I will sell him. And he will be punished for disobeying you, if you insist. That is my decision, citizen. He was a gift to me, and if I choose not to formally accuse him further, that is my right as owner, I believe. This way he will have time and reason to repent.'

I was about to speak – hardly knowing whether to thank him or protest – but he held up a hand to silence me. 'Enough. This is my daughter's wedding-eve and I have spent sufficient time

on other things. I must now go to her. You Paigh, take this
miscreant away and lock him up – with his young companion,
since there is no other cell. Tomorrow I shall dispose of him
as well – by handing him back to the authorities. Citizen
Libertus, make my home your own. I will have you called for
cena. Until then, farewell.'

And with that he turned and left the room, followed politely
by the messenger.

There was a silence, and Aigneis tiptoed in, from the inner
corridor. 'I have been listening,' she murmured in her native
tongue to Paigh. 'So it was decided that the steward was a fraud?'

'I am almost sorry,' Paigh replied. 'Except that it means that
I shall be your attendant after all. In the meantime, I must lock
this slave away.'

Aigneis shrugged her shoulders. 'I'm rather sorry, too.
Gnaeus was most impressed by the way he served last night.
And now he's to be sold and will not be seen again. I suppose
he has a name?'

I did not answer. What answer could I make?

'Citizen Libertus?' she insisted – not addressing me. 'You
were the one who brought him here. What does he answer to?'

The pretender looked startled and seemed to be considering
a name, but it was his dark-haired attendant who replied.

'He was to be your servant, call him what you like. Think
of something interesting – Venibulus, perhaps. Now, if you will
excuse us?' He led his master out, followed by Aigneis and the
little page.

I stood like an idiot, staring after them. And then – at long,
long last – I saw what I should have realised hours ago, and
the last pieces of mosaic slotted into place.

Too late! For there was no one I could tell. Even Paigh refused
to listen. He was in a hurry to attend the rituals. He seized my
arm and, despite my efforts to explain my thoughts, he hustled
me out, down the steps and over to a hut, smaller than the dye-
house where I'd been before. There, without another word, he
pushed me in, locked the door and left me in the dark.

TWENTY-EIGHT

Trinculus was already in there; I could hear him whimpering my name. This was clearly the detention hut for wayward slaves. As soon as my eyes grew more accustomed to the gloom, I groped my way over and huddled close to him.

'Citizen? Thank all the gods you're safe,' he murmured, with such heartfelt relief that I felt touched – and guilty, too. I had been so busy with my own concerns that I'd scarcely thought of him. 'They've not mistreated you?'

'I have fared a great deal better than you have, I suspect,' I replied. I might have been treated as a slave, but I was well-clothed, and last night had slept and eaten well – though I was hungry now. He'd been locked in semi-darkness all that time, probably with bread and water as his only meal – and from what little I could see, still in a skimpy Celtic tunic with my damp cloak over him. And it was unlikely that matters would improve.

I tried to cheer him, as much as possible, by pointing out the only merits of our present plight. The hut was dry and – though smelly and certainly not warm – there was none of the dank and stinking chill that many cells exude. There was even, when one was used to it, the faintest hint of daylight filtering through thatch. But he was not comforted.

'What do you suppose they mean to do with us?'

'I can't tell you that.' It was not entirely a lie. I knew but could not tell him – it would cause distress. Instead I changed the subject. 'But I think I do know why we find ourselves in this predicament. Did they tell you that there's a person here pretending to be me, and insisting that I am just a slave, sent as a wedding gift from Marcus to the bride?'

'What!?' I heard my companion gasp, and then – less tactfully, 'but why? It's not as if you were a wealthy man of rank.'

He had a point, of course. There were stories circulating all round the Empire, of people arriving at the Imperial court with false identities, claiming favours and high posts, because – with three different Emperors in a single year – there were so many newcomers in Rome that personal networks could no longer vouch for everyone. But this was different. 'If I'd been more wealthy the ruse might not have worked. I'm just obscure enough. We are playing-pieces in a very clever game – played by one of the cleverest minds I ever met.'

I felt a thin hand in the darkness reach for mine. 'So who is this imposter? And how could he pretend that he was you?'

'He tampered with my documents and produced his own.' I outlined my theory of when this had occurred.

'You're not suspicious of Crassus Posthumous? But why? You said that he was on the curia. Has he fallen out of favour, like your poor patron, and been trying to evade exile?'

I shook my head, although he couldn't see. 'I was wrong about my patron, he is safe and well. And this man was not a councillor at all. Just a slave from Glevum – though he had not always been a slave. I think I know his story. His father's business failed – horses, I believe: my informant told me they could not be made to pay – and the whole family was sold to slavery to repay the debts. Freeborn Latins, too.'

Trinculus drew his hand away. 'So how can he be here? If he were a runaway, the army would have heard – there is always a tremendous search – and even in Uudum we would have been put on alert. And how could I have figured in his plans? No one in Glevum has ever heard of me – though he might have some reason for selecting you.'

'He didn't. It was nothing personal,' I said. 'Simply that we happened to present ourselves. That is the nature of his cleverness – he can grasp an opportunity and make a plan at once, and then be quite ruthless in his pursuit of it. He has a talent for instant strategy, and a courage so reckless no one dreams what he has done. It was only when he gave a perfect description of the colonia to me, and I saw his damaged hand, that I realised who he was. He was right in one respect – he was wasted as a slave. He would have made a splendid general.'

Trinculus wriggled and I sensed that he had turned towards me in the gloom. 'A damaged hand? So what, exactly, do you think he did?'

'In the beginning,' I said, 'I think he simply saw a chance to "die" – and quite heroically – when there was a fire at his master's house. I doubt he set the blaze deliberately – he could not have predicted how far and fast it spread – though once it started he may have encouraged it to burn: there was mention of vats of oil having been upturned. Either way, there were several people killed: some of the kitchen staff were never found, and three important guests were overcome by smoke – so he, the steward, rushed back in to "help" and perished in the act.'

'But surely that was a noble thing to do?'

'Only, of course, he did nothing of the kind.' I laughed at his inability to grasp it, even now. 'He had seen an opportunity to disappear, in such a way that there would never be a search. He feigned his death, of course. I think he found a body that was already dead – probably the kitchen slave who was "never found" – and dragged it to close to where the dead patricians lay. Then he put his own insignia on it and set the corpse on fire, having drenched it with oil so it would be entirely destroyed. I should have realised, when I first heard the tale, that something was amiss. How could the councillors be simply "overcome by smoke", when the steward's body – lying next to them, and coming afterwards – was burned away to ash?'

'But everyone believed that it was him, because the ring survived?' Trinculus had begun to understand.

'More than that,' I said. 'I think it wore his slave collar as well. I believe he forced the drawer or cupboard where the keys were kept. As a steward he would know exactly where they were locked away. Probably the hiding-place was already well on fire, and that's why no one thought to check the contents afterwards. I suspect he coolly braved the flames to seize the keys – certainly he burned his right hand horribly – so he could rid himself of the slave collar which betrayed his name and who his owner was.'

'And paused in a burning building to put it on a corpse? You really think so, citizen? He would have run the risk of being killed himself.'

'It can't have been near the centre of the flames – the other corpses were not damaged by the fire, and by then the wind had cleared the smoke away. It took a cool head and utter ruthlessness,' I said. 'But after that he could rush out into the street by a side-gate and lose himself with ease. It was dark by then. Lots of people would be scurrying about – too occupied with trying to put out the fire to pay much attention to anybody else. And no one would be seeking him. He was – apparently – accounted for.'

There was a silence as Trinculus considered this. 'I can see how that might work. But it was dangerous.'

'He was not working entirely alone,' I said. 'He had the assistance of a relative – another slave – who caused a distraction by panicking the horse and letting it escape. It may be that the steward captured it and rode it out of town. They were good with horses. It was the family trade.'

'So two of them escaped?'

'Not then, but af—'I began – but my companion clutched my arm.

'There is someone coming. Listen! Footsteps!' He was whispering.

I listened, but my untrained ears could not detect what he had heard. The soldier, though, was right. A moment later there was a rattle at the door, the latch clicked open and a ray of light burst in – so bright and sudden that it blinded me.

When I had rubbed my eyes and half-regained my sight, I made out the figure who was standing there. It was the dark-haired slave, to my surprise, and he was carrying a bucket and a hunk of bread.

'Your food,' he grunted and put it on the floor. 'That's all you get today, so make the most of it. There's water in the pail – and when you've drunk that, don't try using it for other purposes. You'll have to drink from it tomorrow, too – though that doesn't matter much. There'll be times when you look back on this as luxury!'

'I'm surprised that you were sent with this,' I remarked. 'The slave of a so-called important visitor. Surely Darturius has others to do such menial tasks?'

'I volunteered.' He gave me a gloating look. 'They're busy with the preparations for the wedding feast and I wanted to come and take farewell of you. Unfortunately by the time you're taken out and sold, my father and I will be on our way to Gaul.'

Beside I heard Trinculus give a little moan, but I did not turn to him.

'Your father?' I said sharply, to the slave. 'I realised that he was a relative. I didn't know how close. Sold into slavery together, I presume?'

He didn't answer, but went to shut the door.

'Oh, come, Venibulus!' I called, and was ridiculously pleased to see him turn, instinctively. 'That's your name, isn't it? You should not have suggested it for me – if you had not done so, I might not have guessed the truth. I was still thinking that the courier was dead, the victim of the taxman's murderers. But of course he wasn't – he was one of them. You had played your father's trick and found another corpse to take your place. Without a head it would look like Druid work, and ensure that it was not identified. Only this time I think he was not already dead – you murdered him on purpose. Who was it? The deserter? I know you had his sword.'

There was a silence, followed by a laugh. 'You think yourself so clever, citizen. Of course it wasn't him. How could we have got his corpse up there, unnoticed, on a horse? And we couldn't take the carriage, we'd just covered it with pitch and it would have been noticed on the road. I just rode up there myself and chose a likely spot, found some peasant setting bird-traps, and then murdered him. I wanted an inconspicuous tunic anyway – and of course he had to wear the courier's uniform. Did they find the belt-clasp? It had been much admired, and it was additional proof that it was me.'

I nodded. 'And you cut your hair, and dyed it, completing the disguise? Using ink you stole from Flauccus, I presume?' I'd even noted it was inky-black!

'Only roughly then, but afterwards my father did it properly. Blonde curls are distinctive and I never liked them much. Though I was sorry, in some ways, to lose the uniform. It had served me very well – allowed me to ride anywhere I chose and with no questions asked. No one thinks it odd to see a messenger. But we'd killed Acacius by that time, and I wanted to be dead. The soldier's outfit was of no use at all. There would have been questions all the time, and we could not have stopped at any mansio, despite the documents.

Besides, it didn't fit. I had sufficient trouble with the peasant's clothes.'

'Which were too big for you! And yours too small for him. That's why you had to slash it from neck to hem like that,' I said, seeing the answer to something which had puzzled me. 'I wondered why, when there were no wounds below the shoulder area. I presume you strangled him? It seems to be the method you prefer, and chopping off the head would obliterate the marks.'

He laughed, but didn't answer, except to say, 'Enough!'

'Venibulus,' I said. 'I don't have long to live. A man of my age does not survive the mines. Indulge me by explaining something. Why the soldier? I don't understand. I realise how you plotted to steal the tax money – you knew that Acacius Flauccus had been ill, and that he was applying to resign. The curia were discussing it in your master's house the day the fire broke out, and your father – as steward on duty – must have overhead. And you were then promoted to carrying official messages – which you read, of course. Not all of them were sealed, I suppose?'

He smirked. 'And even if they were, there are ways of melting wax which are difficult to spot. It was very easy to discover when Acacius planned to bring the gold, and to arrange that we should both be in Uudum on that day. We'd even discovered he was going to be alone – the slaves were going to market. He'd written to the Glevum curia asking for their help in obtaining new ones – and my master answered him, offering to sell him my father and myself.'

'But how did you know that? That must have been when your father was still thought to be alive? And you were not a courier then.'

'It was written the morning of the fire, before the curia met. My predecessor had not yet dealt with it, so it was passed to me. I never delivered it to Uudum, naturally – and I think it was forgotten afterwards. But my father saw the high priest writing it (he never considered that a slave might read) and it confirmed his fears that he would never gain freedom by any normal means. When the fire broke out, that's what goaded him to act.' He shook his head. 'But I don't know why I'm telling you all this. No doubt you've worked it out – you have a reputation for deductive skills.'

'Most of it,' I said.

'That's why my master was so afraid of you. The plan was first that he would take a room nearby, and I would join him in a moon or so, and we'd use the money to begin again. No one was looking for him, we supposed. But as soon as he heard that you were being sent to Uudum to investigate – I took the message, so I let him know – he decided that we had to disappear at once, preferably by taking a ship for Gaul. So I staged my disappearance, we disguised the coach, and fled. And then we found you staying at the mansio.'

'But you didn't kill me?'

'Oh, I wanted to – when you have done it once, it's easier every time. Acacius was simple, he was feeble anyway. The hardest part was getting him hung up convincingly, especially when Father only had one working hand. How did you deduce that, anyway? I thought we'd made a splendid job of it.'

'You should have realised that Acacius couldn't reach the hook.'

He snorted. 'I knew I should have killed you when I had a chance – but father insisted that would simply set your patron after us. Better, this time, to make you disappear. And so he has – or will do very soon.'

He turned to shut the door and move away.

'And the soldier?' I insisted.

He shook his head. 'That was an accident. He was on fatigues and guarding a checkpoint on the road. He saw the carriage and he challenged us – if he'd simply let us pass I could have let him live, even though he saw my father driving it. But he would insist on opening the door, and of course there was no Flauccus – only money bags. He would have reported it to the army instantly. So I had to strangle him. We put him in the carriage and carried him for miles, until we found a useful spot to bury him. But I kept his sword-belt, because it showed his name and rank, and I hoped it might delay them in finding who it was, even if they happened on the corpse. And then, of course, we met you – and the rest you know.'

'He became Libertus, and you became his slave – hiding in

plain sight at a wedding feast! While I become the steward offered in the note – I presume you kept that and made use of it? – and poor Trinculus was cast as the deserter from the ranks, although there had never been one. The missing man was dead.'

'Exactly, citizen. I think you have the picture perfectly. But you will never prove a single word of it. There are no witnesses to any part of this – and by tomorrow morning we'll be safely gone, and nobody will pay the slightest credence to anything you say. A runaway slave and a deserter – who could be surprised? Anyone would swear that black was white to escape your likely fate. So farewell, gentlemen, I wish you luck of it. Sleep well and enjoy your meal – it may be your last.'

He slammed the door too and thrust the lock across. I heard him whistling as he walked towards the house.

In the darkness Trinculus had began to sob. I tried to rally him – reminded him that he was a military man and urged him to take a little bread and drink to keep his courage up. But he refused all comfort, and in the end I cradled him as though he were a child, and held him, trembling, as he wept all night.

TWENTY-NINE

We did not see the wedding, though we heard the flutes and trumpets, and the cheering afterwards. And Trinculus was able to discern that there were carriages – rattling on the causeway and stopping at the shore. 'Two, by the sound of it,' he said. 'And at least one extra horse.' Events had roused him from his misery and he groped towards the door, where I found him trying to peer out through the crack. 'It's no use,' he reported, 'I can't see a thing.'

We almost did not need to. A moment later it was clear – even to me – that the bride and groom had got into a coach and wedding guests were shouting the usual rude jokes and yelling coarse suggestions after them. Trinculus said he heard a whip crack and the sound of wheels. Someone was presumably throwing walnuts too, because there was a lot of scrabbling and laughing cries. Then it subsided and the voices faded in the direction of the shore: presumably the procession was following the bride, at least across the causeway, even if – this time – it could not accompany her all the way to her new home.

Then nothing. We sank back on the unforgiving floor. After a little while, Trinculus exclaimed, 'Do you think they are going to feed us anything, or leave us here to rot?'

'It's probably not as late as it appears to us,' I said, still trying to control my anguish by assuaging his. 'Everything here is dependent on the tide. I think it is still morning – but the wedding's taken place so that everyone can cross the causeway while it's dry. But now its over and the guests have gone. Someone may bring us something very soon.'

I spoke without conviction, but – as if my words had summoned magic from the dust – a moment later there was a rattle at the door. I looked up, doubtfully, to see who it would be. I knew it wasn't Paigh – and the strangler and his father would have gone as well – free to be wealthy and undisturbed in Gaul.

'Well!'

To my astonishment it was the sulky messenger. I looked at him without affection. 'Well, indeed!' I said, 'I hope you're satisfied. It's you that put me here.' (Not altogether fair, but there was some truth in it!)

'Paigh said the same, but what I said was true. I did not remember you. But when I considered it, I did remember someone on the road. So I offered to come and feed you – they are busy at the house. I wanted to have another look at you.' He pushed the door open to its ultimate extent and looked me up and down.

I was filled with sudden hope, but he dashed it instantly. 'As I thought, I could not have changed my oath. He didn't look like you. He was dressed as a citizen, more like that other man, who I'm pretty certain must be what he claims. He's sent a personal message to His Excellence. I'm to deliver it as soon as I have finished here, while the causeway is still passable. Another day of galloping from dawn to dusk.' He sighed, thrust in a loaf and half-refilled the pail. 'Meanwhile – there's bread and water and you are to eat it fast. They are going to send you on the salt cart to the port and sell you straight away, so Aigneis can have the proceeds as her wedding gift. So let's hope you sell – though I expect you will. There are always shipowners looking for more slaves.'

I gave an inward groan. I loathe the sea. I would almost prefer consignment to the mines. But the youth was going to Glevum, and there was something that I had to know.

'What message?' I demanded. 'Does this "Libertus" send?' Of course, it was a gamble. He should not tell me that.

He did, though. 'Nothing personal. Only to say that he would report again when he got back from Gaul.' He shrugged. 'His patron will be simply furious. He has already told him not to go – with the wedding over he wants him back in Glevum instantly – he's even sending his private gig to bring him home.'

'Marcus is to send his private gig?' I said, feeling as if the world was spinning round my feet. I had visions of Victor, who could rescue me – if I had not already been taken off and sold. 'When is this to happen?'

'It is already on its way. And Libertus knows that. I brought him a private message from Marcus yesterday. But he's ignored it, and gone driving to the port, following Gnaeus Verus and his bride. There's talk of him hoping to take ship today – he's found a captain who is willing to risk the passage, for a price.' He shrugged again. 'None of my business, but I was surprised.'

'And well you might be. And you are right in saying that Libertus knows. Because I am Libertus, I told you that before – however much that wretch declared the opposite. And if Marcus sends his fast gig, as I suppose he might, there's a chance the driver might arrive in time to tell you so. He knows me very well. You remember Victor?' I said to Trinculus, who had been standing behind me all this time, obviously listening and afraid to hope. 'He could vouch for you, as well.'

But the sulky messenger was frowning. 'I would not wager on that, though it's a clever thought. Marcus has sold his driver on to someone else – the Priest of Mercury – whose driver-courier was attacked and murdered by Druids recently. Not encouraging, when I'm to ride that way myself.'

I did not enlighten him. I had more urgent things to say. 'You are certain about that?'

'Quite certain. And Marcus made a splendid profit from the sale, according to the gossip in the servants' hall. He has acquired a new driver in his place, though this one's very young – some stripling whose father sold him as a slave, but who is talented with animals. Took to the position like a fellow twice his age – so good that one of the chariot-teams is making overtures – but he will never have encountered you, even if you are Libertus, which I'm beginning to suspect.' He did that sulky shrug. 'If so, I'm very sorry, citizen.'

It was days since anyone had called me by my rank, and it was oddly comforting, even though the news and situation was so dire. I thanked him for the information, and he briefly smiled.

'Well, I must go, and you must eat your food – quickly, if you propose to eat at all. You'll have to be loaded on that wagon very soon. Another few minutes and it will be too late – the causeway will be covered and you won't get away.'

I wanted to gain time, but I was powerless. I made one last, despairing, try. 'Will you take a message to Marcus Septimus from me, as well? I cannot pay you, they've deprived me of my purse, but he will recompense you, I am sure.' (I could only

hope that I was right.) 'Just tell him that the prisoner – tell him
who and why – before he was taken to the market to be sold,
told you to ask if Marcellinus had yet learned to whip his top.
That should assure him of who I really am. Even if they've
sold me, he might buy me back – or find a way to nullify the
sale.'

I was not really hopeful. If I were on a galley, I would not
be seen again – and much the same could be said about the
mines. Those who were slaves there had no identities, they were
simply living tools, to work until they died.

'I will do that. If you are rescued, remember that I helped.'
The courier seemed tempted to offer me a bow, but instead he
simply nodded and shut the door again, bolting it behind him.

I felt for the bread and water and was in the act of sharing
the meagre meal with Trinculus, when the door was opened for
a second time that day. This time the arrival was a bearded,
heavy man, dressed in Celtic trousers and a cloak like Paigh's.
In his hand he held a whip and he was pointing it at me. 'You
first then, come on – up onto the cart. We've only a few minutes
if you don't intend to swim.' He spoke in Celtic, but the meaning
was quite clear, even to Trinculus, who scrambled to his feet.

'Hands together and behind your back!' our captor barked,
and when I reluctantly obeyed, he bound them firmly together
at the wrists. Then, having done the same to Trinculus, he
prodded us across the courtyard and down the slope towards a
heavy wagon which was standing on the shore – the causeway
stretching out in front of it across the mud. In the middle I
could see the water starting to encroach.

'On the cart!'

It wasn't easy without one's hands to help, but threat of
whipping is a potent spur, and I managed to spill myself onto
the floor of the device, where I lay shaking as my companion
joined me there. The driver took his place and was picking up
the reins, when he let out an exclamation of dismay.

'Dear gods, who's this? And in a vehicle. They'll fill the
causeway up – and we shall not get past. Get back, you idiot!'
He stood up, making gestures with his arms.

I managed to raise myself an inch or two by leaning on my
elbows and straining up my neck. It was just enough to get a

glimpse ahead, and I saw what he was shouting at. A gig was rattling merrily towards us on the path, being pursued by a gesticulating horseman in a cloak. I could not hold the posture, there was too much strain, and I was forced to lie back and await developments. I was secretly not sorry if we missed the tide. By tomorrow my patron would have heard my message, and – I hoped – would be sending a reply. Though by tomorrow there would also be another daylight tide, and I might be on my way to Portus Abonae. If indeed, I did not go today. Our driver seemed intent on leaving anyway – we were already rattling towards the marsh. I wondered what would happen when the two carts met – but to my relief he pulled the horses to a stop.

I craned my head again, and saw what he had seen. The horseman was none other than Darturius himself – his hood thrown back and his fine cloak flying as he rode. He was gaining quickly on the other vehicle, though of course he could not safely pass. And the water behind him was rising all the time.

The approaching cart was almost at the shore by now. I just had time to verify that the sulky boy was right – the driver clearly was not Victor, it was someone small and slight – before I slid back on the boards again. Trinculus looked enquiringly at me, although he dared not speak.

I shrugged and, raising my eyebrows mouthed silently, 'Blockage.'

I am not sure whether my companion understood, but it made no difference now. The vehicle was close and Darturius – having evidently reached sounder ground where he could overtake – was closer still. I could hear him talking to our driver now. Even from here I could detect that he was furious.

'I'll have to stand you down and take the prisoners back to the confinement hut. We can't safely take them till tomorrow, now. It's that wretched gig-boy's fault. He was waiting for us at the mansio, where Libertus and his slave had left their vehicle, and was supposed to intercept him and take him back, on the orders of Marcus Septimus. But he didn't do it. He just let them drive away, and the next thing that I knew he was dashing over here. And now, I suppose, I'll have to entertain him overnight and try to be fairly civil while I do it, too – since he comes direct from Marcus Septimus, and I've already rejected his generous wedding gift. Just at a moment when there's much to do, and Paigh's not here to help. But it cannot be avoided now, the tide is turning fast. You'd better get those prisoners back where they belong, and I will deal with this.'

I did not need the gesture with the whip to know that I was expected to stand up but Trinculus, of course, had not understood. I nudged him helpfully, and he rolled onto his knees and from there contrived to force himself upright. I was not so lucky, I could not raise myself, however much the driver threatened with his whip.

In the end he gave an exasperated sigh and clambered back to me. 'Oh, very well. You can't escape, now, anyway.' He rolled me over, drew his knife and cut my bonds – none too gently. 'Now, get up on your feet!'

Thus freed, I did so – rather shakily – and found myself standing in the cart. From here I had a splendid view of Marcus's precious gig. Ironic that I would never ride in it again, though he had sent it here for me. I could hear Darturius explaining matters to the driver now, with frigid courtesy.

'I fear that you have missed him, by your own mistake. The arrangement was that you would meet him at the mansio. But you somehow failed to do so, and now you're stranded here. It was never the plan that you should drive across. I may be able to arrange for you to go the other way, but it's a slow road to Portus Abonae on the ancient route, and even with fresh horses you won't arrive for hours. By the time you get there Libertus may have taken ship for Gaul. I'm sorry that you missed him. I thought that someone would point him out to you.'

'Oh, they tried to,' a familiar voice replied. 'But they muddled, somehow – it wasn't him at all.'

It was the goat-boy! I could not believe my ears. Or my eyes, in fact. Gone was the scruffy tunic and the homemade boots. He was dressed in splendid scarlet uniform and looked as though he had been born into the role. I was so startled that I stumbled with relief and he looked up and saw me on the cart.

'It's no wonder that I didn't see him,' he exclaimed, lapsing into Celtic automatically. 'Of course Libertus wasn't at the mansio, that's him over there.' He pointed with his whip.

Darturius turned towards me and I saw that he'd turned pale. 'You're sure?' he muttered, weakly – as he realised what he had done.

But the goat-boy was smiling, quite oblivious. 'I'm absolutely certain. He spoke to me before, on the road to Glevum, when he was being accompanied by the local guard. He did his best to help me – it's probably because of him that Marcus purchased me. Of course I'm certain. I'd know him anywhere.'

Poor Darturius. He was incoherent with embarrassment – and very, very anxious to make amends, to myself and Trinculus – and to the goat-boy, too. And there was almost a full day before the causeway would be passable again!

I now know what it is to be a really honoured guest.

EPILOGUE

The goat-boy – or Caprigulus, as Marcus had named him when he purchased him – proved to be as good a driver as the sulky boy had said, almost as skilled as Victor, though (for my taste) much too fast. I cannot pretend the next two days were comfortable ones, I am too old for dashing through the countryside at speed, and the halfway mansio we stayed at overnight did not offer me the 'Emperor's room' this time.

It was quite amusing, on returning to the shore, to see the reaction of the people at the inn which had held us prisoner a day or two before. Grovelling is not an adequate description of their attitude: nothing was too much trouble if we cared to stay, and of course our luggage was restored to us. Though it was sad to say goodbye to little Trinculus, who had been promised transport to return to his post.

The guard who had tormented him was nowhere to be seen – he had been returned to headquarters and "stripped of privilege", meaning that he would spend the future cleaning the latrines. Though that did not remove the bruises he had inflicted on my friend, whose dormouse ears looked still more evident when he was back in uniform – and who was still without his proper sword-belt as he stood and waved me off, but happy to be returning to his regiment.

(Darturius had already returned my purse, of course, rather heavier than it had been when I'd been stripped of it. I was to buy a present for my wife, he said, as an apology for having kept me there so long.)

I was not sure of my reception when I got back to her – I'd been in mortal danger, which she would know by now, since Marcus would have passed on what the messenger had said. And she'd been left alone, without a word from me. But I need not have worried. I made Caprigulus stop outside my house, even before we had reported back to Marcus, and her greeting reassured me instantly.

'Ah, you're back, and safe and sound I see. You're looking travel-stained. I'll get the slaves to fetch some water and they can wash you later on. And I've got some stew – and some oatcakes that I made in case you came—'

I walked across and took her in my arms and for a long moment she leaned against my chest, then freed herself and brushed her apron down. 'Foolish fellow! But it's nice to see you home. Now go and see your patron. He'll be awaiting you.'

He was. Delighted to see me, he told me several times, and glad to learn the facts, though disappointed that the killers had eluded him. He had been looking forward to bringing them to trial – especially on the charge of impersonating me – but he was disappointed to have lost the stolen tax.

'But Flauccus's treasure would have covered that,' I said. 'The curia will not be called upon to pay.'

He nodded, thoughtfully. 'Speaking of the curia, I have some news for you. I'm afraid that I've withdrawn your nomination for the post of duumvir.' He looked at me with some embarrassment. 'I thought that was the reason you were running off to Gaul – and I'd rather have you here, than frighten you away. But then, of course, I got the message saying that you were a prisoner and reminding me about Marcellinus and the top – and I realised that I could have put you forward after all. But by then it was too late. I hope you won't be disappointed. There will be other times.'

I shook my head. 'Not really disappointed, Excellence. Although my wife might be.'

He smiled. 'I fancy she will be consolable. Tell her you're invited to a banquet here, in two days' time. A farewell to the Imperial legate, before he moves on to Londinium, and Saturnalia begins. I've told him about you. It will be a grand affair. I think she'll be impressed.'

It was a grand affair, and Gwellia was impressed – though more worried about whether my best toga had been cleaned enough. (I could no longer wear the toga candida, of course.) But it was at the banquet that I heard astounding news. The captain of the vessel which had sailed for Gaul had been discovered, washed up on the shore. Darturius had heard and had sent word at once.

The bodies of Venibulus and his father were never found. To this day I do not know whether they were drowned as well, and the stolen tax is lying at the bottom of the sea: or whether they simply bribed the crew sufficiently to throw the master overboard, and they are really at this moment both alive and well – enjoying their riches somewhere safe in Gaul.

I suspect the latter, but I cannot be sure.